Praise for The Pacific

"A superb tale of decept ... smooth and believable and portrays the dynamic and fascinating characters, keeping them and the reader in suspense and a whirlwind of emotions. Wong will leave you laughing one minute and crying the next, and in between, awestruck by dead-ends that lead to a satisfying finish."
**- Joanne D. Kiggins**, columnist and author, Cleveland.com

"Wong plays his cards close to the vest, only revealing enough of the story to keep the reader hooked ... the reader is left breathless awaiting the main character's choice between two paths and the tension is palpable ... a satisfying and memorable read."
**- Amy Brozio-Andrews**, *J          zine*

"The author deftly steers ... hat most convoluted mystery, that supreme pa... .. and he makes us feel every inch of the journey. ... novel. Bravo!"
**- Liam Jackson**, author, *O          ...mas Dunne)*

"A beautiful and touching ...l. It is the kind of story that I can imagine being n... novie some day."
**- Esther Avila**, author and          riter, *La Verdad, Arrowhead, Porterville Recorder, Mader*

"*The Pacific Between* is like the rising crescendo in Bolero - getting faster, louder, and bolder as it clips along. It took courage to create a character as flawed as Greg Lockland. A lesser writer would have made Greg more likeable, less petulant, and lost the inherent truth encapsulated in the character's flaws. I think Ray Wong has shown us that this is just the beginning of what will be a long literary career."
**- St. John's Recorder**

"Wong's flair for dialogue powers this modern romance. While the hero stumbles in his search for self, Wong's pace never falters."
**- Petrea Burchard**, actor, humor columnist of "Act As If" (Actors Ink)

# The Pacific Between

by
**Raymond K. Wong**

Behler
PUBLICATIONS
California

**Behler Publications**
**California**

The Pacific Between
A Behler Publications Book

Copyright © 2005 by Raymond K. Wong
Cover design by Raymond K. Wong
Design layout by Cathy Scott – www.mbcdesign.com

This is a work of fiction. Names, characters, places, and incidents either are the product of the author's imagination or are used fictitiously. Any resemblance to actual persons, living or dead, events, or locales is entirely coincidental.

Library of Congress Cataloging-in-Publication Data is available
Control Number: 2005903200

FIRST PRINTING

ISBN 1-933016-32-9
Published by Behler Publications, LLC
Lake Forest, California
www.behlerpublications.com

Manufactured in the United States of America

*This book is dedicated to my father and mother, whose love, support, and understanding mean so much to me. I love you, Mom and Dad.*

I want to thank these special people for helping me realize my dream and potential: the folks at Behler Publications, Barbara Bamburger Scott, Catherine Coan, François and Genevieve Pigeon, Stephen Gibson, Jenna Glatzer, Frank Baron, Barbara Tyler, Lori A. Basiewicz, MacAllister Stone, Liam Jackson, Kelly Skillen, Barbara Broz, Pat Loeb, Charlie Stuart, Lisa Abbate, Molly McEvilley, Jeff Swift, Cary Robers, Andrew Lam, Angela Raymond, Ada Yuen, Kitty Wan, James Jackson, Deanna Yang, Ralph Langer Jr., my brother Philip, and my beloved parents.

A soldier lays his head
On a white patch of dead
Roses and thorns
Broken pieces of a sacred heart, torn
Between a life that has gone
And a love that lives on
— *G. S. Lockland*

# Kate

Betrayal makes us do strange things.

By now I've driven over two hours from Los Angeles and another thirty minutes around the block trying to find 1935 Roselyn Drive. It's already after ten in the evening and I'm speeding. I circle around, then back, again and again, making the same wrong turns, up the same one-way streets. Finally I find it. The apartment complex, hidden in the hills and behind two rows of palm trees, is rather small and old for San Marcos, a quiet middle-class neighborhood just outside San Diego. I park the car and grab the cardboard box on the passenger seat, then trudge through the hallways, looking for apartment 206.

Kate's eyes shine like emeralds in the faint light when she opens her door. I let out a sigh and outstretch my arm, demanding a hug.

"Greg, what are you doing here?" she asks.

I take a step back, surprised by how distant she sounds.

"Are you going to invite me in?"

"Of course." She ushers me into her place and closes the door behind us. "Please don't mind the mess. I'm preparing for a case. Can I get you something? Tea? Coke?"

"That'd be great," I say.

"Which one?"

"Uh, tea. Yeah, tea."

She hurries into the kitchen, and I plop myself onto the sleek blue-green sofa in the living room, next to a small rectangular fish tank—a cobalt betta swims by, lazy and oblivious.

Kate has a typical one-bedroom apartment, cozy for a single woman. Heaps of papers are stacked high on the round dining table across from where I'm sitting. An empty Chinese takeout box sits on the coffee table, a fork abandoned in it. On top of one of the piles of legal papers and books lies her security badge: KATE WALKEN, ESQ. On the off-white wall behind the sofa hangs a poster the size of a large window—a striking montage of the 2001 Special Olympic hopefuls, vigorous and vibrant. Knickknacks of all sorts all over the place: an "I Heart New York" snow globe, a

Shrek bobblehead, three wooden ducks, and a fluffy stuffed piranha. The apartment reminds me of how young, at twenty-six, she really is.

Sarah McLachlan's breathy voice seeps through the bedroom door. *Angel.* I lie there, motionless and silent, and let her every note and word speak to me about love, sorrow, and pain.

"I hope you like this. It's all I have right now," Kate says as she comes out of the kitchen with a steaming cup of tea.

"You have a nice place," I say, taking the cup. The fragrance of jasmine surprises me. *Lian used to drink jasmine.* I nurse the cup and sip my tea, like a little boy stuck at a grown-up party.

"Greg, is everything okay?" She sits next to me.

"I've missed you."

She touches the back of her ear and lowers her head. "Why didn't you just call?"

"I did. But I didn't leave a message. I had to see you," I say. "I asked Emily for your address, and she wondered why I wanted it."

"Um, what did you tell her?"

"Nothing. Just that I wanted to send you a thank you card or something—for coming to the funeral, spending the weekend with me. For being so kind." I smile. "For sharing a joint with me at Griffith Park, et cetera."

She laughs. "Oh Greg. She'll figure us out. My mom's not dumb."

"I didn't think she was," I say. "But, why didn't you say goodbye when you left?"

"I didn't want to wake you," she protests. "It's a work day for the rest of us, you know."

"Not trying to run away, are you?"

She hesitates. "Like you?"

I glance at her sideways.

Her short brown hair and freckled face still remind me of the Brentwood High sophomore I first met when I was home for the holidays from UC Berkeley. A spontaneous trip to Griffith Park, where we shared a joint in my red Mustang, secured our bond. Our parents were good friends, but Kate and I became even better friends. A year later, her father died of prostate cancer, and she seemed to have changed. As I ran off to Wharton for my MBA, I told her I would write. I kept my promise. But in every letter, she wrote about her fights with her mother, how she hated her whole life, how she wished she were there with me in Philadelphia. After a while, I started to forget to write back. I wanted to forget about my life in California. I was running off to build my own world, my own sanctuary and I wanted to forget about this little girl who seemed only half my age. I didn't want to baby-sit anymore.

Now, after almost ten years, our friendship has taken an unexpected, romantic turn, and I wonder if she's actually forgiven me. Probably not.

Guilt colors everything.

"I don't know." I look down and hold the cup closer to my face.

"Greg." Her voice turns soft. "Everything is fine. Is everything okay with you?"

I turn the cup and watch the amber liquid trembling between my palms. "After you left, I went to the attorney, about the will. Then I took the keys to Wells Fargo." I let out a slight breath. "And I found these."

From the cardboard box I take out a bundle of black and white photographs strapped with a worn-out rubber band.

"I've never seen them before," I say, trying to hide the jitters inside. "My father hid them. In his safe deposit box."

I hand the photographs to Kate. The rubber band snaps in two. She makes a face, then holds the first picture by its frail edges and studies it closely.

A handsome Caucasian man stands proud and proper, short black hair slicked back and parted on the right. Crisp summer shirt and dark trousers. In the crook of his right arm he cradles a small boy dressed in an adorable miniature sailor's outfit, a white hat, and shiny black shoes. The boy has the man's straight ridge of nose and wild strength in the eyes. And the broadest smile.

A Chinese temple looms in the background.

"Greg, you were such a cute little boy," Kate says.

I shake my head. "Flip it over."

She does. In thick black ink, my father's stubborn inscription: JUNIOR, AGE 2, PO LIN MONASTERY, HONG KONG.

"That was my brother. He died when he was eight."

"What happened?"

"That's funny...I really don't know. I was only four. They never talked about him, his life, or his death. Everybody we knew assumed I was an only child. I remember the funeral, but I don't know a thing about George, Jr."

"George? But your dad's name—"

"Yeah. And you know what? They avoided mentioning his name, too. Come to think of it, my mom's always called my dad by his middle name. It's always Stephen this, Stephen that."

As Kate flips through the photos, I go on telling her about the brother I don't remember and the family I've wanted to forget.

Before my ninth birthday, my father became a surgical lead for the World Doctors program, stationed at different hospitals all over Asia, and my family began to move a lot. He liked to move around, but my mother grew increasingly tired of that. With every move, there were fewer and fewer things to remind us of George. Eventually there was nothing. Not even a book or a teddy bear or a shirt. I've never seen a picture or home movie of him. It's as if he never existed. We not only buried his body, we buried everything about him, including our memories and feelings.

My family had a long history of burying feelings, important feelings. Pain.

To the outside world, Dr. G. Stephen Lockland and his wife Helen appeared to be an attractive, happy, mature couple. He was a lean German-Irish Californian, a marathon runner and swimming champion, his brown eyes sharp and dimples deep. She was a petite, energetic Chinese woman with a knack for gab. To me she was just Mom. Other men saw her as a former Miss Hong Kong runner-up. With her gray hair cut short, she could still turn a man's head. She'd always tell me stories of her many suitors, from Australia to Iceland, from Korea to the Americas. In the great race to win her heart, the American ultimately won the prize.

But appearances never speak the whole truth, and truth in my family was complicated to begin with. Along with the rides at Disneyland and the cotton candy at Venice Beach, the road trips in China and the cherry blossoms in Japan, there was the whiskey in the morning, the shouting matches in the afternoon, the dreadful silence that began in the evening and lasted for days.

The last time I talked to my father was two years ago, when I congratulated him on some achievement award at UCLA Medical Center. He was so drunk that night I doubt that he remembered my call.

Now, everyone is gone. Thirty-two years into my life, for the first time I remember my brother's face. I have no memory of his life, only his funeral—particularly, my father's figure towering over me, tall and grand, a statue of a stoic king. Now, just these damn pictures.

Kate looks up at me. "What does this mean? Why did he hide these pictures from you?" she asks.

"Other than he's a bastard?"

"That's harsh, Greg. There must be an explanation. Perhaps he didn't want you to see the pictures. He didn't want to burden you with the past, or the pain."

"I wouldn't have known any pain. I was only a boy."

She puts down the photos and takes my hand. "I wasn't talking about you. I was talking about your father. Your mother."

I stare at her for a moment. My tea feels cold.

"They were afraid of their own pain," I say. "So what? I have the right to know. He was my brother, for Christ's sake. I hardly remember him. What kind of parents were they?"

"Sometimes people do things, and there's no reason to it. Maybe your mom and dad decided that it was best."

"That doesn't make it right."

"Of course it doesn't," she says, patting my hand.

"Whose side are you on, anyway?"

"Guess." She touches the back of her ear again—she's so cute when she does that.

I stare at my tea again. "One time," I say, "I came home early from a swim meet and Mom was in the kitchen, screaming into the phone at the top of her lungs. It was like, 'I'm going to kill you, George. I'm going to strangle you and stab you a hundred times!' At first, I didn't know who she was talking to. Then I realized it was my father." I pause for a second and suck in a breath. "My mom went crazy for a while."

"No way."

"Yeah, she did. I mean *crazy* crazy. We actually had to medicate her. That was a long time ago. I was about eight, I think. She tried to kill my dad once."

"Really?"

"Really. Something about a knife. I don't remember. The neighbors were there. Nobody got hurt, of course."

"She always seemed so normal, so nice to me. I'd never have guessed. What happened then?"

"I think my dad put her in a program. She got better. She wasn't a monster, Kate. She never hit or hurt me. I never understood what really happened. It just got swept under the rug like everything else."

She shakes her head.

"Yeah, my family was screwed up." I laugh hysterically.

"You seem to have come out all right."

"You know, my dad would have corrected you. I was never good enough for him."

"That's exactly how I feel, with my mom."

"At least you still talk to her."

"Oh yeah. Things are better now between us, but it used to be ugly." She shrugs.

I lean forward to kiss her, but before my lips touch hers, I pull away. I'm thinking of someone else's lips.

"Let's take a walk," I say.

She squints and studies me. "Sure. Wait here."

She disappears into her bedroom, then emerges in a light purple sweater—it reminds me of Audrey Hepburn in *Breakfast at Tiffany's*. Once out of her apartment, I take her hand and we stroll across the street and enter a quiet park around the corner.

The early November air nips at us, so she huddles next to me. We pick a wooden bench and sit by the stone fountain at the center of the park. The sycamores and sequoias rustle their favorite lullabies. With Kate next to me, I should be feeling like the luckiest person in the world. Instead, my mind is going in all directions.

"How are you feeling?" she asks.

"I'm okay," I lie, my voice flat and emotionless.

"Do you want to talk about the pictures?"

"Not really."

She places a hand on mine. "It's okay if you do."

"I said not really."

She frowns and gestures me. "What are we doing here, then? I thought you wanted to talk."

She is astute, and I adore her. What she doesn't know, though, is that the pictures are only part of it, only the tip of the secrecy iceberg. I'm not sure if I should tell her about the letters I found. In fact, I don't want to tell her about Lian at all. It's not something I can share with Kate.

We sit watching the fountain for a while, and neither of us speaks a word. A few times, I open my mouth, trying to say something, but only slight, dry breaths escape my throat.

A squirrel or a chipmunk cracks a branch nearby, breaking the silence.

Kate looks straight ahead. "What's going on?"

"Huh?"

"What's on your mind?"

"I can't tell you now."

"You know what? This is starting to get on my nerves," she says, shaking her head, her voice a little harsh. "You came down and brought me out here at this hour, and I thought you needed to talk. But you're not giving me anything to work with here. 'I can't tell you this. I don't want to talk about that.' What's it with you?"

"What do you expect? My parents died—in a freaking car accident. And the damn pictures..."

"You're reading too much into these pictures."

"Oh, you think?"

"I think you have trouble with the truth."

My body stiffens. I look away and clench my jaw.

Sometimes she is so brutally honest that it's intimidating.

"It's the secrets I hate," I say. She has no idea how secrets have hurt my family. I don't think she can ever understand. Nobody can.

"I hate secrets, too," she says. "So what are yours? What are you not telling me? Why did you come here, and then just clam up?"

"Boy, I didn't know you were a psychoanalyst."

"I want to know what you're thinking—what's really bugging you. I want to help, but give me something here. This silence, don't-want-to-tell-you thing is getting old."

"Maybe it's because we have nothing else to talk about," I snap.

She breaks away from me, moves toward the fountain, and picks up a twig from the rim. She throws it into the water, making a crisp splash.

I don't know what has gotten into me. Maybe I needed a fight. My father can't pick fights with me anymore. Somehow, I'm missing those fights.

But Kate is not my father.

"I'm sorry," I say. "I have so much on my mind right now. I need some time to think it out. There are things you don't know."

"Then tell me."

"I can't. Not now."

"Here we go again. I don't think we're connecting here."

I stare at the fountain.

She lowers her head. "Maybe last night was a mistake."

"What?" I turn to her. "No. Is that what you think? That last night was a mistake?"

She tosses another twig into the fountain, pauses for a long few seconds. A little too long.

"No, last night was perfect," she says, touching the back of her ear. She flashes me a smile. "Except the burnt shrimp and tomato paste. I am the lousiest cook."

I reach for her and pull her close, slipping my arms around her waist, afraid that when this moment passes, this lousiest cook will be gone.

"I'm sorry I yelled at you," I whisper. Her body feels tense in my embrace.

"You've already apologized. But what really is the problem? Tell me."

"I don't like these emotions. Being angry. This rage." I suck in a breath and clench my jaw. "I'm so angry. I'm so angry with my father. I'm so fucking angry that when he died he had to take my mother with him."

"It'll take time. It's part of the process. I remember when my dad died, things were bad for a long time," she says. Her voice is quiet but strong. "I used to go into the garage, pick up one of his drills or something, and throw it. Breaking things. It was a tough time for me, being a stupid teenager and all. I was very close to him, you know. Now I look back, I feel kind of guilty for acting out like that."

"You sounded really angry in your letters. Mad at the world."

"You remember those letters?"

"Sure, I kept all of them."

Her lips tremble, forming a faint half-smile. "You know what? Things are going to be rough for a while," she says. "But you and I are together now, and that can be a good thing."

I lean in and kiss her on the cheek.

She glances at her watch. "We should really go back. I have to be in court early tomorrow. I still have work to do."

When we get back to the apartment, Kate reaches for her keys in her pocket.

"Shoot, I left them in the apartment," she says.

"What are we going to do?" I ask.

"Don't worry." She winks. "Give me a credit card."

I take my American Express card from my wallet and hand it to her. She slides the card down the gap between the door and the doorframe. She wiggles the doorknob about while sliding the credit card up and down the gap until we hear a click.

"Voila. Easy as cake," she says and opens the door.

I mouth a "wow."

"I've learned many things at Berkeley." She beams. "Besides, it's an old apartment—anyone can do this. And don't leave home without American Express."

"You should have the lock fixed. What if someone breaks in?"

"Don't be such a big brother. There's nothing worth stealing here."

"I'm not worried about that."

"That's sweet," she says. "Really, it's a good part of town. I had two years of Karate. I can defend myself. Besides, it's not the first time I've forgotten my keys. This comes in handy sometimes." She throws herself onto the sofa. "It's really late. You should stay over."

I gasp as I open my eyes. Crazy shadows dance across the walls like castoffs from a macabre party. Then I recognize Kate's bedroom and the uneven moon outside her little windows. My heart pounds against my ribcage. And I remember. Exhausted, I fell asleep on Kate's bed, while she was busy with her case in the living room.

I glance over and Kate's now sleeping next to me, her left arm draped over my chest. I stare at the paint bumps on the ceiling and think of my dream. My day. My life.

I take Kate's hand and play with her fingers. She is deep in her slumber, oblivious to the world around us. She wears a wiry, silver ring with a speck of emerald that matches her eyes. Her fingers are wonderful, slender but strong. She could win a fistfight if she wanted to. I plant a soft kiss on her forehead, but she doesn't stir. I slip out from under her arm and slide off the side of the bed, then place her head on a fluffy pillow and pull the patterned quilt over her.

For about five minutes, I watch her sleep.

I tiptoe to a corner and tug my shirt from the top of an old armchair. From the pocket, I take a small envelope and sneak out of the room, slowly closing the door so it doesn't squeak. I sit on the sofa and, in the faint florescent light from the fish tank, peel open the flap of the envelope, pull out a letter, and read it for the third time today:

*My Dearest,*

*Yesterday was your birthday. I wanted to call you very much but I did not know your number. I dreamed about you though, and that was nice. I have always wondered what you are doing at the moment. Yesterday, when I was on my way to work, once again I cried. Not because I was sad that I could not see you at the hospital, but because I felt that I was blessed, especially when I thought about our time together, even though it was so short. It will always stay in my heart. Even when there is the Pacific between us.*

*I want to wish you a happy birthday, and I hope you will live out your life the way you have always wished.*

*I will wait for your reply, with love and patience.*

*Love,*

*Lian*

I found this letter in my father's safe deposit box, under the stack of photographs.

I brush my fingers over the name etched in faded blue ink. Lian. A name I haven't heard in fourteen years. A face I memorized. A woman I will never forget.

Betrayal.

Right then, I make up my mind.

# Angel

Snow. That was what I missed the most about Japan, especially northern Hokkaido, where I'd spent six wonderful days skiing in the mountains the previous December. On those powdered slopes, looking down onto the minuscule villages nuzzled in the valley, the feathery flakes landing on my face and melting in my breath, I'd felt like I was back in the States, somewhere high up in the Californian mountains, close to home.

Nine years was a long time to be away from home.

It never snowed in Hong Kong, however, even on Christmas Eve. In fact, it was a warm night. I was in Tsimshatsui, a harbor-front shopping district, with my friends Choy, David and Martin. Ming-sing Choy and David Kwan, both Chinese and seventeen, tall and scrawny, went to my secondary school, the prestigious Wah Yan College. Martin Cowen was an exchange student from Australia with a stocky build and massive soccer legs—Martin and I sort of had the same looks, except he was one head shorter and fifteen pounds more rugged. We came out of Bulldog's Pub on Nathan Road after a few rounds of beer and whiskey, immediately swarmed by the bustle around us. The whole district was shimmering with illuminations the size of the towering office buildings on which they were displayed: some Jingle Bells here, a blinking Santa Claus there, and "Merry Christmas" everywhere. Madonna was wailing *Like a Prayer* nearby, and the line to a theater, *The Last Temptation of Christ* glowing on the marquee, wrapped around the block. The hypnotic smells of roasted chestnuts and Chinese barbecue, hot asphalt and smoky sidewalks, designer perfumes and pungent exhausts consumed us from all around. We were bombarded with so much life—it was sinful.

I looked at my watch and realized that it was almost eight o'clock. "Shit."

"Shit what?" Choy screamed, his lanky body half leaning on David.

"Shit, shit, shit. I have to go."

"Christmas Eve, mate! Let's go to Lan Kwai Fong. The party's just started," Martin chimed in.

"That's the problem. I'm not allowed to have any fun tonight. I promised my dad I'd be at the hospital by five. Shit! He's going to kill me."

"C'mon, let's go." Martin pulled at my sleeve.

I hesitated. "Really, I can't. Sorry guys."

I went down to the MTR station and hopped on a packed train to Kowloon Tong. Like a school of sardines, hundreds of people and I shoved and crammed into the small can of a subway train. Using my tall, muscular frame, I pushed my way into a tight spot by the door. The lights were so bright, and the train shook so much that I had to squint to make out the route map. The PA system sounded muffled. I couldn't decipher anything that came out of it. Hands were everywhere. I could have sworn that I was goosed by a bespectacled teenage Girl Scout. But I didn't care. I was more concerned about not missing my stop

A beer or bourbon too much had me staggering as I stumbled into Baptist Hospital on Waterloo Road. The outpatient waiting room was almost empty, as if people knew better than to get sick on this holy night. The light gray linoleum floor was shiny with new wax and polish. The bland halls were decked with superfluous pots of poinsettias and red and green paper decorations. In the far right corner behind the white plastic benches stood a fat, brightly dressed artificial Christmas tree with a gold star the size of a basketball jammed on top. Bing Crosby's *White Christmas* flooded the antiseptic air.

*God, I feel sick.*

As I skipped past the nurses' station, a loud, domineering voice barked at the back of my head.

"Gregory Lockland. Good to see you at long last."

I turned around. Nurse Agnes, a tall, mannish British woman in her late forties, stood still with her arms crossed. I gave her an apathetic shrug. She glared at me from two feet away, her wide hips looking ridiculous.

"What's up? What's happening?" I said with a smirk, swaying from side to side, my hands dug deep inside my jeans pockets.

"I personally don't care how charming you think you are, dimples and all. Your father has been looking for you all evening. He's expecting you at the chapel."

"Okee dokee," I said, and turned to leave.

"Greg, for Heaven's sake, go, wash your mouth. You reek of alcohol. Your father's going to be livid."

"Agnes, go home to your pussies."

I walked away before I could hear her scorn. I hated Nurse Agnes. The Director of Nursing reeked of pomposity. She always talked to me as if she were my mother. The nerve! But Agnes was right about my breath. I sneaked into a staff bathroom, grabbed a bottle of Listerine and gargled until the inside of my mouth felt sterile and raw. I splashed a few drops on my neck for good measure. In the mirror, my face was bursting like a ripe red tomato. I sighed.

*My father's no fool.*

I half ran and half hopped into the small chapel on the first floor. It was already packed with about fifty people. Scanning the hall, I found Mom, in her white nurse's uniform, standing on the left side by the third pew. As I marched toward her, I tripped over a stray wooden chair, making a loud thump. Everyone turned to look, so I stopped, grinned, and bowed. Mom was gesturing to me, waving her hands like mad, and I couldn't tell if she was angry or simply apprehensive. When I finally made it over to her, she put a finger over her mouth and frowned. Before I could respond with a smug "Missed me?" she turned me around to face a choir of two-dozen singers, draped in grape-colored robes, standing under the three-paned stained-glass mosaic. They were in the middle of a performance. Rather, I was in the middle of their performance. I spotted Dad standing to the side behind the choir, scowling at me.

I was in more trouble than I'd realized.

I started to twitch, and Mom had to pin me down. This was the last place I wanted to be, at some stuffy Christmas concert performed by some amateurish choir made up of some overworked hospital staff, while I was half drunk. It was a grave mistake. I should have stayed in the bathroom and taken a nap. Now I had to sit, no, stand, through a sorry singing practice.

I was about to lose it when the fluid arpeggio of Schubert's *Ave Maria* came alive from the organ. Though I'd listened to Mom play it a million times on our old piano, the piece always found a way to calm me. I shut my eyes and absorbed the music into my veins.

Then it happened.

A mezzo-soprano voice seized me, seeming to come from every corner of the chapel. It was everywhere, penetrating me from every angle—transcendent, rich and glorious.

If angels had voices, they sounded like that.

I opened my eyes and looked over at the choir. I saw her. A Chinese woman so stunning to me that I froze. I could tell she had a lovely figure underneath the unflattering curtain of a robe, almost as tall as the tallest men in the choir but sleek like a calla lily. Her oval face was graced with the most exquisite features any woman could hope for. Everything was in its perfect place, in perfect proportions—her long, black hair rippled down to her mid-back, coiled at the ends, those big and dark almond-shaped eyes. Mesmerizing.

If angels had faces, they looked like that.

For the following twenty minutes, the creature was the only thing I saw, the only thing I heard. She seemed to be singing to me, just me, and I felt an intense connection. At times, I couldn't comprehend her words, but I understood her songs. When that voice surged to the highest notes, my heart took flight with it.

There was love that gradually grew on you, and then there was love at first sight.

*The angel had claimed my soul.*

# An Old Friend

The Pacific Ocean is just as majestic as I remember—but vaster.

Fourteen hours and an eternity later, I find myself waiting in a long line at Immigration and Customs. New, modern, and sterile-gray, the Hong Kong International Airport was built on an island not much bigger than the airport itself, among the rolling hills and ragged South China shorelines, some twelve miles away from the heart of the central metropolis. Still, it's hard to miss the city's fervent heartbeats.

Finally it's my turn.

"Business or pleasure?" the officer asks in a monotone.

I don't know how to answer. Certainly I have no business being here and there's nothing pleasurable about this trip. I mumble something that resembles "closure." He takes a quick look at me, then thumps my passport with a large stamp.

The enormity of the region unfolds around me as my quiet taxi ride takes me places I've never been before. The sky is gray with overhanging clouds, and the air is heavy and warm, saturated with the acrid spawn of urban hubs—soot, sewage, and smog. The cab driver is telling me how things have changed dramatically on Lantau Island since the development of the new airport began a decade ago. In my succinct memory, Lantau was a place in my youth where my friends and I would come during the weekends, exploring the beaches unspoiled or trekking the paths least traveled. Rarely a summer would sweep by without at least a few days or even weeks spent discovering Lantau. It was only an hour or so of boat ride away, a quick escape from the fanatical rhythm elsewhere around this narrow nub in the South China Sea. The countryside was always lush with hues of green, and the surrounding sea seductive in deep, dark blue. On those early summer mornings, while we were high up in the hills, the layers of fog lingered in the valleys, forming a contiguous ring around the emerald heaps—scenery straight out of a Chinese watercolor painting, drenched in sublime divinity.

All I can see now are buildings and bridges and factories and construction sites and cars and people and a future without regard for its past.

Progress, I suppose.

On our way in, the taxi crawls through the thick traffic on the west side of Hong Kong Island, and I notice how things actually haven't changed much here on the strip, only more people, more stores, more cars, more cell phones, and less room to breathe. Gone are the Union Jacks. Instead, proud Chinese flags fly. Chaos abounds: loudspeakers, car horns, tram bells, stores brimming with Chinese herbs, dried scallops and ginseng root, side-street vendors and their cheap imitation merchandise, McDonald's, Ah Yee Noodles, obnoxious neon signs, tall glass houses. Hong Kong is like a grandmother—no matter how many more wrinkles she has, you will always remember her face.

The taxi drops me off outside of the Grand Hyatt in the fantastically packed Wanchai. It's a sparkling hotel towering on a prime cut of real estate. I check into a quiet corner room on the thirty-fifth floor that overlooks the spectacular Victoria Harbor and half of the Kowloon Peninsula. Down from my window, the new, mammoth Exhibition Center stretches out on the waterfront, a giant white turtle perched on a flat rock.

Breathtaking.

I sit on the King-size bed and extend my tired limbs, loop my hands around my sore neck, twist and crack it twice, and feel immediate relief. Exhausted, I lie down and shut my eyes for a second, catching my breath. It's so quiet that I almost forget I'm half a world away from Los Angeles and only moments into my past.

When I open my eyes, the night has fallen already. A second must have turned into hours. Darkness has enshrouded the room, and outside my window, the incredible view of the Kowloon Peninsula shimmers with a thousand tints of red, green, blue, yellow, silver and gold, bringing back indelible memories of my youthful indiscretion, somewhere buried in that conglomerate of blinking lights.

After taking a shower and changing into my sand khakis and black pullover, I walk out of the Hyatt and stroll along the waterfront promenade. The walls of people are dissipating, and along come the love-struck couples with their fingers entwined, dreaming of the future.

I lean over the railing and look across Victoria Harbor. It seems much smaller than I remember, but with twice as many boat lights. As two cargo ships sound their despondent horns, getting out of each other's way, I think of my father, my mother, and Lian—they're the reason I'm here, the reason I'm standing here, feeling an intense solitude.

And Kate, the only meaning in my life, is now a colossal ocean away. I wish she could see this marvelous sight.

I wander for about an hour, all the way to Causeway Bay, where endless streams of cars and people pour in and out, like lava spilling over Pompeii. It's more frantic than I recall.

Navigating through the armies of marching bobbleheads, I find my way to Ho Lee, a small Chinese barbecue and noodle shop, wedged between the Sogo Department Store and HMV Super Records. My chums and I used to come here after school once in a while for a steaming bowl of noodle soup. It's a pleasant surprise that the restaurant survives: the same cheesy markings, the rich and greasy aroma of roasted duck and wonton soup. I'm instantly seduced by the window's succulent display of five fat birds, hanging by their wiry necks, their skins gleaming golden and crisp.

The place is packed belly to butt. A spot opens up, but I have to share a round table with a young family of four and a stone-faced police officer in his early twenties. The intense mix of garlic, onions, oriental spices, chicken grease, barbecue and cigarette smoke is oddly scrumptious.

The bubbly and busy waitress seems genuinely impressed with my command of Cantonese. She can't decide whether I'm Chinese or a *gweilo* (foreign devil) so I tell her I'm coffee cream: half and half. She bursts into a blasting laugh and promises me the best bowl of homemade wonton noodle soup with roasted duck in the world. She's right. Ho Lee has the best wontons, and Chinese food in Hong Kong is a joy to begin with. When the bowl arrives, I dig in with gusto.

I'm savaging a piece of plump roasted duck breast when I hear a voice: "Greg Lockland?"

I turn my head and look up, my lips moist with grease. A man in an impressive gray suit stares at me with a surprised but amused look. I can't believe it. It's Choy, my buddy from Wah Yan College.

He looks as lanky as he was back then, but his wild, long hair is now cut short and slicked back, parted neatly on the right, and a dark pair of glasses sits squarely on the narrow ridge of his long nose.

"It is you. Oh my God! I am wondering...this *gweilo* looks familiar. Gweilo Greg! It has been years, you know?"

"I'm surprised to see you, too. What are you doing here?" I say as I wipe my mouth with a paper napkin.

"I am about to ask you. I work around here, you know, and I have been coming here every Friday night for the last five years. But what about you? What are you doing here?"

"I'm in town for a visit. You look exactly the same."

"No. Got a lot more wrinkles, and gray hair, and a fat beer belly. But you look good, real sharp, you know? Life has been treating you very well."

"Choy, why don't you sit?" I move over a bit and pull up another green plastic chair.

"Don't mind if I do." He plunks himself down. "I am actually waiting for my wife, Wendy."

"You're married?"

"I am thirty-two, you know. What do you think? I take it you are still single?"

"I am—well, actually, I'm in a relationship."

"Good for you. Good for you. I always thought you were the player type, you know?"

"So, what happened to you?"

"You mean, since Wah Yan? Well, where do I start? Okay...I went to Vancouver for seven years, and then I came back, and got married two years later. Wendy and I actually met in this restaurant, you know? Can you believe that? I am now working at the Hang Seng Bank. My branch is right around the corner, you know, and I live a few blocks away. You should come over for a visit. Our place is small, but we have a beautiful view of the harbor, you know. Anyway, work, eat, shit, work, pretty boring life. Enough about me, what about you?"

"I'm doing all right, all things considered." I glance away for a second. "My parents died. Three weeks ago."

"Oh God, I am so sorry."

"That's okay." I shrug. "Other than that, I'm just hanging in there. Happy to be alive."

Having said that, I stare into my bowl of noodle soup. A thick layer of fat has caked on the surface, and the lone duck carcass lies choked in the clump of egg noodles. The noises around me rush in.

"Are you still keeping in touch with David Kwan?" I ask.

"Oh yes. He teaches at the UST—you know, the University of Science and Technology. What a beautiful campus. Anyway, a group of us gets together once or twice a year. David is very fat now, you know? Humongous, and bald, too. You will not recognize him."

"Really? Uh, what about Martin? I suppose he went back to Australia?"

"No, he started working for the museum. He married a local girl and ended up staying here. Listen, if you are here for a while, we should get together some time, you know? Actually, we should have a party in your honor next weekend. A reunion. It has been such a long time. I know they would love to see you again. You know, you kind of just disappeared."

Choy hands me his business card: *Choy Ming Sing, Senior Financial Advisor.* Impressive. Everybody is building a life. Everybody has built a past.

A young woman walks in, and immediately I know she's Wendy. Besides the fact that she's twice as wide as Choy, their faces look the same. They could easily be twins. As Choy introduces us, a table for two becomes available. They argue whether to sit at my table instead, but my tablemates refuse to leave. As the baby screams, I tell Choy and Wendy I should really get going. I promise him I will call soon, but I can't promise anything else.

I walk out of the restaurant, feeling optimistic about my chances of finding Lian. The Causeway Bay MTR station is only three blocks away. I travel down two levels of steps and through the underground labyrinths of purple tiles and advertising banners. Once I get my metro-card from the vending machine and continue further down an escalator into the netherworld, I hop on a packed subway train going north. The lights in the subway car are so bright that I have to squint to make out the route map, and the PA sounds muffled. The size of the crowd seems to have tripled over the years. I count five stops and push myself through the herd of half-corpses in time to alight at the Kowloon Tong station. I easily get a little disoriented when I emerge from the exit. As I make a turn onto Waterloo Road, I finally feel an extraordinary sense of homecoming, looking at the fourteen-story building of the Baptist

Hospital three blocks ahead—its name in four enormous Chinese characters hung high on the side, suffused in a warm flood of spotlights, so warm perhaps to deflect the fact that people do get sick and die here.

To my surprise, the main entrance has been sealed off. What was once a double glass door is now a large wall of concrete, with a spread of moss crawling over it and a small, shriveled shrub crouching next to it. I track my way around the corner and to the west side of the building, head up a long, wide, serpentine driveway and find the main entrance with a hefty, ornate façade and two red taxicabs parked right out front. It used to be the much more obscure but busier entrance to the ER, where I more than once saw a great pandemonium unfold—fire engines, ambulances, and a cast of hundreds. Now it is hushed, like a midnight showing of *Ishtar* on Super Bowl Sunday.

The automatic door slithers open with a crisp swoosh, and I'm greeted by a bright glow of interior light. Gone are the tacky wall paintings and elevator music, but the stone-gray linoleum floor is waxed and polished to the same spiffy standard. Some things never change.

Right in front of me is a patient registration counter, behind which a young woman in a floral blouse sits idly, chewing on her nails. She offers me a rigid smile. "You want help?"

"Um, yes, actually. I don't know if she still works here, but I'm looking for a nurse, Ms. Lian Wan."

"I am sorry. I don't know."

"Can you check the staff roster for me?"

"I am sorry, no roster."

"I understand. Okay, well...then, do you know if Dr. Howard Cape's working tonight?"

"I am really sorry. I don't know."

"That's okay," I say, getting annoyed. "Let's try this, then. Can I get an attending nurse? Maybe she'll know?"

"I am sorry. Office hour over. If you want talk to nurse, come back tomorrow morning."

"I'd really like to talk to someone now."

"Is it emergency?"

"To me, yeah."

"The Emergency Room on the other side."

"Good Lord, does anyone know anything here?"

A familiar voice startles me from behind, "Is he causing any trouble?"

I turn and follow that voice. There she stands, about five feet away from me, hands anchored on those incredible hips—rounder in stature, grayer hair, and more lines on the face.

But it's her, no doubt.

# Dr. Drop-dead

I tore through the swinging double doors to the cafeteria, and the first person I saw was Agnes. She was standing by the doors, behind a small folding table, handing out little red raffle tickets. She narrowed her eyes, faked a smile, and pointed at the kitchen behind her. I shrugged and walked around the table. About forty people packed the cafeteria, most mingling near the dining tables with white tablecloths and poinsettia centerpieces. I looked around, hoping to spot my dream girl, but she hadn't shown up. *Maybe she won't.*

I dragged my feet into the kitchen. Dr. Howard Cape saw me and nodded. Dr. Cape was about thirty-two, tall and handsome with slightly graying hair and gold-rimmed glasses, somewhat bookish. The nurses loved him. Dr. Cape and I had even played hoops a couple of times in the summer. Something jelled between us.

"Hey, Doc," I said, almost completely sober.

"Greg, what are you doing here?" Howard asked, handing me a pair of kitchen mitts. "It's Christmas Eve. Why aren't you out having fun?"

"Two words: my dad." I dropped my shoulders. "He always has a way of ruining my life."

"Don't be so dramatic. It's not so bad here. And the nurses adore you."

"They're all so old. And they love you, not me, Dr. Drop-dead."

Howard laughed. "Well, I'm off the market," he said. "Hey, can you help me with the lasagna in the oven?"

"Sure." I walked over and pulled one of the large trays out of the lower oven. I buried my nose in the steam of the concoction of tomato and meat sauce and cheese and spices. "Why are we here, anyway?"

"It's late, so the chefs went home for Christmas. They did make the food, though. We just need to serve it." Howard took out another tray and laid it on the kitchen counter. "No, I'm afraid it's just you, me, Agnes, and Theresa over there."

"That sucks," I groaned. "So, who's the lucky girl?"

"What lucky girl?"

"C'mon, the cat's out of the bag. You're off the market, you said. You have to tell me now."

"Some other time, kiddo."

"That's cool." I put the fourth tray of lasagna onto the kitchen counter. One of the good things about the hospital kitchen was that it had big ovens. You could put a whole person in there and nobody would notice.

"What about you? Any sweetheart for a good-looking kid like you?" Howard asked.

"Not really. My dad put me in an all-boy's school. I don't get around much."

"Dr. Lockland's pretty tough, huh?"

"Tell me about it. I can't get him off my back."

"My dad was like that," Howard said. "And you know what I did? I came here, all the way from Pittsburgh, Pennsylvania."

"That's a long way from here. I was in Pittsburgh once, a long time ago."

"I know, your mom told me. She told me all sorts of things about you."

"I can't believe her."

"Relax, I'm just kidding. But moms do that. You're still young. Let her have some fun until you're too old like I am. Then you'll want her to talk more about you and less about having grandchildren."

"She didn't tell you anything embarrassing, did she?"

"To tell you the truth, I don't think she knows what you're really up to," Howard said with a wink.

"Good." I tossed him a grin and went out with two trays of lasagna.

I returned to the kitchen and slipped the mitts under another tray.

"Be careful. That was the last one. It's really hot," Howard said.

I turned, trying to tell Dr. Cape that everything was under control. Howard wasn't talking to me. Instead, he was standing in front of the ovens, taking out a long tray of golden scones. Leaning on Howard was a nurse with black hair braided up and tucked under her white cap, her long, svelte legs extending from her uniform. She turned toward me.

I almost fell over. It was her.

# Nurse You-know-what

"Nurse Agnes," I shout.

"Gregory Lockland, fancy seeing you here," Agnes says, sounding uncharacteristically sincere.

"You remember me?" I ask.

"Do I remember you? Is that a real question or are you taunting me?"

"Agnes, no one can ever taunt you."

"What are you doing here? I thought you were in California."

"I've taken a leave and decided to give good old Hong Kong a long overdue visit. This city has grown so much—I can't believe it."

"Hasn't it really? Good gracious, so have you. My oh my, all grown up and devilishly handsome."

"Agnes, you know you can't make me blush."

"Still obnoxious, I see." She glares at me, but there's a glint of warmth in her eyes. "Really, why are you here at the hospital?"

"Um, don't ask me why, but I need to find Lian Wan. Do you remember her?"

"Lian Wan. Let me see." She rubs her chin. "Pretty girl, long black hair, used to go out with Howard Cape. I might be a bitter old hag, but my memory still serves me well."

"So, do you know where she is?"

"You mean now? No, I don't. She left Baptist a long time ago."

"Do you know where she went?"

"I believe she went to Q.E. Hospital. Only one way to find out for real. Come with me."

I follow her down the hallway. We make two lefts. I don't recognize anything at all. The whole floor must have been remodeled from the ground up. What was once the ER is now a maze of white walls, wood trim and bland offices.

In silence, Agnes marches forward in quick, long strides, and I follow closely. She pushes open a door and leads me down a flight of stairs, and I remember this space. I must have had gone up and down these stairs a thousand times. The harsh florescent lights feel oddly comforting, and the hollow echoes of our footsteps conjure nostalgia of flirtations and secret handholding.

When we are on the first floor, I recognize the generic hospital décor, the rows of exam rooms with little white doors and plastic curtains, and the lingering antiseptic smell. The lights are off, and it's silent as a mortuary. I feel like I'm going through a ghost town, every door and floor tile etched with distant history.

As we round a corner, I recognize the large, old oak door to the chapel. I stop in front of the door and close my eyes. I can see Lian on that choir stand, in that purple robe, and I can hear her angelic voice seeping through that solid wood.

I run after Agnes. Eventually she stops in front of an office door. The silver nameplate on the light wood door reads: SUPERVISOR, AGNES E. CUNNINGHAM.

"What happened to the Director thing?" I ask.

"They always prefer some younger broad," she says, inviting me in and closing the door behind me. "I was once the younger broad. Believe it or not, Theresa Lee is running the show now."

"Theresa? You mean Tiny Mouse Theresa?"

"She's not tiny anymore." She laughs irreverently. "We're old friends, so I was happy for her. And to be honest, at my age, I don't need the politics. I'm grateful."

She pulls out the bottom drawer of a gray metal file cabinet and sifts through a thick mass of documents. "Let's see what we have. It's like a time capsule in here...Wan...Wan...Wan...Lian... Ah ha, here it is."

She studies a piece of paper, then looks up. "I was right. She transferred to Q.E."

"You mean Queen Elizabeth Hospital, right?"

"Precisely. Let me see. October first, the same year you left."

"That's great. If I take a taxi now I should be there in about twenty minutes," I say, turning toward the door.

"Wait a minute. Not so fast. What's the hurry? What is it that you want from Lian? Did she owe you money or something?"

"You're so nosy."

"You know me. Good old Nurse Cunt—"

"What?"

"Think I didn't know? Remember, nurses talk," she says. "You never really liked me. And that's fine, because I never really liked you either."

"You're always so damn blunt. I didn't really dislike you that much."

"You're also such a terrible liar. The contempt you had for me. Goodness gracious!"

"I was only fifteen."

"Youth is a marvelous scapegoat. It doesn't matter. I'm almost sixty-four now—too old to hold any grudges." She frowns, realizing something. "By the way, are you here by yourself? Where are your mom and dad?"

"Agnes, I don't know how to tell you." I let out a sigh. "They both died a few weeks ago."

Her face freezes as if she's just seen the devil. Then she lets out a long, agonized sigh. "Oh."

She covers her face with her hands and starts to wobble. I put my hands on her shoulders, steadying her, and guide her to a chair. I sit her down.

"Stephen and Helen? How did that happen?" she says, catching her breath.

"A car accident. I'm so sorry, Agnes."

"No, I'm sorry. You poor thing."

She pats my hands solemnly. I'm startled by this gentler side of Agnes. The hard edges of her personality seem to have dissolved completely. All of a sudden, she seems like an old friend.

"What happened?"

"He had a heart attack, and his car crashed into my mom, outside their house."

"Oh Jesus." She sobs.

I had no idea the news would hit her so hard. I hold her stoically, letting her have her moment. After a while, her wailing starts to quiet down. She reaches for the box of Kleenex on her desk, pulls out a big wad, and blows her nose loudly.

"It's okay. At least they didn't suffer much. And they're together in heaven now."

"Rubbish. You never believed in that religion nonsense."

I shrug.

"I want to show you something," she says, pulling herself up on my right arm, grabbing it tightly. She drags me toward a wall and points at eight framed pictures.

They are all black and white eight-by-ten photographs, marvelously composed. Simple architecture juxtaposed against complex and intriguing life objects: a wilting orchid framed by a stone arch, two old men playing chess in front of the Hong Kong City Hall building, a younger, frowning Agnes hunching over the geometric lines of the linoleum floor, her face twisted with disgust. Next to that is a high-contrast portrait of an old, diminutive Chinese lady, sitting on a foot-high three-legged stool in a small stone-paved alley, her face dry like a shriveled prune, laden with deep, crisscrossed lines of life's rich tales. Her eyes droop with sadness, as if she has been waiting for something or someone for most of her life. She's still waiting.

"That's my old land lady, Po Ma, in Wanchai. She's long dead now, but somehow her spirit lives on in this picture," Agnes says. "Your father was a great photographer."

"He took these?"

"He had such steady hands. Such strong and precise hands. He's, was, a phenomenal surgeon, Greg. He also had a great eye for things. People, really. Very perceptive. He took many of these."

"I never knew."

"He didn't take them with him when he left. They just got thrown out over time, or stacked with the other rubbish. A shame. So I framed some and hung them on my walls," she says, and tears start running down her cheeks. "I'll miss Stephen so much."

"Good god!"

"What is it?"

"Is that Lian?" I ask, pointing at the last picture on the far left, the one with a young woman draped in a white sheet, posing as a goddess against two Greek columns. I see only the contour of her sleek body, and her eyes through the crevice of the sheet—I never forgot those eyes.

"I'll be darned. It looks like her. I never even noticed."

"Agnes, did he ever talk about Lian at all?"

"He was a quiet man. He never talked much, especially not about any particular nurse. No, I don't think so, other than a passing comment about what a pretty girl she was, or something like that."

"Thank you, Agnes."

"What for? What did I do?"

I smile and swing my arms around her shoulders. She looks at me as if I'm possessed. I realize I've desperately needed some kind of continuity in my life. Strangely, I'm finding it in a person I so despised all those years ago. Agnes is a link to my past, and to my father, my mother and Lian.

"Greg, where are you staying?"

"The Grand Hyatt in Wanchai."

"That's like a thousand dollars a night, isn't it?"

"Something like that, why?"

"You will cancel your room tomorrow and come stay with me."

"Agnes?"

"That's not a suggestion. I have a nice, cozy spare room in the back."

"Wait—"

"Shhh—it's settled, then. Done. Come back here tomorrow and pick me up. I get off at ten in the morning. If I don't see you here, I'll come to the Grand Hyatt and hunt you down."

"Do I have any say in this?"

"No."

"God, you're so—"

"You know me. Good old Nurse You-know-what."

When she puts it that way, I have no choice but to comply. So goodbye mini-bar and hello crammed two-closet apartment. And cats—conniving, ugly, smelly, hairy, evil cats.

# Lian

"Hey, come over here. Meet Lian," Howard said.

I dropped the tray and leaped over.

"Lian, this is Greg, Dr. Lockland's son," Howard said.

"Hello," Lian said, her voice as soft as she looked. She spoke in exceptionally fluent English, a slight British accent. "I have heard a lot about you."

"Lian. Such a pretty name," I said to her. "What does it mean in Chinese?"

She nodded. "It means *lotus*."

"How old are you, anyway?"

"Greg, that's rude," Howard interjected.

"I am twenty-one," she said, regardless. "And you?"

"He's seventeen. Only a kid," Howard said.

"Old enough," I said, ignoring Howard.

"Old enough to drink, too. I saw you at the concert. Quite an entrance," she said.

"Oh, God," I grumbled.

"What happened?" Howard asked.

"Everyone was getting bored, and you walked in and made that noise with that chair. It was funny when you bowed," she said. "The funniest thing was I heard your father curse behind me. I had never heard Dr. Lockland curse before."

"Yes, he curses. Trust me," I said.

"And I missed the whole thing," Howard said.

"Yes, where were you?" she asked, elbowing him.

"I got tied up with a patient, then I had to come down here with Agnes to get things ready. I'm sorry I missed the concert. How was it?"

"She was perfect," I said. "Magnificent."

She shook her head with grace.

"She is perfect," Howard said, cocked his head, smiled and winked at her.

"Well, people are waiting for the food," I said.

I rushed back to the dining hall with the last tray of lasagna. I felt funny. I felt warm. I felt sick in my chest. I was sick in love with this magnificent woman. I was sick in love with Howard's girl.

One of the custodians came over, slapped his large, calloused hand on my shoulder. "Merry Christmas! *Nay ho ma?* Where your Pa?"

"I don't know, Old Chow. He should be here soon," I said, unable to keep myself from glancing at Lian where she stood, now, behind the counter with Howard.

"You like?" Old Chow asked.

"Yeah, I like," I said with a laugh.

Old Chow, as everyone called him, was in his early fifties, almost as wide as he was short, strong as a bulldozer, with slickly pomaded gray hair and tobacco-stained teeth, two of them missing. Sometimes when I was waiting for my parents to finish their shifts, Old Chow would chat with me in his broken English, telling crude, dirty jokes. Married with four children, he wanted six more but his wife wouldn't put out. Time to time, he would smuggle me condoms and Marlboros. A good guy.

"Beautiful girl. No like ma wife. Eh, ma wife ugly."

"No, she's not that ugly," I lied, knowing that Old Chow spoke the truth.

"You ask girl dinner."

"She must have eaten already."

"Ask her go dinner."

"Oh, you mean ask her out. Old Chow, she's already taken."

"What you mean?"

"She has a boyfriend."

"So?"

"What do you mean by 'so'? You don't ask someone out if she's already seeing someone else."

"Who say?"

"That's just the rule."

"Rule? You too young believe rule. Live! You see something you like, you get."

"Is that what Confucius said?"

"Smart boy. But no smart here," he said, pointing to his heart.

"What do you want me to do? Go over there and ask her out in front of Dr. Cape?"

"No?"

"It doesn't work that way."

"I think something. You wait." Old Chow patted my shoulder, then walked out of the cafeteria.

# Welcome Home

After I get back to my hotel room, I call my best friend Patrick in Hartford, Connecticut.

"Bud," Patrick's voice booms in my ear. "Haven't heard from you since the funeral—are you all right?"

"I know why he had the letters."

"Who? What are you talking about?"

"The letters. The letters Lian wrote. The letters that brought me here. The letters."

I go on telling him the story about Lian, the letters I found, the reason I'm here in Hong Kong, and the picture on Agnes's wall.

"Lian and my father definitely had an affair," I say.

"Did you talk to her already?"

"God, I'm so stupid..." I breathe hard. "I kept hoping that she actually wrote me, that the letter was for me. Maybe because I left her—so completely? That's why she ran to my father...oh shit."

"Okay, calm down. You don't know anything yet. You need to find Lian and ask her."

"I know there was definitely something between them."

"Where are you now, by the way?"

I look at the alarm clock. "It's after three."

"Are you drunk?"

"I had a couple of Jack Daniel's at the bar. Why?"

"You need to get some rest, bud."

"I'm all wired. I can't sleep...Patrick, I haven't called Kate yet."

"What? She didn't know?"

"Well, I told her I had to go away for a bit. Personal business or something."

"You have to tell her."

"I don't know what to say."

"Tell her you're safe and tell her where you are. Tell her everything."

"I can't."

"Why not?"

"I just can't. She won't understand."

"What won't she understand? Try her."

"I can't."

"Bud, try her."

I pick up the phone and dial the first four digits, then put it back down. I just don't think I can talk to Kate. Not now, not when I realize what a fool I've been. I'm so obsessed with Lian now. How can Kate ever understand what I'm doing here?

My suspicions and jealousy make me realize how much I still feel for Lian.

How much I still want her. Maybe love her.

How can I ever tell Kate that?

I am startled by a loud banging on the door. I slit my right eye open and am besieged by a bright glare that stuns my senses. The room spins in a flush of white light. I might have died and gone to who-knows-where. Then a brash voice brings me back to Earth.

"Greg, open up."

I drop my left foot on the carpeted floor and manage to push myself up with a right arm that seems unattached to my body. I'm aching as though I have been sleeping on a rock all night. My head. An unbelievably pinching, throbbing headache. I drag myself to the door. "Who—eh, what?"

"Have you forgotten our date?"

It's Agnes.

"Just a minute."

"Open the door, Greg."

"I'm not dressed yet."

"I don't care. Open the door. I don't want to wait out here."

"Agnes, give a guy some privacy, would you?"

"Open up." More banging.

"All right, all right. You don't have to wake up the whole damn floor." I open the door.

Agnes barges in as if she's a jealous wife sniffing out a cheating husband. She's wearing a frumpy yellow shirt and black polyester Capris. Here I am, half-naked in my underwear, gruff, unshaven, and thirsty like a blind bat dying for blood.

She takes a quick look at me. "Terrible night you had?"

"You can say that. I guess I had a little too much to drink."

"You drink?"

"Sure. Who's there to yell at me now that my dad's dead?"

She pushes me into the bathroom. "Hippity hop. Get yourself all spruced up and spiffy now. We have to go."

When I get out of the bathroom, wearing only a terrycloth towel around my waist, she's already packed my suitcase and set it on the bed. She sits in an armchair by the window, pressing her thin lips on a coffee mug. The TV is mumbling in the background, images from CNN flashing on the screen.

"They call this tea?" she says, puckering her lips. She gets up and turns off the TV.

I unzip the suitcase and find my clothes ruffled and crinkly all over the place. I take out a green polo shirt, a pair of white briefs, and some black socks.

"Do you mind?" I say.

"Pardon me." She turns toward the window. "You have a great view here."

"Well, thanks to you that's the last time I'll see it." I drop the wet towel on the floor and pull on the briefs.

"It'll save you money. A few weeks will run you broke here."

"A few weeks? Once I find Lian, I'm out of here."

"That's what I said. A few weeks," she says with a snicker.

"Agnes, I didn't think this would ever happen, not in a million years. You, me naked, alone in a hotel room."

"Life's full of bizarre twists," she says, staring thoughtfully out the window. "I never imagined not seeing Stephen and Helen again."

I frown. I take two tablets of Advil from a bottle and pop them into my mouth.

"Tell me something about my father," I say, then take a sip of water from a glass on the dresser and swallow the pills.

"You know your father."

"No, tell me what you know about him."

"Your father was a very serious man."

"Tell me something I don't know already."

"He was also a very dedicated man. Unlike so many other doctors, he really cared about everyone who came into his care."

"His job was his life."

"His family was his life."

I study Agnes as I put on my khakis. Her eyes are fixed on something outside.

"He was so young when we first met. He was younger than you are now," she says, her voice turning soft.

"I thought he didn't start at Baptist until he was forty-eight."

"We knew each other way before then, when he lived in London."

"That I didn't know."

"Suppose you didn't know this either, that we shared a flat in Soho, above a small bakery. A flat straight out of a Dickens novel. Every morning the smell of freshly baked bread and scones and coffee would wake us up."

"What was he doing in London? I thought he was practicing medicine in California then."

"He was. He was also quite a dreamer. He took a sabbatical and went to Paris first, then came to London, to study photography. He sure was a charmer—so handsome and articulate. And talented. You remind me a lot of him." She turns toward me. "He went back to the States after three months."

"Why?"

"Family. His family needed him. That's all he said before he suddenly packed up and left. We stayed in touch every now and then over the years. Eventually I came to Hong Kong, and one thing led to another. He was here with his young family and took up residency at Baptist."

"How come I never knew about this?"

"You never paid attention. You never asked. You were always running about, playing havoc like some little bugger without a leash. You just thought I was an old useless hag, a thorn in the side of your young, exciting life."

"But my mom hated you."

"I know. I said your father and I were good friends. I didn't say anything about Helen. To this day, I still think your mother thought I had an affair with your father in London."

"Get out of here."

"Can you just imagine, me and your father? That would be a big laugh. But your mother thought otherwise. She was very insecure."

"That's fucked up."

"I liked your mother though. She was a wonderful mother to you."

"She was."

I close my eyes and see my mom in her white uniform. I draw a deep breath. "Tell me more," I say.

"Maybe some other time. We have to go now."

"What's the hurry?"

"We have a hospital to visit."

She slams my suitcase shut and zips it up. She lifts it off the bed with her strong arms and drags it to the door. I struggle with my left shoe as I chase her down the hall, her incredible rump disappearing around a corner.

Twenty minutes later, our taxi stops in front of a hospital, and Agnes tells the driver to wait. "He's paying," she says to him and winks at me.

"This isn't Queen Elizabeth," I say.

"Who said anything about Q.E.?"

"But I thought we're looking for Lian."

"I already checked. She quit Q.E. ten years ago. Nobody knows where she went."

I let out a dejected breath. "What're we doing here, then?"

"We need to pick up somebody."

I follow Agnes into the hospital lobby. It's one of those small, crowded, outdated public hospitals situated among the slums in central Kowloon. The walls are peeling and an odd, pungent, almost sulfuric odor of Chinese medicine pervades the air. Compared to this, Baptist is like the Ritz-Carlton.

We exit the elevator on the third floor. As I follow Agnes into a tiny room at the far end, I'm surprised to see Old Chow, the custodian at Baptist, sitting on the edge of a bed.

"Finally," he says.

"Old Chow? What're you doing here?"

"Sick stomach."

"He had diverticulitis," Agnes says. "It's all that meat he eats. I told him to lay it off for a few months."

"Kill me la," Old Chow grumbles.

"I told him to go to Baptist but he wouldn't listen," she says, and turns to Old Chow. "You never listen."

"Why spend money? Free here, and Chinese medicine."

"I'll never understand Chinese medicine. But, if it works for you," she says, nudging him.

I stare at them, puzzled. Agnes catches a glimpse of my face, and she bursts into a deafening laugh.

"Old Chow and I are together."

"Since when?"

"Since divorce. Goddamn wife rob me," Old Chow says.

"He caught her cheating with another man. Can you believe that atrocious bitch ever finding someone else? Pigs sure can fly," she says. "So he divorced her, and she took everything. She was the one cheating, and she got the apartment, the money. It's a sick world. Thank God the children are all grown."

"I'm so sorry, Old Chow." I pat him on his back.

"Happy see you." Old Chow flashes me his dark yellow teeth. He is almost bald now, only a few white hairs sticking out here and there. His arms are just as big and strong as before, though, and his laugh as hearty and sincere.

"So how did you two?" I gesture vaguely at them.

"You know, love at first sight," he says, winking at me.

She shakes her head, grinning. "It's a long process, years in the making," she says. "He needed a place to stay after he moved out of his apartment. It just happened."

"Wow," I say.

"And you thought I was a dried up old maid." She breaks into a coarse laugh.

"She tough lady," Old Chow chimes in. "We go?"

"Let me get you a wheelchair," I say.

"This is not America. You walk here," Agnes says.

I put Old Chow's right arm over my left shoulder and lift him up from the bed. For someone his age, he's solid and heavy. Agnes takes a brown paper bag from his hand and carries it for him.

"I walk," he protests. We walk out of the room and toward the elevator. He turns to me. "Greg, you want find Lian?"

"Yeah, but it seems like my luck's running out. Agnes told me she left Queen Elizabeth a long time ago. I don't know where else to look."

"Get P.I.?"

"What pie?"

"Private Investigator," Agnes says. "You'll need a good one."

"I know people," he says. "Greg, I find Lian."

I wink at him in appreciation. Even with his heavy body leaning into my side, I feel as if a grave weight has been lifted off my shoulders. I know Old Chow will find Lian for me. He always keeps his promises.

The taxi makes its final stop in Homantin. I look out of the window and realize it's parked on Princess Margaret Road, right in front of a gated, five-story residential building with large black-framed windows, concrete walls and balconies with rectangular parapets—quintessentially sixties. We are at my family's old apartment.

"What the—"

"Your parents never told you I took over the flat after they left?" Agnes says.

"No."

"It was before the housing frenzy in the nineties, and your father was a very generous man. Come on up."

Ten minutes later, I still can't believe I'm standing in our old apartment again. They are all there, exactly where they were years ago: the dull eggshell walls, the triple windows with black steel frames, even the white cabinets and cedar bookcases. I stare out of the windows, watching the traffic go by. The noise is soothing.

"Ahem, Greg, let me show you your room," Agnes says.

"I thought you had cats," I say.

"Old Chow's allergic to cats, so I got rid of them. Hardest thing I've ever done."

"You must really love him."

I follow her into the small bedroom at the back. Out of the windows is the little city park across the street, the trees taller and greener and the concrete benches as deserted as before. In the confinement of these four walls I spent four years of my life, writing stories and listening to U2 and the Police and Queen and Bruce Springsteen, being a lonesome, horny teenager with my private stack of *Penthouse*. Life was simpler then.

"Why didn't you tell me?" I ask as I lean over the bed.

"And ruin a surprise?" She smiles. I come forward and give her the biggest hug I've ever given.

After Agnes returns to the hospital for her evening shift, Old Chow insists that I take him to the park across the street. I protest. He won't listen, so we end up alone in the park, sitting at a small concrete table. He takes out a yellow wooden box. The box flips over and unfolds into a chessboard, emptying the green and red chess pieces onto the table.

"*Cheung kei?*"

"Oh no, not Chinese chess."

"Very simple. I teach you."

"All right."

"Like American chess. You think, plan, move."

I lay the pieces on the chessboard and sit across from Old Chow.

"So Old Chow, how long have you been with Agnes?" I ask, making my first move with a Pawn.

"Seven years."

"I didn't know you had eyes for her."

"No. First no like woman. Loud mouth and big ass. Ai-yah. But she give place to stay. Sudden she like angel. I treat her nice, too. Flowers, clothes, romantic dinners, massage. She just woman inside."

"Well, I hate to say it, but I think you've softened her. I've never seen her so warm and kind. You've done a great job."

"I no do nothing. She has tough shell. Really beautiful woman, here," he says, pointing to his heart.

"You don't smoke anymore?"

"She lose cats, I lose cigarettes."

I smile as I take his Rook. He swears loudly in Cantonese, then makes a move with his Cannon and takes my Bishop.

"Why you want see Lian?" he asks, pondering his next move.

"I have something to ask her."

"You go dinner like I tell you?"

"Yeah, you old bastard. I finally did ask her out to dinner. That was a long time ago."

"Sex?"

"Old Chow, stop asking these questions."

"What, shy? Come, man to man."

"We did it. Sure. So cut it out."

"Lucky. She beautiful."

"Yeah, she was. I wonder what she looks like now."

"I tell you I find her. I have connection."

"I know. But there are like seven million people here, and God knows if she's still in Hong Kong."

"I find her," he says, and moves in, taking my other Bishop.

"Hey. I don't like that."

"No like to lose?"

"Never."

"Lose chess game? Lose money? Job? Woman? Lose love?"

I look at him as he takes my second Rook. I'm losing fast. The sky starts to rumble, and the tepid wind picks up in earnest.

"I think a storm's coming. We should go in," I say.

He makes his next move, taking my Cannon, and yells, "*Cheung gwun!*" I look at the board and realize I have no more moves. He has my General pinned. The game is over.

"We should really go in," I say, tapping my fingers on the table.

"Greg, one face, many side. See, you lose cheung kei game. But you make Old Chow very happy. You win."

"It's not that simple."

"Simple as you like," he says as we gather the pieces into the box. "Simple as you like."

It starts to pour. Hard.

# The Writer and the Nurse

When I returned to the kitchen, Howard and Lian were whispering to each other. They stopped and looked at me, then at each other, smiling.

"What's so funny?" I asked.

Lian came over, some paper towels in hand. "You have tomato sauce on your face." She gently wiped the sauce off my cheek, and for a moment, I wished I were drenched in tomato sauce.

"Greg, your mom told me you're going back to the States for college. Is that right?" Howard asked.

"I don't know. I sent in a couple applications, but I haven't heard anything yet. I know for sure, though, that I won't be in Hong Kong this fall."

"Where then?" he asked.

"Somewhere in California. UCLA, USC, Stanford. I have a good feeling about Berkeley, though."

"Medical school?"

"No way. I'm thinking maybe journalism or communications."

"Yeah, your mom told me that you wrote. That's pretty cool."

"Well, not if it doesn't pay the bills." I mimicked my father's deep, stern voice: "You must be responsible for yourself and your family. Writing is a dream. And dreaming is so Bohemian. And Bohemian doesn't pay."

"Don't listen to him. Follow your heart."

"What did your parents want you to be?"

"A doctor."

"Ah ha!"

"But that's what I really wanted anyway. Don't be such a smart ass, kiddo."

"What about you, Lian?" I turned to her. "You always wanted to be a nurse?"

"Since I was four," she said. "But I also wanted to be an opera singer."

"An opera singer," I said. "Wow. And I thought writing stories was cool."

The PA came on and we heard a nurse's voice: "Dr. Cape, please come to Outpatient. Dr. Cape, please come to Outpatient."

"Got to go. You kids think you can handle yourself here?" Howard said.

He took Lian's hand and gave it a gentle pat, then smiled and left.

Lian and I stood in awkward silence. I couldn't help but look over at her from time to time. I was never nervous in my life, but there I was, knots in my stomach and tongue in my throat. My mind was going in circles, trying to find something to say. Something witty, something smart. Nothing came out. I kept myself busy getting the scones into a big metal pan as she put the butter cookies in another pan. We were standing no more than three feet away from each other, but at different ends of the world. Two pans, two worlds.

I glanced over again, and our eyes met. A jolt of electricity. I grinned at my silliness, felt my face warming, and turned back to the scones, which seemed to take me forever to finish. *Oh that tension.* I decided I must say something to break the ice, even if it sounded stupid.

"So, what do you think of Dr. Cape?" Immediately I realized how stupid I sounded. Dr. Cape's perfect, she would certainly say.

"I am very sorry, did you say something?"

"What do you think of Dr. Lockland?" I asked instead.

"I think he is a brilliant surgeon. Angry sometimes, and very tough, but I am glad to be working for him," she said. "I admire him a lot."

"You work for my dad?"

"Yes, I am one of his assisting nurses at the OR."

"He never mentioned you."

"I am sure he doesn't know who I am."

"Sure he does. You're very beautiful. The most beautiful girl I've ever known."

She smiled. "So the rumor is true."

"What rumor?"

"That you are a big ladies' man. You say nice things to girls."

"No, not really," I said, tittering. "You've heard about me?"

"A little." She shrugged.

"Don't believe the other nurses. They like to tease me. I'm really a nice guy." I knew she didn't believe my defense. I didn't either. "How come I've never seen you around here?"

"I usually work the early morning shift. I am here tonight because of the Christmas concert, and I don't have to work tomorrow."

"That's right. You know, normally I won't even wake up until like two in the afternoon, and the last thing I want to do is to come down here and look at sick people."

"You are funny," she said. "And aggressive."

"You think?"

"Oh, I am sorry if I am too forward."

"Look, modesty and politeness don't work for me. If you ask the other nurses, you'll find out that I don't believe in any of that. I'm probably one of those...what do you call them? Yeah, 'Ugly Americans'—loud and obnoxious."

"You are not obnoxious. You are sweet."

"Thank you," I said. "And Dr. Cape is a very lucky man."

Silence fell between us again.

Jealousy crept up my chest. I wanted to throw away every caution and chivalry, ask Lian out on a date, right there, right then. *Screw Dr. Cape. Screw him.* Lian deserved better. Yeah, someone like me.

But that moment of envious rage whisked past as quickly as it struck. Howard Cape was my friend and he always treated me like an equal, a brother even. And brothers don't steal from brothers.

"Greg, may I ask you a question?" Lian broke the silence between us.

"You can ask me anything."

"What do you like? Small things, big things, anything at all."

"Why do you ask?"

She smiled instead of saying anything. That only made me want to tell her more about myself.

"Well, for one thing, I like the smell of coffee when I wake up."

"That is nice. I don't drink coffee."

"Oh, I like only the smell of coffee, not the taste of it."

"I see. What else?"

"Let's see...how much time do you have?"

She laughed, like distant whispers of a waterfall—I was definitely in love.

"I like to write," I said. "I'm writing a children's story now. It's called *Oscar and the Potbelly Pig.* I know. The title is stupid."

She gestured me to go on.

"Well, I like singing in the shower—screeching is more like it. I like shrimp marinara with garlic and basil. Lemon iced tea. Coca Cola. Asian food. Yeah. I love Asian food. I like the ocean, the Pacific in particular. Red Mustangs. I like movies, good ones, bad ones, especially the old ones with Audrey Hepburn and Cary Grant, and *Star Wars*, *Aliens*, and all those movies that scare the bejesus out of me. Listen to me, going on and on. What about you?"

"I—"

"Ay..." a voice interrupted her. It was a short man in light blue scrubs with a buzz haircut. "*Kei ta di sik muk gei si lei la?*" I knew enough Cantonese to know that the man was asking for the rest of the food.

"*Ho fai la*," Lian said. She turned to me. "We should take the food out. These people are so impatient."

I sighed in resignation. As I turned, Lian put her hand on mine. I quivered.

"You like to sing, Greg?"

"Uh, only in the shower."

"Would you like to join us later in caroling the patient floors? It would be fun."

"I can't—I'd love to."

I took the pans of scones and butter cookies and floated out of the kitchen. My parents had arrived. Mom gave me a calm nod as my father talked to Dr. Liu, ignoring me completely, which was actually for once a good thing. I was setting the pans on the table when I felt a tap on my shoulder.

"You ask girl dinner?" Old Chow said.

"Was that you who paged Dr. Cape?"

"Yes. Smart, no? You ask girl dinner?"

"No, Old Chow. I didn't get a chance."

"Why?"

"The timing's not right. Maybe next time."

"Next time no easy," Old Chow said, pointing at the kitchen.

I saw Dr. Cape's back as he leaned over Lian. I was jealous, but I could deal with that now. I had finally met my dream girl. Best of all, I was going to see her again. Singing, of all things.

"That's okay, Old Chow. Really, that's okay," I said, grinning at myself. "Thank you. I have a feeling that I'll be coming here more often. Bright and early."

"Good." Old Chow stretched his hand past me, going for the butter cookies.

# Chasing Ghosts

While waiting for news about Lian, I spend my free time roaming the city, revisiting my youth.

I remember a little record store in Causeway Bay where I bought my first Queen album after searching all over town with twenty dollars in my pocket. To my disappointment, the record store has disappeared. In its place is an ostentatious beauty salon with an oversized poster of some pop star named Fei Wong stuck to the front window, a choking chemical odor oozing out the open door, pervading the air. Gone also are my favorite bookstore—Simon Says, in Yaumatei—and Hing Fai, the best sports equipment store in Mongkok. I run around town trying to find these relics of my past, only to find that I'm chasing ghosts.

However, the sight of my alma mater on Waterloo Road is comforting and real as ever. Fenced within the high granite walls, steel fences and huge iron front gates, the serene campus of Wah Yan College still stands among the blanket shades of oak trees, seemingly untouched by the changing times.

Through the gates I see the red brick school hall, where I had my first social dance with a girl from Sacred Heart. She was a doll—would I have been dancing with someone who wasn't? She was sixteen, a fine blossom with short black hair and glasses, smitten with a fourteen-year-old Eurasian boy who spoke little Chinese but knew a thing or two about slow dancing. There were chocolate ice cream and lemon cakes. Paper stars and moons on the ceiling. Elvis Presley.

I don't remember her name.

I enter the campus, and walk down a narrow pathway to the athletic wing, taking my time in the trudge across the grassy soccer field where many of our fierce matches were won and lost. The cheers are gone now. Between the goalposts on this lush, fresh-cut grass stands only a thirty-two-year-old man in his $250 pair of Perry Ellis shoes.

I pass a vending machine and stop to buy myself a pineapple cream bar. Wandering back to the classroom complex, I instantly surrender to the familiar scents of perennials, palms and banana trees. Classes are in session. I sit on a shaded stone bench by the principal's office, licking the popsicle and listening to the thumping sound of a few basketballs nearby. Four schoolboys in their handsome dark green uniforms romp in the parking lot, shouting at each other. My eyes follow these stray cads who don't seem to belong to any classrooms, and I see my shadow. How young and wild I once was.

A mild lift of wind ruffles my hair. I start to hum the school anthem and surprise myself by remembering every word. I never felt like I belonged here. I was a half-breed in a foreign city—an outcast in its old school.

I get up and toss the popsicle stick into a trashcan. I walk around the corner, toward one of the three teacher's rooms. I reach for the door, then decide against calling on the old teachers. Half of them have probably retired already, and I don't know what to say to the half that's stayed. I turn to leave.

"I remember you."

I recognize the owner of that voice. Mr. Frank Hong, our Oxford-educated World History teacher, stands by a pillar and nods at me. With gray hair and a creased face, he must be at least fifty-five now.

"I don't remember names. Not anymore," he says. "But I remember your face. You were the team captain or something."

"Aquatics."

"I remember you and that other boy from Australia."

"I haven't been back for a long time," I say. "I'm surprised that things haven't changed much here."

"A new gymnasium. Did you see it? Where did you go after graduation?"

"I never graduated, actually. I went back to California."

"America. Horrible, horrible place."

"Why?"

"Your so-called culture now. It's getting worse. Children nowadays listen to that rap rubbish. And the hip something?"

"Hip-Hop."

"Hip-Hop. When I was younger, we had Elvis Presley and the Beatles."

"I love the Beatles."

He smiles.

Mr. Hong and I find a long bench in the shade, and we talk for a long time, about the school, the changing times, the coming and going of teachers and administrators, and most of all, our love for the school.

For the first time, I feel like I belong here.

At the end of the afternoon, I leave my alma mater. This has been my last visit. I've found what I came for.

On the second muggy morning, I take a ferry from the Central Piers to Lantau Island. As the boat cuts through the murky sea, the skyscrapers on both sides of the harbor disappear into the converging lines of white foam. A speck of sunlight peeks through the slate mesh of clouds, dappling the choppy water with narrow strips of gold. Sometimes a seagull or two glide above the stern, flapping their long white wings against the salty breeze, uttering only occasional, faint cries. Their mournful, broken songs echo the secret sorrow of a man passing to another shore, bound by the sea, lonely, only a few birds his companions.

At the fishing village in Mui Wo, I get on an air-conditioned bus and ask the driver to remind me when he makes the stop at the Po Lin Monastery. He tells me I can't miss it. As the bus climbs along a twisting road that wraps around the hills, the sea comes into view. This part of Lantau seems the least disturbed of any I've seen. Rustic houses and broken sheds spread along the way, and they are welcome sights as the burgeoning satellite cities rapidly devour the northern side of the island.

The bus gets around a long bend, and a great brown statue of Buddha rises through the thick woods. The bus driver turns his head, his eyes glinting with pride and appreciation, and tells me this is the Tiantan Buddha, the largest seated bronze Buddha in the world.

The bus makes its final stop at the Ngong Ping terminal, only yards away from the central plaza and the white entrance gate to the Po Lin Monastery—a majestic span of temples with aged, golden tiled roofs, large carved wooden doors, towering pillars, and manicured gardens. Looming over us is a long flight of stone steps—the ornate "hundred steps" that lead to the top of the Muyushan Mountain and the superlative, two-hundred-fifty-feet-high Sakyamuni, who looks peaceful and loving sitting on his lotus pedestal. I have never known much about Buddhism. However, in the presence of this magnificent symbol, somehow the unrelenting ideology and its universal teaching of love, kindness and self-enlightenment seems to me to be what's carried these remarkable Chinese people through centuries in hope, comfort, and faith.

I wish I had such faith.

I follow a small flock of Japanese tourists into the monastery. Passing under a wide ancient lintel, we reach the middle of the main courtyard and stand before its *ding*—a bronze tripod the size of a giant man. Inside the *ding*, hundreds of incense sticks burn fervently.

I recognize this place. I take three steps back, lean against a white stone banister, and take the picture of my father and George Jr. from my shirt pocket. As I look back at the Main Hall in the center, the Veda Hall on the left, and the *ding* in the central courtyard, I can make out the exact spot where they stood. My mother, with her camera, stood right where I stand now.

I shut my eyes. I can almost feel my mother's hand.

Just then, the bells, distant on the mountaintop, start to toll. Their long, hypnotic tones echo throughout the valley. I walk up the steps and enter the Main Hall. Inside, three golden Buddhas sit among the solemn wish-makers. As the crowd moves around me, I notice how quiet and peaceful it is inside the temple. Except for the light sound of gongs and cymbals, and the steady and low chants of *namo-amita-bul*, there is hardly any noise.

I, too, step forward to the center Buddha, then take an incense stick from the hand of a young monk and kneel onto a crimson praying pad.

Before the golden Buddha, I make a wish.

# On the Town

When I return at four-twenty in the afternoon, Agnes has been waiting for me. She has the day off, so she's been busy managing the little project called "kitchen remodeling"—meaning she's been barking orders at Old Chow as he handles the tools, extensions of his fingers. Old Chow does everything: fixes the sink, builds a new spice rack, paints the cabinets, organizes the pantry, cleans and scrubs, and prepares his favorite peppered shelled shrimp and Chinese hodgepodge with beef, sausage, and lamb chunks. Greeting me at the door, Old Chow confesses that Queen Agnes is a slob, but a fine slob. I think they've found a perfect match.

"There you are. Hurry! Change into something nice," Agnes says.

"What's up? What's happening?" I ask, wiping the sweat off my forehead with a soaked handkerchief.

"We're going out. A night on the town, how about that?"

"What's the occasion?"

"You, of course, our royal highness. I've been working all this time. Tonight's a good night. Besides, I've got tickets."

"What tickets?"

"It's a surprise. Hurry, we haven't got all day."

Agnes, Old Chow and I take the long way, a leisurely Star Ferry ride from Tsimshatsui to Causeway Bay. She has a reservation at an upscale, New Age-inspired Thai restaurant called Arloi Dee by Times Square. Agnes is out of character in a turquoise silk dress—she could have been rather a hot number when she was much younger and thinner. As for Old Chow—well, Old Chow is simply Old Chow. Wearing a tie is a big deal for him already. "Only for big date," he says.

As we wait for our Mee Grob and shrimp toast at a quiet corner table next to a white jade elephant, Agnes pops the question: "Why didn't you tell me you and Lian were together?"

"Old Chow has a big mouth," I say.

"Me?" Old Chow squints and shrugs.

"Don't change the subject," Agnes says. "Why didn't you?"

"It didn't come up." I toss two fried peanuts into my mouth.

"I asked you."

"Honestly that's none of your business. Besides, all you asked was what I wanted from Lian."

"Technicality."

"Sometimes that's how a case is won. Right, Old Chow?"

"I no involve," he says, taking a swig of his Löwenbräu.

"Agnes, it doesn't matter," I say. "I told you. I have something to ask her, that's all. So leave me alone."

"I thought she was with Cape."

"She was. Then she wasn't."

"I didn't know that."

"Do you need to know everything?"

"Why are you so evasive, Greg?"

"Why are you so nosy?"

"We want to help, but you need to tell us the truth."

I look her in the eye and sigh. "You know what? Sometimes even I don't know what the truth is."

"How long were you together?" She presses on.

"We weren't really together. We went out. We had dinners. We talked. We had a frigging picnic on Cheung Chau."

"You shagged?"

"Yeah. Right." I look at Old Chow and he shrugs again. "*Shag* would be the word. Very good. Are you happy now?"

"Oh, I'm not trying to pry. I don't really care who and what you slept with. I just want to know what went on between you and Lian. I want to understand why there's such an urgency to find her. That's all."

I take a sip of my beer.

"Okay, I lied." I shrug. "Lian and I were together for a few months. I was really fond of her, if you want to know. After I left for the States, I never heard from her again." I smear the condensation on my beer glass with my fingers. "I just need to know what happened."

"Chasing a ghost, aren't we? After all these years—"

"I suppose."

"We'll find her," she says, patting the back of my hand. "We'll find her."

"Thanks," I say. "So, tell me more about my father."

"What do you want to know?" she asks.

"What was it like living with him in London?"

"Actually he was a hoot. That was the sixties, of course, so things were a little different, you know?"

"The sex and drugs, flower power thing?"

"The whole enchilada, as you Yanks would say." She laughs. "I was quite a dish myself, mind you. It was all about free love and the pursuit of happiness. I bet you didn't know that about your father. He was an artist, after all."

"I suspected that much. He sure knew a thing or two about pot when he tried to lecture me. And he had this weakness for whiskey, something he couldn't shake."

"I'm worried you're picking up that old habit as well."

"I'm only having a beer, so get off my back, really." I push my glass away. "You said he was a ladies' man. What exactly did you mean?"

"Women fell for Stephen all over the place."

"I'm not surprised. He was God-awfully handsome."

"It runs in the family," she says. She looks away for a second and I sense that she's trying to say something, but she hesitates.

"Did he have any affairs?" I ask.

"I wouldn't know." She looks the other way.

"He did, didn't he?"

"I'm not at liberty to say."

"Oh come on, Agnes, don't be coy. Tell me the truth."

"Stephen was a good man. I just want you to know that. But yes, he was quite a charmer, and the sixties. That's all I have to say."

"And he was a doctor. Women love only three things in a man: his looks, his pocket book, and his status."

"Aren't we cynical, here?"

"It's true."

"I have no looks, no pocket book, no status," Old Chow chimes in, pounding his own chest. "Women love Old Chow."

"Oh shut up," she says, slapping his arm hard. "Consider yourself lucky that you have me."

Old Chow smirks and winks at me. He knows.

After dinner, we take the Star Ferry back to Tsimshatsui. I lean over the railing on the top deck, taking in the splendid magic hour, when the city lights start to outshine the cobalt sky.

When we step off the pier, the partying crowd has crawled out and the fun has begun. A street vendor calls out to me: "Chestnuts, chestnuts! Big and nice chestnuts!" I'm tempted by the sweet and toasty aroma of the kettle, but Agnes shakes her head and pulls me away. Two young boys do a Britney Spears dance near a lamppost to the music of Eminem. An elderly woman sells some cheap made-in-China plastic toys next to a middle-aged couple with an assortment of incense and lucky bamboos. I'm glad that the local police haven't chased them out. They're part of what makes Tsimshatsui such a colorful, chaotic place.

We stroll past the famous Clock Tower—the sole remnant of the red brick, colonial train terminal, where young lovers like my parents once romanced—and on to the Cultural Center on the promenade. Erected next to the egg-shaped Planetarium and Space Museum, the Cultural Center has two curved, windowless structures that spread out like mammoth angel wings, encased in a sleek shell of geometric lines and patterns. Two Rolls-Royces, a Mercedes, three Porsches, and a yellow Lamborghini are parked on the arched driveway under the porte-cochere. It's looking like a big event tonight.

Agnes leads the way, and soon we're inside the expansive, avant-garde atrium of the Grand Theatre, ceiling-to-wall contemporary art everywhere we turn. Agnes takes three blue tickets from her purse and hands one to me. Five bold words are printed across the ticket: A NIGHT AT THE OPERA.

"Opera? A little highbrow, isn't it?" I say.

"We all need a little culture," she says. She looks around at the walls, then points her fingers at the ceiling, counting the number of crystals in the three chandeliers.

Old Chow nudges me and whispers, "I hate the shit. Like pigs slaughter. Hee-hee haw-haw." I can't help but laugh out loud.

"What's so funny?" She scowls at us. "Show some respect."

Soon the doors to the theater open and we're slowly let in. A keen sense of luxury—the long tiers of burgundy seats, the incandescent skylights, the triple layers of red and gold trimmed velvet curtains and the golden carpet. Andrea Bocelli's sweet *Sancta Maria* transcends the air.

A red-uniformed usher guides us to our third row, center seats. She hands me a program booklet.

"These are expensive seats," I say to Agnes.

"Old Chow paid for them," she says.

"Old Chow!"

"I make good money." He laughs. "I no like the shit, but you can."

We are settled in our plush velvet seats when the lights dim and the curtains are drawn. The 101-member Hong Kong Philharmonic Orchestra fans out and spans the entire tilted stage in a broad arc, framed by a three-story-high backdrop of rectangles, circles and triangles of red, blue, and white, subtly suffused in nine strategically-placed spotlights. After the orchestra adjusts their instruments and quiets down, a silver-haired, Japanese gentleman—Maestro Kin Takeda—sweeps onto the stage, takes a long bow, and in the warm flood of applause, gives the baton in his right hand a flick. The overture to Verdi's *La Traviata* starts to lift the air.

# L'amour est un Oiseau Rebelle

"I have to pee," I whisper to Agnes. It's ten minutes into the program. Some Italian tenor named Marcello is belting out *Nessun Norma* from Puccini's *Tunadot*.

"Now?" she hushes.

"I had too much to drink at dinner."

"It just got started. Can't you wait?"

"I can't or I'll have a bad accident. Would you excuse me, please?"

I squeeze myself past three indignant, snobbish middle-aged Chinese ladies, each of whom gives me a knotted frown and a dead stare. I sneak out of the theater through the back. I need some air and, desperately, to release myself. I find the marbled restroom near the left end of a long hallway past the cash bar. I should have a drink when I return. Marcello's voice continues to seep through the PA even as I check out my reflection on the sparkling urinal. He ends his aria on a haunting note. Appreciative but reserved applause follows.

I'm washing my hands at the marble sink when the familiar tango of *Carmen*'s *Habanera* begins. Roaring cheers drown out the swelling strings. As the warm water runs through my fingers, Carmen's electric voice bursts through the PA.

My heart skips a long beat.

In the mirror, my face quivers—it's the face of a seventeen-year-old boy haunted by an angel's voice.

The same voice that is haunting me now.

My hands still wet, my dress shoes slipping on the floor, I gallop back toward the theater. I push through the heavy teak door and look up at the stage. There she is.

Lian, in a full length, bright red, shoulderless sequined gown, poised at center stage. My Carmen.

I stop breathing. She's more stunning than I've remembered.

I stand by the door for the longest time. I just watch her. She looks so small on the stage, but she is all I can hear. She is all I can see—how her hands sway, how her hips swing, how her long, black, wavy hair ripples down her right side, all the way to her waist. As her lips move, I surrender to the glorious resonance of *L'amour est un Oiseau Rebelle* ringing around me. I'm instantly transported back in time and space, back to the third pew in a chapel, where a girl in a purple robe sang to a half-drunk boy for the first time.

Then she sees me. Our eyes meet for a split second across twenty-five rows of hushed audience. She doesn't miss a beat, but her voice trembles slightly when her glance touches my face. I can feel her Carmen turn fiery: her cadence burns, her words savage, her pauses ache.

She never looks my way again.

As Lian exits the stage amid vociferous reception, I pull the door open and scurry out of the theater. I pace the perimeter of the atrium until I find an exit door hidden behind a large-fronded palm. I toddle down four flights of stairs, no idea where they are leading me, and continue down a narrow passage where exposed pipes snake above my head and machineries hum behind chained fences on both sides. After about two minutes, I stop for a quick survey. The backstage should be on my left if I continue that way, so I make the first left I can. I'm correct. I push open the door with a big red BACKSTAGE sign at the end of the narrow passage and climb two flights to yet another door. I step into a small waiting room and am immediately stopped by a security guard stationed across from the door.

"*Ay, nay hai bin goh?*" the guard commands.

"Excuse me. I'm with the newspapers." I extemporize, brandish my passport, then shove it back into my suit pocket. "I need to get backstage."

I suppose my presence and my stature startle the guard. He doesn't know how to respond, so I press on: "I'm with the *South China Morning Post*, and I'm doing an interview with Ms. Lian Wan. She's expecting me. Would you be kind enough to show me to her dressing room, please? I'm already late."

He presses a button on his walkie-talkie, and the feedback shrieks through the small room. He speaks into the walkie-talkie in low Cantonese. "There's a reporter here to do an interview. A foreign devil..."

"Foreign press?" a man's voice replies in Cantonese. I look away, pretending I don't understand a word.

"Yes, sir. Should I stop him?"

"Foreign press is trouble. Let him through."

"Thank you, Sir."

He turns to me. "Yes, sir. You may pass." He points at the door to my left.

Easy so far. Beyond the door, a long hallway, lit by soft floodlights, extends and bends around. On each side are three doors, one with the name "Victor Marcello" on it. I follow the bend and find Lian's name on the second door on the left.

My heart thumps against my chest. My pulse throbs in my veins. My tongue parches in my mouth. I stand still for a moment. Then I knock.

No answer. I knock again. Still no answer. Lian's either not in her dressing room or avoiding me. I knock for the third time. Silence. I turn to leave.

I jerk backwards.

The creature before me seems to have materialized from the pale overhead lights. Her face is radiant, glamorous in makeup that only accentuates her natural beauty. She has not aged at all—her complexion shows neither wrinkle nor blemish. Her dark brown eyes are fixed on mine.

And mine on hers.

Time has stopped and pinned us.

"Hello," I finally say.

Down the hallway, a door opens and shuts—muted sounds of laughter and violins sputtering, footsteps fading in and out.

We haven't moved.

"Hello," I say again, with a little swagger this time. "It's great seeing you again, Lian. You're still the most beautiful woman I've ever known."

She bites her lower lip. "It really is you."

"I saw you out there." I grin. "You're magnificent."

"What are you doing here?"

"I came here to see you."

She tilts her head at me, her gaze cool. "You are very late."

I titter, lowering my head and putting a hand on the back of my neck. It feels like a warm stream back there. From the corner of my eye, I see her stepping forward, then back again. I look up. She is exactly where she was a second ago, her hands resting at her sides. Her eyes continue to be fixed on mine.

"What do you want, Greg?" She leans back on one high heel.

"I'm not sure," I say.

"It is a long way from California and you are not sure?"

I keep rubbing my neck. "I made a wish," I say.

Her eyes lock on mine.

"I made a wish that I'd see you again. That wish comes true today," I say. "But here I am, standing in front of you, and I don't know what to say. I guess you still have that effect on me."

"You want to see me after all these years? Why?"

"There's something I want to ask you."

She tilts her head, waiting for me.

"You see, my parents passed away three weeks ago."

Her face turns blank for a second before her brows tether into a knot. For a moment, I don't think she understands what I've just told her. Then she brushes her hand over her face, lowers her head and turns away. After a few seconds, she lifts her head, slowly turns toward me.

"I am so sorry," she says. She opens her mouth and lets out a sigh. "I am sorry. The grief—"

She frowns again. A door slams shut down the hall. I look over her shoulder toward the sound, breaking our locked gaze.

She cups her chin with one hand. "I don't know what to say. After all these years."

"And here I am."

"Yes, and here you are." Her lips twist, finally, into a reserved smile.

As she moves to open her dressing room door, I catch a whiff of her perfume. It's the same scent of jasmine that used to drive me crazy.

"Please come in," she says.

I follow her into her dressing room and close the door behind me. It's a plush and intimate space, about the size of a bedroom, but the mirrors on the walls create the illusion of a larger suite. Bouquets of anthuriums, glory lilies and heliconias, vases of red roses and jade orchids are all over the dresser and in all four corners. We can barely hear the orchestra playing the overture from *Faust* in the background. The lights are dimmed. Three candles flicker on a round coffee table, their gentle glow reflected in its marble top. The room effuses a summer garden. Tangerine. Her perfume.

"It's so nice seeing you. Your English is more eloquent than ever," I say as I succumb to a cradling green armchair by the coffee table. Lian rests as well, draping her long legs across a blue chaise next to me. "How long have you been singing?"

"You know I've been singing all my life."

"I mean the opera."

"It will be six years this New Year's Eve."

"You told me you wanted to be an opera singer. Look at you now. You're a star."

"Actually, I have you to thank."

"Me? What did I do?"

"I read *Oscar and the Potbelly Pig.*"

"You did? When?"

She brushes a stray hair away from her face. "Do you remember what Pig said to Oscar at the Village of Shoes?"

"God. No."

"Oscar needed a pair of shoes to continue on his journey after the river swallowed his old pair. There were exactly one hundred and twenty three pairs to choose from, made of every material in the world: iron, gold, silver, cloth, paper, feathers...and Pig said to Oscar, 'Choose your shoes wisely.'"

In spite of myself, I continue: "If they are too tight, they will hurt your feet. If they are too heavy, you will have to carry that weight for the rest of your journey. If they are too thin, the rocks will cut through them and break your skin. If they are too thick, it will be too hot for your feet."

"So I decided it was time for a pair of my own." She smiles. "Trust me, we women know how to pick shoes."

"They're perfect for you."

"What about Oscar?"

Her question catches me off guard.

"He did all right. Pig wasn't there to help."

"What did he choose?"

"The money shoes. What else? He's now a management consultant. Very exciting and lucrative. Oh yeah, what a dream job."

"You're not writing anymore?"

"I never did write."

She drops her smile. I shift uncomfortably in my chair.

We stare at the candles, rapt in the trembling flames. I look up and watch the shadows waltzing on her exquisite face. I'm mesmerized by the crimson rose petals that are her lips—lustrous and soft. Her impossible perfection.

"I remember the tangerine candles. You used to love them," I say with tenderness.

"I still do."

"And origami, raindrops falling on your head, red roses, little Brazilian red-ear turtles, Japanese castles, first snow, chocolate, *Carmen.*"

"You remember."

"And long walks on the beach."

She looks away. I know she remembers that walk.

"It was March. A Tuesday, your day off. It was a cloudy, chilly evening. We took a bus and got off at Deep Water Bay and there was nobody around. Not a soul. Remember?" I say.

"Why are you bringing that up?"

"The sun had already set and the sky was beautiful with that rich blue." I shift again in my chair, watching her face closely. "It was cold. So I took your hand to warm you up, and I didn't let go of it for the entire evening—"

"That was a long time ago."

"We walked for a long, long time, from one end of the beach to the other, and back again. We talked. We laughed. We stood by the railing near a creek. You were wearing my pullover. I wrapped my arms around you. You were shivering. I held you close. And I knew, at that moment, that I was completely in love with you."

"Look at the time. You should go now." She rises from the chaise.

"What?"

"I have to get ready for my next number."

"But I have to talk to you," I say. I've forgotten what I came here for. "I have something to ask you."

"Maybe some other time. I have to get going."

"I can wait here."

"No."

"Why not?"

"You really must go now," she says, and reaches for the door. She turns the doorknob and pushes the door open. She's determined to get me out of there.

"I'll see you after the show, then?"

She bites her lower lip and gestures me out. I walk out of the dressing room, and she shuts the door behind me. I turn and knock, but she doesn't answer. I knock again.

"Lian," I shout. "I have questions for you. Lian?"

A man's voice booms behind me: "Who are you?"

I turn. Victor Marcello. He's a barge—six-foot-five, two hundred and fifty pounds at least—a robust forty-something Italian in a tuxedo with the mean looks of Robert De Niro in the overtly theatrical makeup of Faust. Though I'd like to laugh, I know he's not someone to mess with.

"I'm here to see Lian," I say. "I'm a friend of hers."

"I heard her slamming the door. Looks like she doesn't want to see you," he says in a perfect American accent. His voice is rich but tender, not at all threatening.

"She's just a little flustered by what I said."

"Therefore you should leave now."

"But I must talk to her."

"You heard me. You should leave now," he says, folding his bulky arms across his bulky chest.

"Can you tell her that I'll be here after the show?"

Victor doesn't say anything. He just scowls at me as if I'm a pest. I had no idea Italian tenors could be so intimidating. I'm not about to test him, though, so I relent.

Back in the theater, Agnes and Old Chow have no idea that I've already seen and talked to Lian. Agnes is fiddling about, clearly agitated that I have missed Lian's entrance. I keep my face straight, not giving them the slightest inkling what I'm up to.

When Lian comes on stage for the second time, they cock their heads and steal a glimpse of my face. I know they've been planning this all along, and I don't want to disappoint them. I drop my jaw and bug out my eyes. My reaction is so over the top that they crease their eyebrows and give me dubious looks. Then Agnes starts to crack. Right at the beginning of the solemn *Un Bel Dì, Vedremo* from *Madame Butterfly*, she quacks like a duck. It's so bizarre that I start to laugh, too. This doesn't sit well with the three prudish ladies next to me. They hiss at us discreetly, and it only makes matters worse. I shake my head and howl.

Now in a classic ruby and ivory kimono with gold chrysanthemum embroidery and a sapphire obi, Lian is immune to the madness Agnes and I are conjuring in the audience. She's naturally poised, graceful, her long sleeves swaying. Maestro Takeda feverishly waves his baton, and the expressive orchestra manages to drown the boorish interruption without much effort. But madness is contagious. At the end of the divine brilliance that is *Madame Butterfly*, a middle-aged, balding man in the sixth row suddenly stands up and bellows: "Bravo! Bravo! Bravo! We love you! Jesus loves you! Bravo! I love you! Jesus loves you!" I start to crack up all over again. Fortunately, the audience seems equally infatuated with Lian, and their wild reception quickly surmounts my impudence, even though I know that there is no bigger fan of Lian than I.

I simply can't stop laughing.

"Did you see Lian?" Agnes asks as we're getting out of the theater after the concert. She has a gift for pointing out the obvious.

"Of course I saw her. Even a blind man could have seen her."

"What do you think? Isn't she fabulous?"

"Why didn't you tell me?"

"I told you this was a surprise."

"When did you find out?"

"Old Chow's very good at what he does," she says, squeezing Old Chow's arm. He winks at me. "He found out about the concert just this morning."

"And I buy ticket," he says. "Four hundred dollars for hee-hee haw-haw. I find Lian, see?"

"I'm forever in debt to you, Old Chow."

"And?" Agnes says, narrowing her eyes.

"And you, too." I kiss her on the cheek. "You're a sweetheart. I'm completely grateful."

"Why don't you go see her now? Don't muck around here. Hurry."

"I already saw her."

"You devil. When?"

"When I was in the bathroom. I sneaked off and found her in her dressing room."

"What did you say to her?"

"Not much."

"Don't be coy now. Tell me."

"That's the truth. She kind of kicked me out. I have to go back."

"Then go. Old Chow can take me home."

"Do you mind?"

"Go. That's what we brought you here for."

I kiss her again and pat Old Chow on his back.

The backstage area is already crawling with reporters and adoring fans, waiting, wanting to get through. I gesture at the security guard, and he nods and points at the door to the dressing rooms. I mouth a "thank you" and enter.

"Here you are again." Victor greets me in the hallway, holding a small white towel. His bowtie is hanging loose around his neck, but his black hair is slicked back, revealing a classically handsome face without the gaudy makeup.

"Well, I promised Lian I'd be back."

"I'm afraid she's left already."

"Really. I don't believe you."

"You don't?"

"No. I want to see for myself."

"What makes you think I'm going to let you through?"

"Because...because...I think you're a brilliant tenor?" I say. He doesn't budge.

I sigh, and continue: "Because I know you're a kind and understanding man. Because you know that the greatest tragedy is when we forsake ourselves and let our lives pass us by, sitting on our hands and not doing anything. You really care about Lian, as a true friend, and she needs to hear what I have to say. If she doesn't, I—she—will regret it for the rest of her life. Because you know that regrets are what break a man's spirit. Because—"

"You are good."

"I write speeches for executives."

"Okay, go ahead. But I tell you, she's already gone."

Victor's telling the truth. There's nobody in the room. The flowers remain, and the kimono hangs on the rack at the back of room. The candles have gone out, and her makeup box has disappeared from the dresser. The only sound is the quiet hum of air from the vents.

"See, I told you," he says.

"Do you know where she lives?"

"I can't tell you that."

"Come on, Victor."

"Oh? I didn't know we were on a first-name basis. I don't know you. I don't even know your name. I can't give you her address. You might be a damn stalker."

"You know, there is someone else who can find that information for me."

"Go ahead, my friend. But I don't think that's a good idea."

"Why not?"

"You'll definitely freak her out and get yourself arrested."

"Well, then, I'll come back tomorrow night."

"It won't do you any good. It's our last show. She won't be back tomorrow."

"I'll find a way. I'll die trying."

"You're a dramatic guy, aren't you? You should be in our business."

"Ozzy Osbourne sings better than I do."

He breaks out into a high-pitched belly laugh. He says, "Guess what? I'll do you a favor. I know where she'll be tomorrow and perhaps you can catch her there."

"You'd do that for me?"

"My dear friend, I too have regrets."

He grabs a pen from the dresser and scribbles something on a scrap of paper. "Don't tell her I did this."

I take a quick look and am astounded by what he's written:

*Dr. Howard Cape, Drake Building, 10:30 a.m.*

"Thank you. You have no idea how much this means to me."

"Go easy on the girl, okay?"

"I will," I say. I start to walk away. Then I turn. "Victor, what made you change your mind and trust me with this?"

"Your eyes. I can see the passion in your eyes. And passion, my friend, is what makes a grown man weep."

In his great passionate tenor voice he starts to sing *L'amour est un Oiseau Rebelle.*

# Bulldog's

BULLDOG'S PUB. The painted-over gold-on-black sign still dangles on the front window. The solid oak door has great iron hinges and a brass horseshoe for a knob. A peeling yellow sticker reads *Legal Only*, next to an orange-red neon sign in the shape of a cigar-smoking bulldog, soldered above the door. The same old place. Bulldog's has always been a dump.

I enter and am greeted with a wind of stale beer, fried oysters, cigar and cigarette smoke. Bulldog's is configured like a submarine, long and narrow with a low ceiling, rusty pipes and water-stained walls. From the cheap, scratchy speakers in the corners, a husky voice sings a jolly Irish song about a drunken sailor named Kyle and his port girl Annie Mae. There are about thirty people in the pub, mostly men, mostly in their forties and fifties, mostly in clumps of three or four, mostly drunk out of their wits.

I squeeze past two older gentlemen who are taking turns spitting chewed tobacco into a shot glass. I get to the back of the bar and claim a stool with a ripped red vinyl top.

The bartender, a muscular man in his mid-forties, comes over and greets me with a firm, greasy handshake. His shiny bald head and thick beard look familiar. I order a double Johnny Walker on the rocks. As he turns to grab the bottle, he stops and gawks at me for a second. "Have I seen you before?" he asks.

"I suppose. I used to come here years ago."

"I remember now. There's a bunch of you beardless pups. There's a tall skinny one, I reckon."

"That's right. You've got a good memory."

"Here ya go." He thumps the tall whiskey glass down on the counter. I empty the glass in one gulp. The whiskey burns in my throat. "Martin, right?" he asks.

"No, it's Greg."

"Olie." He again offers his hand to me. "Been here since '82. Came from the Australian outback. Never left, never will. What brought you here, mate?"

"Just a couple of drinks in a familiar joint. I'll have another one, Olie." I tap my glass. Olie pours again. "This joint hasn't changed a bit. I remember that same damn jukebox back there."

"It's still playing the same damn songs. That's for sure. Hold on, I'll be right back." He turns and caters to a man with a baseball cap.

David, Choy, Martin and I got wasted here a few dozen times. Martin first took us to Bulldog's for some carousing after our win in the soccer tournament. We'd sit by the big gas pipe next to the bathroom and not mind the stench. We'd put a few dollars in the jukebox and listen to Fleetwood Mac and Bruce Springsteen and the Who and Pink Floyd, break a few glasses and manage to have a grand time being young and obnoxious. No one seemed to mind. I felt comfortable here, where everyone had an intimate relationship with cold beer and hard liquor.

I down my second glass of Johnny Walker, then hop off the stool and cross the bar to the jukebox. I pull out three one-dollar coins from my pocket and slip them into the slot. Olie's right: they have the same damn songs. I scoot back to the bar and signal Olie for another drink. *Born in the USA* starts to blast in the background. I stare into the glass and let out a long sigh.

"A hard day, aye?"

"Not the best."

"What happened?"

"Eh, I'm thinking, love is a bitch. It never leads anywhere."

"That bad, huh? Here, my friend, Olie's got a good ear."

For some odd reason, I trust Olie, so within two minutes I tell him the story. Not everything, and nothing about my father, just enough to keep him interested.

"Who's this Howard Cape character?" He sinks his right elbow onto the counter, his face only inches from mine. I can see pools of red in his eyes and smell the residual cigar on his breath.

"An old flame of hers. I can't believe she's back with him again."

"You don't know that. Maybe she's there for a physical."

"I don't know. He's very handsome and well-to-do and a damn nice guy. Why wouldn't she?"

"Well, you're a goddamn handsome guy and you seem goddamn nice to me. Guess you'll just have to go to the good doctor tomorrow and find out."

"I don't know. I'm beginning to think this is a huge mistake. I should just go home, back to California."

"Now listen, mate. It might sound stupid coming from a loser working in a fuckin' dive like this, but I tell you, you didn't come all the way here just to fuckin' give up."

"Olie, have you ever gone to a Chinese banquet?"

"You mean like a wedding? No."

"Well, it's usually about ten to twelve people sitting at a round table. The host or head of the family sits in the north position. And you know who sits opposite him?"

"The guest of honor?"

"No. It'd be the secondary host, like the wife. The guest of honor sits on the right side of the host. And you know what they say when they make a toast?"

"That one I know. *Gan Bei*."

"Yes. When the host bestows a *Gan Bei*, the rest of host family follows, one by one. It's always the mistake for a Westerner like you or me to think we should follow right after the host."

"Okay, you lost me. What's your point?"

"The point is I'm not even invited to that table this time. She didn't want me there. I used to be the one sitting next to her. Now it's Howard. And maybe there was someone else—Anyway, I ran away. There's no *gan bei* for me. I don't know why I'm here. What I'm doing here."

"You know, I almost became a pilot once," he says while drying a glass with a dirty rag. "Fuck. Took my lessons and ready to take the test. And you know what happened? I goddamn chickened out. I fucked up. I didn't think I had what it took and I didn't go. You know what the moral of the story is? Hell, take a fuckin' chance."

"You don't understand. She hates me."

"Did she tell you that?"

"Not really."

"Then you don't know, do you?" He takes away my glass. "Go home. Go to the girl. Find your truth. You don't belong here."

The goddamn bartender kicks me out, and I'm not even finished with my third drink.

# Howard Cape

Dr. Howard E. Cape's office is on the twenty-seventh floor of the Drake Building on Connaught Road, right across from the Central Piers. In fact, you can see part of the piers from the huge glass windows. I had a rough night, trashed and disoriented. It's just after eleven in the morning by the time I get there. The waiting room is wallpapered in a lily pattern, and twelve light gray leather chairs are lined up in a U-shape, surrounding an oblong white coffee table on which spread a few copies of *Vogue* and *Cosmopolitan* and some Chinese tabloids. I pick up a copy of *Ming Pao Weekly* and flip through it. I can't really read Chinese, but at least I can look at the pretty pictures of pop stars and celebrities I don't recognize. There seems to be an abundance of advertisements for luxurious cars, fine jewelry, Viagra and other male enhancement supplements.

In a corner, a Chinese mother in her early twenties is having trouble making her little boy behave. He has a cute round face, a long bowl-cut down to his eyebrows, and voluminous lungs. He seems to have no comprehension of what the word "quiet" means and proceeds to run about and scream at will. I look at him with amusement, then wink. He takes a long look at me and stops screaming. His mother smiles at me as if I've just performed a miracle. I smile back, and the little boy starts to giggle. A vigorous, loud, affecting giggle. I hide my face in my hands and play peek-a-boo with him, and he laughs even louder in delight.

"What's your name?" I ask.

He tilts his head and puckers. I ask him again. He runs around, puts his arms around his mother's right thigh, and buries his face behind her knee.

"Franklin, this gentleman is asking your name. Say 'Franklin' and 'How are you, Mister?' " she says.

He refuses to oblige. Instead, his curious eyes peep through the cave of her bended knee, like a little groundhog checking out his shadow.

"Hi, Franklin, I'm Greg. How are you, buddy? How old are you?" I extend my hand to him.

He slowly comes out of his shadow. He puts his hands around his belly and twists a corner of his yellow striped shirt into a bunch.

"Do you know how old you are?" I ask.

"Two," he says and runs back behind his mother's leg.

"He's such a cute little boy."

"Thank you. He is a lot of work. Do you have children?"

"Me? Oh no. I'm not even married."

"Sorry," she says. "I thought you are waiting for your wife."

"No, I'm here to see Dr. Cape."

"Yes...but...he is a gynecologist."

Now I'm embarrassed. I had no idea he specialized in that particular field.

"Howard and I are close friends," I say. "I'm taking him, eh, to lunch."

"Oh, I see," she says with a lift in her voice, as if she has learned something significant. "I understand."

"What's that?"

"Dr. Cape is a very handsome man."

"He is."

"It is a shame to my girlfriends that he is not available. They all like him. Now he loves only opera," she says with a snicker, tossing me a sly glance. "He is lucky."

"Do you know Li—"

"Mrs. Wong," a nurse calls out in Cantonese at the reception window. "We are ready for you now. Please come in."

Mrs. Wong smiles at me. She gathers her belongings, grabs Franklin's tiny hand, and tugs him toward a door next to the window.

After sitting in the waiting room all by myself for another ten minutes, I approach the window and tap on the glass. The young nurse peeks over her computer. "May I help you, Sir?"

"Actually, can you tell me if Ms. Lian Wan's still here?"

"She has gone already."

"She has? When?"

"About half an hour ago."

"Damn," I whisper to myself. "Do you know where she went?" I ask her.

"I am not sure, but I think she said she was going shopping at the store."

"What store?"

"Windsor's, I think. It is two blocks away."

I find the small supermarket with a red and white striped awning exactly two blocks away. On the front windows are all kinds of decals—royal crowns, carriages, horses, cloverleaves, and Union Jacks—that tell of its continental affiliation.

I find Lian at the back of the store with a large white straw tote bag hanging at her side. She's checking out a red sweater, and her back is turned to me—she has no idea I'm spying on her. She looks relaxed in a light blue blouse and dark gray khakis, and I don't want to disturb her. Actually, I don't want her to think that I'm stalking her.

I pick up a copy of *InStyle*, hold it up my face and follow her around the store. Lunchtime and it's bustling with customers, allowing me to lurk in the corner.

I am a damn stalker.

She puts a bouquet of white roses in her shopping basket. She then picks up a small box of Guylian chocolates—if she ever had a weakness, it would be chocolates. She used to be much like Eliza Doolittle, weak at the sight of those "brown or white pieces of heaven," as she once put it. Of course, there was no Henry Higgins to tempt her. I was much too young even for the role of Freddy Eynsford-Hill. Besides, I'd already sold my soul to the devil to be on the street where she lived.

Perhaps Howard Cape is indeed her Henry Higgins.

I follow her, from a safe distance, out of Windor's, up the skywalk and across the street. She has a slow and lithe walk— almost as if she's dancing on air. Before long, we're in front of Pier Four at the Central Piers. She gets up to the ticket booth, then disappears into the terminal through a chrome turnstile. Once she's out of sight, I run up and ask the ticket clerk, "Do you know where that woman's going?" Without hesitation, he replies in a monotone, "Cheung Chau. Twelve o'clock ferry. Twenty dollars."

Inside the terminal, I quickly locate her near the metal gate. I hide behind a concrete column in a corner but never let her out of my sight. It's impossible for me to get my eyes off her.

From her tote bag, she takes out a paperback: Toni Morrison's *Paradise*. She opens the book to the middle and starts to read. I watch her read.

She's always loved to read. In her closet-sized apartment on Waterloo Road, just blocks away from the hospital, there used to be just enough room for a single bed, a dresser, a stack of opera records on top of a turntable, and three bookcases full of old books, some of them covered with tea stains, mostly classics and poetry: Forster, Austen, Dickens, Hemingway, Morrison, Eliot, Shakespeare, and famous Chinese authors such as Ba Jin and Bing Xin. Some nights she would sit by the bed and, while I stroked her long hair and ran my hand along her bare back, tell me the story of a book she'd just read. *Sula* was her instant favorite.

That all the more inspired me to write. I wrote in spurts, imitating the masters. I knew I could never measure up to her expectations as a writer, but I was dying to impress her.

I never showed her any of my scribbling.

I have no idea how she came to read *Oscar and the Potbelly Pig*.

She's startled by the horn of the docking ferry. She lifts her eyes off the page and looks my way. My heart thumps fast as I retreat into the corner, behind the concrete column. I don't think she's seen me. If she has, I'll just have to make up a story.

When I look again, she's already gone. With my back hunched and my head tucked between my shoulders, I walk among other passengers past the gate and up a long, slanted boardwalk onto a blue and white vessel that resembles a large steamboat without a paddlewheel. At the sound of a somber horn, it leaves at twelve o'clock sharp.

There are three decks on the ferry, and for a few extra dollars you can get on the top, which is air-conditioned and has a small snack bar and an outside deck. I have a feeling that Lian will be sitting outside, nose in her book, pampered by the soothing wind and the hypnotic sound of the breaking waves.

I'm right. She's sitting on a green plastic chair on the outside deck, facing the stern with her back to me and a lucent blue scarf wrapped around her hair. I watch her from behind a glass door. I have an intense desire to walk up and introduce myself to her. Start all over again, like a new person, with a new attitude and a new purpose. But I can't. I just watch her, from afar. I just watch her.

I hear a faint cry and look up. Two seagulls circle, gliding above me, like leaves falling from an autumn tree, against an ashen sky that meets the sea only at a fine gray line. As they soar past the stern, I catch a glimpse of Lian again, and I am comforted to see that she, too, is captivated by the immediate grace and coarseness of these white scavengers. Perhaps the sky speaks to her as well.

I keep watching her.

# Cheung Chau

The ferry sounds its long horn, edging its way toward the island. Piers, docks and row houses pack tightly together in a stretch along the shore. Twirls of smoke ascend from a temple at the far end of the village. On the near side of the island, the rocky hills give rise to a green plateau on which tiers of red-roof condominiums and houses spread out like icing on a cake. The water is a dark, murky turquoise of quiet undulation, with frequent parades of wooden sampans and motorboats cutting languidly through. Time seems to slow down on this jagged bump of an island and fishing village southwest of Hong Kong. A mosaic of at least three hundred boats and junks, large and small—their long masts and ragged, batten sails wavering about—drifts in the sheltered harbor. The breeze is damp with the smell of salt and fish.

Cheung Chau is almost as ageless as Venice. The dumbbell-shaped island was once two small islets rising from the sea with their crags dropping straight down to the water as if they were carved off of something grander. Over the years, sand and rocks deposited, forming an isthmus and connecting the two islets into a single island. The narrowest part of the isthmus, which carries the centennial village on the west side and the Tung Wan Beach on the east, is no more than two hundred and fifty yards across.

Lian took me here fourteen years ago, and I'll never forget the whiffs of incense down the narrow, zigzagging alleys hidden amongst the two- or three-story houses with small balconies, iron bars, peeling paint, and undergarments flying high like international flags on crisscrossed chicken wires and bamboo poles. You can easily get lost here, turning every corner just to find another. There's not a single car on this island—only boats, bicycles and the things we call feet. Simple people smile and speak in various tonal, southern Chinese dialects. Their conversations were at once urgent and friendly, even though I had no comprehension of a single word they said.

Once off the ferry and out of the wharf, Lian strolls across to the Praya (Portuguese for *Square*), picking at papayas, mangoes and kiwis at the stalls lining the main street. The locals ride by on their tattered bicycles, occasionally ringing their rusty bells to get us out of the way. A teenage boy bumps into me on his bicycle, then hands me a flyer of some sort. I casually fold the flyer into my back pocket, and as I turn, I almost trip over a plastic tub of swarming tiger shrimp. The elderly woman sitting by the tub opens her toothless mouth and lets out a loud crow. I apologize.

I look up. Lian has disappeared. I hurry around the corner and am relieved to find her in a narrow alley, a few houses down, chatting with three small children playing in front of a doorstep. The children flutter their arms and giggle around her, eagerly touching her hands. She speaks to them attentively, and once or twice places her hands on their heads.

She eventually waves goodbye to the children. I follow her through the maze of alleys to the far end of the village, which opens up to a clearing that has a small playground with a whirligig and two broken swings. Sand crunches under my shoes. I walk up a set of steps onto a paved walkway about two feet above the ground, and from that vantage point, I can see the panorama of the sapphire sea and a broad, ivory beach. In the distance, three cargo ships complete the setting with part of Lantau Island in the background.

Two bikinied Caucasian women sunbathe near a tuft of rocks on the right, though there are hardly any rays peeking through. Lian has trekked halfway down the beach toward a low cement platform under one of the scattered trees. Her scarf ripples in the wind, dancing ballet with her hair.

She hops onto the platform and puts down her tote bag. Out of that magic bag, she pulls a small white cloth. She lays it on the platform and sits down on it. She then pulls out the roses and a Saran-wrapped sandwich and lays them on the platform next to her. Next comes a bottle of wine and two plastic cups. She takes off her blue scarf and wraps it around the handle of the tote bag. Then she just sits there and watches the waves washing over the sand.

I watch her. After a while, I take off my Nikes and socks and step off the walkway onto the sand—it feels warm, dry and coarse. Lian doesn't see me until I'm about five feet away. She turns toward me and slowly wipes her cheeks with the tips of her fingers. She has been crying.

"I know I was a jerk last night. I'm sorry that I followed you here. I didn't mean to upset you. Please don't cry."

"Greg, not everything is about you."

"What is it then?"

She presses her lips together and looks away.

I hop onto the platform and sit next to her, hugging my knees.

"How did you find me?" she asks.

"A little bird told me."

"I see," she says with a faint smile. "That little bird is a big man with a soft heart. I should have known."

"Don't blame him. I was very convincing."

"What do you want from me, Greg?"

"I just want to talk to you." I pick up a rose and gently bend its thorny stem with my fingers. "I remember you liked to come out here."

"I still do."

"Lian, why were you crying?"

She stares at the sea. The waves are responding without an answer.

"And these roses?" I ask. "What was that you were doing?"

"You ask too many questions."

"I have more."

"Why are you here? What do you want from me?"

"Now who's asking too many questions?"

"Greg, you have not changed at all."

"Yes, I have. I have gray in my hair now. I'm not a boy anymore."

"I'm not so sure about that."

I look down and notice the tuna melt sandwich.

"When did you start eating fish?"

She keeps staring at the sea. Then something strikes me.

"My dad loved tuna melts—and the Merlot, the white roses. What are you—you were crying for my dad, weren't you?"

I pull a piece of paper from my shirt pocket and wave it in front of her. "Recognize this?"

She stares at me, her expression blank.

"It's a letter. It's the reason I came back here. I came back here to ask you this—did you have something going on with my father?"

"What are you talking about?"

"'My Dearest, Yesterday was your birthday. I want to call you very much...' " I start to read the letter, then hand it to her. She takes one look. There is a strange glint in her eyes. "Your letter to my father," I say.

"Why would I write him such a letter?"

"You tell me."

She narrows her eyes. "I don't know what you are trying to do," she says. "Believe whatever you want." She reaches over to her tote bag and starts packing things up. "Have a nice life."

I grab her hand. "Tell me."

"Tell you what?"

"How long had you been with my father?"

"Greg, that is sick. I haven't seen you for years, and now you have come back and gone mad."

"I don't believe you."

"Believe whatever you want. But I am telling you the truth. It was a letter to you. I sent it to your apartment."

"On Princess Margaret Road?"

"Yes. I used one of the envelopes you left at my place."

"The one addressed to G. S. Lockland?"

"Yes."

"Those were my father's." I let go of her hand.

"Your father's name is Stephen."

"No, George. His full name's George Stephen Lockland. Same initials as mine." I sigh.

She frowns. "Greg, believe me or not, I sent you the letter on August eighteenth. I didn't know where you were in California, so I hoped your parents would forward it to you. You never replied."

"I never got it."

"You didn't?"

"No. I never saw it until a few days ago. I found it in his safe deposit box."

"Why did he—", she says, and sighs. "I understand now."

"What?"

She shakes her head. Suddenly, I know what she means—if she's telling me the truth, then my father did a cruel thing.

"Fucking bastard," I say.

"Greg..."

"Fucking bastard ruined my life." I grab the sandwich and squeeze it into a large lump. I stand up and hurl it like a baseball toward the sea. It travels in a long, great arc and falls into the water like a rock. A thud, and it's gone. I wish my anger could disappear like that. Instead, it swells like the waves.

"Greg, he loved you," she says.

"He loved ruining my life. That's all."

"There are things you don't know about him."

"I don't want to know anymore. The more I find out, the more I despise him."

"It is not what you think."

"Lian, what do you know?"

"I knew him—more than you realize."

I stare at her and draw a long breath, my face tightening.

"Tell me, why were you crying for him?" I ask.

"He was very good to me."

"How so?"

"He helped me find a job at Q.E. and put me through the conservatory."

"It doesn't make any sense. Why would he do something like that? He barely knew you. There's something you're not telling me. Why did you pose for him? I saw the picture he took of you. The white sheet and Greek pillars."

"That was a long time ago. He just asked me to pose for a picture. That was all. It was a very innocent thing."

"What did you want from him, then?" I say, and take the green envelope from my shirt pocket. I hand it to her. "I found this with the other letter."

*Dear Stephen,*

*You are the most wonderful, kindest man. I don't know what I would do without you. I feel ashamed, however, to have to lie to Helen. She starts to ask questions. I really need to talk to you. Soon. Can you come to my apartment after your vacation? It is very important. Please come.*

*Lian*

She reads the letter, then drops it to the side.

"What did you want from him?" I ask.

"Greg, please don't ask any more questions."

"Why not?"

"Everything is in the past. Why do you want to dig up the past? Why did you come back?"

"I need to know. I have the right to know."

"You should go back and get on with your life. Your life is in America. Not here."

"Answer me." I rub my hand over my eyes. "Did you and my father have an affair?"

"You are truly insane." She stands up, gathering her things. "What has gotten into you?"

"You didn't answer me."

"What are all these accusations about? You are out of your mind."

"What was so important that you had to see him? Behind my mother's back?"

"That was between your father and me. It had nothing to do with you."

"Answer me." I grab her by the shoulders and shake her. Her eyes widen with terror.

"You are hurting me!" she shouts and pushes at me.

I let go of her and step backwards, miss my footing and fall onto the sand. I look up at her and shout, "Answer me!"

"You are a madman."

"Answer me!"

"No. The answer is no."

"I don't believe you."

"Then don't. I don't care." She puts everything inside her bag and hops off the platform. "You have no right to badger me with all these questions after disappearing for fourteen years."

"But it's not my fault. I never got that letter."

"Nothing is ever your fault, Greg. Nothing. It is always someone else's fault."

"What do you mean?"

"You knew where I lived. You could have written. You could have come back and seen me. Christmas. Summer. Autumn. Anytime. But you never did."

I hold my breath.

"You didn't even leave me an address or a phone number," she says. "You never wrote. You just disappeared. It was as if you wanted to run away, as fast and as far as possible."

"Is that what you think?"

"It doesn't matter now."

"Lian."

"Just leave me alone."

She picks up her bag and starts to walk away, back to the village.

I sit on the sand and stare at the breaking waves, a tight knot in my chest.

*Nothing is ever your fault.* Her words haunt me.

It was a mistake to come back to this ghost land of my past. There's nothing for me here. Although I had my suspicions, I have no choice but to believe Lian—she couldn't be lying to me, could she? What else could I do? My father's dead. My mother's gone. And the woman I once loved has this tremendous hatred for me. All I could do was to shake her by the shoulders. What kind of a madman have I become?

I bury my face in my hands. I sink into the sand and let it swallow me whole and the world crumbles around me. I feel small and tired.

Then a hand rests on my right shoulder. I turn. Lian's face is all I can see. Her brown eyes. Her soul.

"You remember my birthday..." I whisper. She nods, then places her hand on my cheek.

# Sai Wan

Lian and I haven't spoken a word to each other since we left the beach. She's asked me not to talk about my father, and I'm fine with that. For now.

For about twenty minutes, we trek along Peak Road, a winding, tree-canopied path off the north side of Tung Wan Beach. As we head up the hill, on the right, between the nets of trees, clusters of red and blue tiled roofs swarm beneath us. On the other side, glimpses of the sea.

Soon we come across Cheung Chau Cemetery, spreads of gravesites ensconced in the woods on both sides of the path. Heavy thickets shelter the gated entrance. Behind a tranquil resting area, a couple of cement benches huddle a bronze drinking fountain. Four elderly men rest in the shade of a grand oak tree, puffing at their pipes, holding their bamboo birdcages like they would fat glasses of cognac, occasionally gossiping with each other: deep war scars, erstwhile love affairs.

"I remember this place." I point at the Victorian gas lamp by the benches, painted red and green, a little rusty at the top. "That's where I tried to kiss you. And you pushed me away. Not respectful to the dead or something."

"Spirits. Always be respectful around the spirits."

"Superstitious."

"Spiritual. Remember that bench?"

"No."

"I don't believe you. You were wearing white shorts that day."

"Oh yeah. Gosh! The melted chocolate. I walked all over town with this big, brown stain on my ass."

"I thought that was funny. Disgusting, but funny."

"We had some good times together, didn't we?"

She keeps walking, past the iron gates and up a few steps. She stops in front of one of the gravesites, looks around, and decides that it is where she wants to be. She kneels on the grass and starts tidying up, tossing away the wilted mums, pulling out wild weeds.

These gravesites are all alike. Most headstones are gray granite, each a traditional monument the size of a small file cabinet, adorned with ornate Chinese façade, pillars and stone lions, the name and picture of the deceased engraved in each face. There are a few hundred of them, lined up in staggered ranks. This particular plot belongs to a Mr. Yee Man Sun, 1928-1994.

"So many graves here," she says. "Generation after generation, many of them were born, lived and died on this island."

"Forgotten by time."

"And it isn't a bad thing," she says. "I always come here. It gives me peace."

She pulls a stubborn weed out of the ground. I help her straighten up a white ceramic urn, small as a dove, three burned incense sticks planted in the ashes.

"So much sadness here," she says. "And forgotten pain."

"Do you know this Mr. Yee?"

"No." Her face tightens. "After all these years, some of these graves are abandoned and uncared for. It is nice to come here to pay some respect."

"My mother has a nice grave."

She stops what she's doing. I grab a small leafy stalk and pull hard, uprooting it, leaving a hole in the grass.

"I know I'm not supposed to talk about him," I say, "but I'd like to talk about her."

"I miss her."

"Me too." I sit next to her. "She had a beautiful funeral. She really did. It was a perfect day. Sunny, warm, clear sky, light breeze." I grasp a small twig and bend it, snapping it in half. "It reminded me of the time she took me to a park next to her hospital. I was, what, six or seven and I don't remember much, except that she was so beautiful in her uniform. I waved at her and she smiled and waved back."

"I am sorry, Greg."

"It's been three weeks. It's still hard talking about her—the memories of her." I place my palm on my forehead and shut my eyes. I'm spinning around on a merry-go-round, and every time I turn, I see my mother in white, sitting on a bench, waving and smiling at me. "I miss her so much."

"You know what she said to me once?"

"What?"

"Before she knew about us. She said, 'Greg is a big baby, but he is my big baby.' "

"Wait. She knew about us?"

"Eventually. Yes." She shrugs.

"What did she say?"

"About us? To be honest, she wasn't very happy."

"Why?"

"You were only seventeen, for one thing." She stands up and wipes the dirt off her khakis. "And she thought you were a bad influence on me."

"Me? She said that about her own son?" I push myself up. "How come she never told me?"

"I asked her not to."

"Why?"

She pauses. "You promised me."

"What are you hiding, Lian?"

She picks up her bag and looks around again.

"Lian." I study her as she heads toward the entrance. I follow.

The road becomes more and more deserted—first a jogger or two, then three old men with their wooden canes, then only Lian and me. Occasionally some birds croak from deep inside the coppice. The thick scents of trees and vines and wild flowers and wet soil consume us. I imagine myself deep in a tropical forest, parrots and monkeys hooting. The foliage rustles as a light breeze sweeps past. A squirrel wriggles by, skipping from crackling branch to crackling branch, a large acorn in its mouth.

I pick up a black chestnut-shaped pebble from the ground, tossing and catching it in my hand. "Ever think you'd see me again?"

"Someday. I thought someday. But not yesterday. Not today." Her voice is so soft I can barely hear her.

"And here we are again."

"But everything has changed."

The pebble falls into my palm. I clasp it, feeling its smooth contour with the tip of my thumb.

"Are you happy with your life?" I ask, glancing at her.

She bends down to pick a dandelion on the side of the road, where another path splits off and disappears around a bend.

"Are you happy?" I ask again.

"Yes," she says.

My feet glue to the ground. Then I fling the pebble into a bush. It makes no sound. I expected, or wished for her misery. That way, I could sweep her off her feet. Rescue her.

"That's absolutely great." My chipper tone betrays me.

"How about you? You seem so sad." She continues down the main road.

"What do you expect? My parents just died."

"That is only part of it." She turns to me. "You scared me."

"I wasn't myself." I scuttle forward a few steps and leap at a high branch, missing by about an inch. "I'm sorry. There's...There's so much I don't know. So much I want to know." I scoop up a handful of pebbles. They clatter in my grip. "I want to know everything."

"Such as?"

"Everything. Like, what about the opera?"

"Opera is great. It is what I love. I liked being a nurse, but opera is something else. Imagine—the pageantry, the art, the passion, the drama, the characters, the human condition—everything that is great about life."

"A dream come true, too. Didn't waste your life waiting for something to happen."

She tilts her head and tosses her hair over her right shoulder, exposing her smooth, white-jade neck.

I haven't kissed that neck for a long time.

"What's your company again?" I ask.

"The Grand Republic Opera. We are based in Shanghai, actually. It is a great company, and the people are exceptional."

"Marcello's very good."

"He is a wonderful friend."

"Ever gone to the States?"

"Yes. Four times. Mostly the West Coast."

"And you didn't look me up?"

"Greg, please."

"Sorry." I shrug.

We come around a sharp bend, going deep into the hills.

"You didn't answer me yet," she says. "Are you happy?"

"Uh. Sure."

"Greg."

"I'm happy here. It's so quiet and peaceful. And I remember all these things." I pitch the pebbles into the deep umbrage. The sound of rain. I glance at her again. "I don't know—for one thing, my father and I had it bad until the end."

"He loved you."

"I want to believe that. I really do." I fling another pebble into the woods. "And Mom—stuck between us." I stop and look at the gray sky. "I thought we weren't going to talk about him."

"What about your own life?"

"What life?"

"Your own life. You are, after all, thirty-two."

"I have a good job, if that's what you mean. I have some money, a great condo, a kick-ass convertible. Toys galore. Things."

"Do you have anyone special?"

"I had you." I smirk.

She looks away, picks up her pace and passes me.

Watching her sleek back moving away, I think of Kate. I want to tell Lian about her—the piece of tomato on her cheek, the burnt shrimp, her purple sweater. Her rants. But it feels so good walking next to Lian now. What does that mean? I'm not sure anymore.

"No," I say.

"No?" She turns and looks at me.

"I have a private life, of course." I run past her again. The road bends around, sloping downhill, leading somewhere but nowhere. "I obsess over nothing important. I have no passion. A lot of times, I just want to be alone."

I turn around and walk backward, fixing my eyes on her. "But then, sometimes I hope for someone to come along and make me happy."

"I used to feel that way."

"And now?"

"I am not so sure." She shrugs. "What a burden on the other person. You agree?"

"So, we're supposed to be lonely?"

"We still need people, of course. We are best when we are around others. But to depend on someone else to make us happy?"

"What's the point of finding someone who loves you, being with someone you love?"

"To give."

I stop.

She stops.

*To give.*

Some creature wriggles by again, crackling another branch.

"Have you? Found that person?" I ask.

"Greg."

"Have you?"

She glides past me. "Have you?" I turn and follow her. She walks faster. I follow closer. "Have you?"

She doesn't answer.

"Have you?"

"Yes."

*I don't believe her.*

I bolt ahead. The road opens on a small plaza. A blue sign— "Sai Wan" in English and Chinese characters—welcomes any passersby who happen to stumble across this tucked-away village.

Sai Wan, or West Bay, is on the quieter, more secluded part of Cheung Chau. Tight grids of two-story houses, darkened walls, and rooftop antennas poking out like fish bones, the village is almost completely desolate at this hour, a ghost town in an alternate universe. Outside a small temple, throngs of steel beams, red tiles, bricks, wires and sand bags scatter. A hardware store with a red-on-white sign sits in a corner, its doors and black gates shut and locked.

I skip down a long flight of steps toward the other edge of the village. A curving railing spans a humble harbor. I lean over and count—five tugboats docking at the piers, twelve random sampans tossing around. I sniff the air. Fried tofu is cooking somewhere.

A few minutes later, Lian saunters down the steps. "Hey," I holler. "I remember this harbor. We walked around for a couple of hours. I remember the fried tofu and rice crackers. Didn't we get some white sugar cakes, too? You were so happy."

"You mean these?" She holds up a brown paper bag.

"You didn't."

"At the food store around the corner."

"I love them." I take the bag from her. Nuzzling inside are two wedges of pearl-white spongy cake, semi-translucent like fogged glass, each the size of my fist. I take one out, and its warm, moist crust sticks to my fingers. I tear off the tip and shove it in my mouth. The smooth, gooey texture clings to my palate and the subtle sweetness melts instantly on my tongue.

Lian's smile exudes such tenderness that I forget we are not young foolish lovers anymore. I touch her cheek. She steps away.

Leaning against the railing, she stares at the surf, her eyes trailing the anodyne rhythms.

"Thank you," I say.

"You are welcome. Save me some."

I laugh. That's exactly what she said fourteen years ago when I started to hog the whole bag. *Save me some.*

I did.

I will.

"Isn't there a pirate cave somewhere around here?" I ask.

"The Cheung Po Tsai hideout? Yes, it is nearby."

"Should we check it out?"

"Now? It is getting late. We should go back to the Praya."

"Come on. Let's check it out."

"Greg, it is quite a hike."

"I got sneakers on."

She shakes her head. "You are such a boy."

I cross my arms, spread my legs and strike a pose.

"I'll never grow up. Come on, Tinkerbell. Let's find some pirate cave."

I grab her hand and fly.

# Another World

A short walk from the edge of the harbor, along a narrow dirt path, takes us to a rocky cove. Not a boat or a soul, only the distant blankets of scud. The ocean ridges up rough in frothy white crests, gathering into an expansive pool embraced by random heaps of rock. Driftwood scattered here and there. The breakers crush against the jagged cliffs, splattering my face with algid, thick brine.

I lift Lian by the waist onto a large, flat piece of limestone teeming with coarse honeycomb holes and fossilized seashells. Her black hair capers against the swollen turquoise. I grin widely.

I am seventeen again.

We find the cave hidden among some chaparrals, behind a broken steel fence. It's not a large crevice, only a few shapes bigger than a grown man. A hundred or so years ago, when the pirate king Cheung Po Tsai discovered this place, how excited he must have been. A perfect hideout, shielded from the rest of the world, with a gorgeous view. Imagine the exotic adventures, swashbuckling tales, and tragic love epics. Not the throat-cutting, gut-spilling truth of the pirate life.

"Let's go inside." I climb over the fence. "It looks okay from here."

"You are not serious."

"Yup. I can get through."

"Please don't go in."

"Why not?"

She leans against a post and frowns. "I was trapped inside once."

"What happened?"

"Some boy took away my flashlight and ran out. He left me." She presses her lips together and frowns. "It took me a long time to find my way out."

"I'm sorry. That bastard." I come forward and put my hands on hers. "I'd never do that."

"It is dangerous inside."

"Danger? I laugh in the face of danger! Ha! Ha! Ha!" I do my best pirate imitation, but her brows burrow deeper. "It's not so bad. Cheung Po Tsai brought his treasure here, and I'm going to find it."

I put my hands around my eyes and peer into the opening. "Doesn't look that deep."

"Greg, please."

"Oh, come on, Lian. Live a little," I say. She leans closer to the pole. "Fine, tell you what, you stay here."

I grab hold of a boulder and lower myself into the cleft. Twisting my body like paper into a curved slit, I slip through, hobble down a few feet, and make my way completely inside the hollow.

As Kate would say, *easy as cake.*

Lian calls my name, but I ignore her.

The cavern opens up into a chamber large enough for me to stand without hunching over. A dreary space, nothing but limestone and the sour odor of old sod, a New York sewer without the stench. Where are the stalagmites and stalactites? The pirate booty? I slog forward about twenty feet, step into a musky void. A shred of light drifts into the abyss from far ahead. A few seconds to adjust my eyes, and a passage appears, lodged between clumps of rocks jutting in all directions.

What am I doing here? I don't even have a flashlight.

"Greg, please come out." Lian's voice is distant but tense.

"I can do this," I shout. "Meet me on the other side."

I edge my way through the passage, feeling ahead with my hands. I bump into crags, scrape a finger, then an elbow. I love a good challenge. But, damn it, why wasn't I an Eagle Scout or something? I have absolutely no idea what I'm doing. All I know is that I must move forward to the dim light. That's the way out. I don't know how far it is, or what is in the way. I can only hope that there are no vampire bats. Or rats. Or spiders. Or snakes.

The passage becomes much narrower as I crawl deeper, until the rocks are pressing on me on all sides, allowing me only a tight gap to squeeze through. In this enclosure, all I can breathe in are loam and foul, brackish wafts of moisture. Something creeps across my neck. Frantically I flick it away. I hear some critters, their exoskeletal legs or claws tap-dancing around me.

Lian was right. This is a stupid idea. Why do I always do such stupid things?

Suddenly, the light goes out and a rumble ricochets through the cave like a muffled blast. I jerk, slip, trip over something. A sharp pain. Struggling to regain my footing, I find myself stuck in a fissure. My left calf burns.

"Shit." I groan. "Lian." I have no idea how deep I'm in— possibly a few dozen yards. She can't possibly hear me.

I push myself against the jagged wall and struggle up, enduring the pain. I'm all turned around. The only guide I have is the occasional rumble from where the light used to be.

I put most of my weight on my right foot. "Lian!"

In the darkness, I can move forward only a few steps at a time without rubbing my legs against the rocks.

"Lian!" I grunt.

"Greg." Lian's voice comes through from a distance. Twenty or thirty feet. I can't tell. It's such a relief to hear her voice.

"Are you all right?" I yell.

"Yes. Are you?"

"Stay where you are." I hop twice, pushing my left hand against the wall. "Damn."

"What is wrong?"

"Nothing."

"Let me come to you."

"No, stay where you are. It's dangerous here." I move toward her. "What's going on out there?"

"A thunderstorm."

She sounds near. I crawl out of the passage back into the chamber near the entrance. Eventually her face emerges in a pale glow. Her hair and clothes are drenched.

"There you are." I lean forward and touch her hand. It's cold like stone.

"I was worried. I came looking for you."

"You're soaked."

"It came very fast and hard. It took me by surprise."

Thunder roars outside. She flinches.

"I'm sorry. I know how you hate thunderstorms."

"It is okay. Only a flash storm. Why are you hopping?"

"I scraped my leg."

"Let me take a look."

She crouches down. There is a rip in the left pants leg. She gently rolls it up, exposing a gash about three inches long, halfway between my ankle and knee.

"You are bleeding." Her finger grazes the skin around the wound.

"Ouch! It hurts."

"Let's see, we might have to cut off your leg."

"Very funny."

She takes a bottle of water from her bag and spills some on the cut. I bite my lip. She pulls out her scarf and pats the gash with the tip, cleaning off the blood and grime, then swathes the scarf around my calf, spreads the silk and ties two tight knots. I grunt a little. She unrolls the pants leg. "This should stop the bleeding. I hope it doesn't get infected."

I help her up. "It'll ruin your scarf."

"It was cheap."

"You know? My mom used to spit on the wound when I split something open."

"No, she didn't."

"Yes, honest to God. The miracle spit."

She shakes her head.

The thunder and wind and rain grow louder. A boulder perches about four feet away, large enough for both of us to sit. I limp toward it, pulling Lian behind me.

"I guess we're stuck here," I say.

We sit close together, my right arm brushing against her left. Her blouse clings to her thin bra—her breasts round and full, nipples pushing against the cotton. I steal a long look and hold my breath. She quivers. I take off my black pullover and put it over her shoulders—it's marked with muck, but it's dry and will keep her warm.

And keep me from gawking.

"I'm sorry," I say.

"At least we have shelter now."

"No. I'm sorry." I stare at the ground. "I'm sorry I disappeared."

"That was a long time ago."

"Will you ever forgive me?"

"There is nothing to forgive."

"Yes, there is." I sigh. "You must've hated me. I ran away. I ran away as far and as fast as I could."

"Why?"

"I don't know." I fiddle with a corner of my undershirt. "It was my old man, I thought. Teenage angst? Who the hell knows?"

I kick at the gravel on the ground. "I've just been running. From my father, my family, my dreams. Myself."

"From me?"

"I idolized you." I rub my neck. "But I suppose I got a little scared."

"I got too close."

I let go of the crinkles in my shirt.

"I'm so sorry."

"Greg." She places her hand on mine. "It was in the past. I am an old woman now. I don't have time to wallow in past regrets. And I don't hate you."

A clap of thunder invades us, distant but muscular. Her hand trembles. I grab it and hold it tight.

"Have you ever thought about us?" I glance at her.

"My mother always says, 'Time is like a river. It flows in only one direction,'" she says. "You must always look downstream, not up."

"Is there something downstream for us, you think?"

Her face is still in the muted light.

I lean over and kiss her cheek. Her skin is cold against my lips. An image flashes in my head—that Tuesday evening at Deep Water Bay. I kissed her for the first time. She was wearing my pullover.

In this dark cave, she pulls away again.

Our eyes meet. There's something strange about her eyes— large and green, as green as the most sublime emeralds. Freckles sprinkle both her cheeks against her wavy brown hair. The most wondrous half-smile.

Kate.

"Gosh darn it!" I edge away from her. "Shouldn't have tossed that sandwich. I'm hungry."

"We have white sugar cake left. And chocolates."

"Guylian."

She raises an eyebrow.

"That was always your favorite. Those little pieces of heaven," I say, fidgeting.

"You remember."

"I remember everything. Everything I know about you. I just don't know everything there is to know about you."

She hands me the last piece of white sugar cake.

"I saved it for you," I protest.

"I am not hungry. You are." She puts the bottle of water next to her, folds the brown paper bag in half, then stows it in her straw bag. "And you? I don't know anything about you either."

I shrug and take a large bite of the cake.

"You are the mysterious one," she says. "Do you lead a good, happy life?"

"Why do you keep asking me that?"

She takes a sip of water. Waiting.

"Like I said, I have a good job, make good money," I say. "I'm very comfortable."

"But you are not happy."

I'm transparent before her. I look away and stuff my mouth with the last lump.

"Because you have no passion, you said." She hands me the water bottle. "You have given up writing."

I take a swig to wash down the mash in my mouth. "Writing?"

"That was your dream, Greg. You talked of being a famous author. That was all you talked about."

"I did." I stare ahead at the dark space. "You know what my real passion is?" I take another sip of water. "I'm still hung up on you."

I fling the empty water bottle on the ground.

"I never seemed to be able to hold on to a relationship. Now I know why," I say, laughing at myself. "The biggest irony. I ran away from you. And then I kept looking for you. Or a facsimile of—"

"There must be a wonderful girl out there—"

"Don't interrupt me, please." I place a hand on my forehead. "Now I know you wrote me that letter, I have all these questions— And guilt."

I lean forward.

"Guilt." I take her hands. "Sadness. Regrets. Guilt. I didn't even say goodbye. I never realized before how much I must have hurt you. Since the letters, I just wanted to see you, to hold you again. To be with you."

"You can't step into the same river twice," she says.

I kiss her hands.

"I am married." She pulls her hands out of mine.

"To a good man."

"A very good man."

I stand up. I back away.

I skip over a large puddle of turbid water and hop around the opening and look up and see a darkened sky. Rain sprays my face and it's as chilly as the deep null in my heart and I just wish I had not come back.

"Greg."

I turn. She looks at me, a soft glint in her eyes. She is perfection—the only perfection—and I lost her. Now I've found her, I know. She is not mine.

"Come sit with me," she says.

And I know. I still want to be here.

In the dark cavern we wait for the storm to cease. Tentative at first, we talk, anecdotes of our separate lives. She asks me about college. I tell her all sorts of things—mostly bad, naughty, foolish things.

Like how, on a camping trip in Lake Tahoe, my pals and I sank our boat by jumping about with the big fat trout I caught. Tripped over and went under. The fish got away, too—hook, line and sinker. We swam half a mile to shore and faced the scorn of the burly boat owner, who insisted on charging us six hundred and fifty dollars for that ramshackle piece of shit. It was a rip-off, but what could we do? I was too high to punch his face.

Then there was the warm February afternoon I streaked across campus at Berkeley. Friday. Three o'clock. Incessant honking. I got a citation, a three-day suspension and an inbox filled with email from dozens of adoring women and half a dozen men.

Lian tells me some of her stories, too. She was in Munich four years ago, shopping for chocolates—what else?—losing track of time. She got flustered trying to find the subway station, halfway across town, half an hour before call time. She didn't speak a word of German and became uncharacteristically frantic. Eventually she found it. She took the train, not knowing she had to pay—there were no gates or turnstiles or ticket counters. She barely made it back to the concert hall in time, and was horrified to learn later that she had, in fact, broken the law. After the show, she ran back to the station just to pay for the ride she'd taken four hours earlier.

Then there was San Francisco, with an impromptu trip to Berkeley, a stroll near the Campanile, amid barefoot, dark-soled hippies and bra-less, tattooed feminists. At the end of the sunny afternoon, she took off her bra as well—keeping the blouse on, of course—possibly the wildest thing she'd ever done.

We talk about many other things: the Dalai Lama, Buddhism, poverty in Middle Asia, the conflicts in North Korea and Indonesia, operas, paintings. And books, we talk about books. We talk for a long time about Arthur Golden's *Memoirs of a Geisha*—the last book I read—and how it moved us. Lian thinks the world of Sayuri is a metaphor for the oppressiveness of our minds. I think it's a reminder of how our common struggles persist through time.

Perhaps we're both right. Perhaps I'm wrong.

Every time I'm around her, I pretend to be more sophisticated and polished than I really am. She always fascinates me for being so articulate, intelligent and cultivated. Her beauty. Her compassion. Her grace.

I built a pedestal for her. I kept her up there.

I had to run away.

Our conversation circles back to relationships, and she asks about mine. I stick out my tongue and hop away. I have nothing to tell. I've been single my entire adult life. Even Kate—I just don't know. And Lian's a happily married woman. The ugly wound starts to show.

I look up the opening and see only blackness. Night has sneaked up on us. The wind continues to wail, strong and constant.

"We're still trapped," I say.

"Greg."

I turn. She's only a dark shadow now.

"My marriage has failed."

"What?"

"We are getting a divorce."

"But you told me you were happy." I skip back to her side, trip on a rock and almost fall on my face.

"I am. It has nothing to do with my marriage."

"What are you saying?"

"I have found peace."

"Peace?"

Her smile sparkles in the dark. "A monk once told me a story. Do you want to hear it?"

I lean closer.

"There once was an Emperor who lived alone in his palace. Every morning, afternoon and evening he would come out on the balcony to enjoy the exquisite view. One day, as he ate a peach, the Emperor dropped it on the ground. A beautiful finch appeared and began picking at the remaining fruit. As it feasted, it sang a glorious song. That delighted the Emperor very much. The next day, the Emperor had another peach, and once again, the finch came, feasted on the fruit, and sang a glorious song for the Emperor. Day after day, he and the finch kept each other company on the balcony. The finch would get the peach, the Emperor a song in return.

"One day, the Emperor became very ill. For the entire day, the finch would come and find no peach. Sadly it left. The next morning, the Emperor recovered from his illness and came out on the balcony again. He dropped a peach on the ground, but the finch didn't come. He dropped another peach, but the finch still didn't come. When the ground was littered with peaches, the Emperor became very sad. He closed and locked the doors and never came out on the balcony again. The sun set and rose as usual, the view glorious. But the Emperor never saw it again."

"And the moral of the story is?"

"Have no expectations."

"You've got to have expectations. At least that's what they taught me in business school. Expectations motivate you."

"Do they really?"

"No?"

"Expectations stifle happiness. Expect nothing in return and you will find that peace, even when life deals you a bad hand."

"Is this one of your Buddhist teachings? I don't get it."

"I hope you will." She pats my hand. "I hope you will. I have always wished for that."

I lean even closer. "Even when I dealt you a bad hand?"

She smiles.

"You're amazing." I take her hand in mine and gently rub it.

"It doesn't mean I am a saint," she says. "I still have moods."

"And get mad. Man, you get mad."

"You were yelling at me."

"Yeah, and you pushed me. I got a big mouthful of sand."

"No, you fell," she says. Her hands quickly warm in mine. "Anyway, I was sad. I suppose I still have some expectations. About you."

"I don't want to make you sad. Disappoint you."

"Greg, it isn't about me. You. It is about you."

"But—what about your marriage? What happened?"

"He is a good man," she says. "But he isn't happy. Not for a while now. He wants to sail to Europe. He wants to paint. He wants to spend five years in Africa. All by himself."

I roll my eyes.

"I do believe he loves me, and I love him very much," she says. "But there is a time when you must do what is right for yourself and the person you love. We have come to an understanding. We don't know when the divorce will happen."

"Then he doesn't really love you."

"So, you didn't love me either?"

"Don't be absurd." I let go of her hands. "How can you let him go? You still love him?"

"If you love somebody, set them free."

"Hey, I love that song."

"And I love Sting." She elbows me.

I chuckle. "But how does that work? Tell me."

"Maybe some other time. Over a glass of lemon iced tea," she says.

I cock my head and gaze at her. Perfection. "Howard's a fool."

"Howard?"

"Dr. Cape. Your husband."

"No, no. Not Howard. Whatever gave you that idea?" She frowns. "Howard has been with someone else, for seven years now."

"Who's your husband, then?"

"His name is Martin."

"Martin?"

"Martin Cowen. He works for the museum."

Martin Cowen? The Australian farm boy? The Soccer King? My best friend?

"How did you two meet?" I ask with a hard shrug, pretending that I know nothing about Martin. I stare straight ahead, my face taut. I honestly want to know. How our lives are all linked together by fate's depraved sense of humor.

"He had a motorcycle accident. Nothing life-threatening, just a concussion and a broken leg. The ER resident looked at him and gave him something for the pain. Maybe that had something to do with how he approached me."

"How?"

"He started to talk to me. I couldn't really understand his accent—maybe the Vicodin had something to do with it, too. We talked while I was putting a splint on him. He wasn't the smartest person, but he was very charming. When I was about to leave, he grabbed my arm. Then he said the sweetest thing."

"What?"

"Marry me."

"How corny."

"I thought it was very sweet."

"Then what happened?"

"We were married six months later."

It all seemed like a fairytale, and they did have some kind of a fairytale wedding. St. Paul's Cathedral. Ten-layer cake. Honeymoon in Osaka. He stayed in Hong Kong and got a job at the Hong Kong History Museum as a curator...

"Then what happened?" I ask.

"Did you expect 'happily ever after'?"

"I was just asking."

"He was good to me. But, no, there was no fairytale."

"He is a lucky guy." I stare at nothing.

I clench my jaw, quietly crushing the edge of the boulder with my left hand.

I could anticipate Howard Cape. I could deal with that jealousy—I did deal with it, long ago. Howard could have taken good care of her and I would have been fine with that. But Martin? He had no right to claim this prize. He was a hick, good with his hands but not much up there. He was not good enough.

*Then again, you gave her away. It was all your fault.*

Guess what? They're splitting up. Things are looking good. Now is my chance.

*What are you talking about? Jesus Christ. What about Kate? What you feel about her is real, isn't it? What's now in front of you is not real. It's your past. Your ghost. Why are you still so hung up on Lian? What has gotten into you?*

Go away.

"Listen," I say, holding up my right hand.

We hush and listen.

"Water?"

"Exactly. Just water running. Sounds like the storm has passed." I let out a breath. "We should go."

　She gathers the empty water bottle and chocolate box into the tote bag. In the dark we slowly track our way to the opening. The rain has indeed stopped. A chill creeps down my neck and beneath my undershirt. The boulders leading up are slippery, overflowing with mire. I struggle up, pulling Lian close behind me. By the time we get out of the cave, both of us are smeared with sludge.

　We look marvelously ridiculous.

# Stay a Night with Me

As we return to the Praya, the rain starts again. The shops are closed, the stalls stowed, and the bicyclists rare. Only the Ho Won Restaurant, in the corner across from the wharf, stays open for business. On its front door, a loose poster of a Chinese boy band, Rage, flaps in the wind. Two tables of somber customers cuddle their teacups in a cozy corner.

The rain quickens. Lian and I run to the wharf. To my dismay, the gates are shut and locked.

"Damn. What happened?" I ask.

"They must have stopped the ferries. What time is it?"

I glance at my watch. "About eight."

"That is strange. Wait. Today is Hing Ping Day. That is right. They were running the holiday schedule."

"What the hell is Hing Ping Day?"

She smiles. "It is a local holiday. Peace Day. Most people stay home to rest and say thanks to their families."

"Ah, like our Thanksgiving, without the turkey and football," I say. "So what do we do now?"

"We…" She glances away. Something is turning in her head. "I don't know. You must go back to Hong Kong."

"You mean we."

Her brows twitch slightly. "Yes."

"We can stay here overnight. It—"

"No." She sounds exasperated. "We must find someone to take us back."

"On a tiny boat in this weather? You must be kidding."

She just stares at me.

"I know," I say. "You have to go home."

I hate that she has a home to miss.

We dash across the street and find shelter at Ho Won.

"Stay here." I tug at her sleeve, pulling her under the restaurant's green awning. "I'll ask."

I walk around in the rain, looking for someone willing to take us back to Hong Kong Island. The locals have gone home for the holiday. Most of the boats at the docks are untenanted, and the few folks I find all shake their heads to my peculiar request—there is a storm out there and no one wants to leave port. Eventually, a short middle-aged man in a bright yellow raincoat agrees to take us in his little junk with a poop no bigger than a two-person tent. But he asks for a thousand Hong Kong dollars for each person—around a hundred and thirty American. I'm not sure if I have that much on me.

I thumb through my wallet. Eighty dollars short. I search my pockets and find half a dozen more rumpled bills, some loose change, and a folded piece of paper. I unfold it. It's the flyer the boy on the bicycle handed me this afternoon—an ad for a local hotel, the Pacific Inn. I have a swift idea. I have just enough cash to cover Lian and myself for the trip, but I tell the man otherwise. He shakes his head and turns away. I let him go.

Lian has cleaned up, dried off and taken a table at Ho Won when I return. The jasmine tea is strong. The hot towel loosens the knots in my face. I drop it muck-sodden on the table, and a waiter promptly picks it up, a moue evident on his oily mug.

"You should really clean up," Lian whispers to me. "And get dry."

"Why don't you order something for us, then? I want hot and sour soup."

When I return from the restroom, there's a scrumptious feast of steaming plates of vegetables, vegetables, and more vegetables waiting for me. Gardens of green, red, yellow, brown, pink and purple bloom in four embroidered ceramic plates.

"What's all this?" I ask.

"I hope you don't mind. I ordered some of my favorites. Hot and sour soup is a little too American, even for you."

"No meat? Not even chicken? You're turning me into a monk."

"You will like these." She hands me a small bowl of soup, definitely not hot and sour, but thin slices of two different kinds of greens in a clear broth, tiny flakes of soft husk floating. To my surprise, it soothes with intricate flavors, slightly sweet, somewhat bitter, silky down the throat, like warm brandy on a bleak wintry night.

"What is it?"

"Winter melon and Chinese squash."

"What about this? And this? And this? And this?" I point at each thing before me.

"These are braised tofu and eggplant," she says. "Be careful of the hot chili sauce. And this is Shanghai bok choy and black mushroom, wrapped in tofu sheets. Pea sprouts with garlic. And my very favorite, lotus root and fava beans."

I make a slurping sound. "Liver and Chianti." I scoop large portions from each steaming dish onto my plate. She sips her tea absently, missing the Hannibal Lecter joke. "Thank you. Smells delicious," I say.

She grins and lifts a slice of lotus root with her chopsticks. She takes a tiny bite.

"You eat like a mouse," I say.

"But I am healthy."

"I suppose. And you have time to stop and smell the roses. Unlike my friends here. Too busy pushing and shoving."

"You still have friends here?"

"Of course. Well, there's Agnes and Old Chow, from the hospital—you remember them? My friends Choy, David."

"Choy?"

"Jesus, these are hot." I swallow the rest of my tea and reach for the teapot. I glance at her—she squints, then slowly sips her tea. Maybe she knows Choy through Martin. "You know what bothers me sometimes? People who choose their own names, as if they just pick something out of a dictionary. Like Bison Wong or Igloo Chan. Or my friend, Bok Choy. What kind of a name is that?"

"I know a girl named Rainbow Chow."

"See what I mean? If I want a Rainbow Trout, I'll go fishing."

"Greg, you are rude."

"Thankya, thankya. Thankya vury much."

She laughs.

Distant whispers of a waterfall on a bright summer day. It's been a long time. It pleases me that I can still make her laugh.

I consume the sumptuousness before me. The eggplant, piquant in luscious violet, titillates with vim, while the verdant pea sprouts, drenched in a voluptuous stock, burst into vigorous rapture. The black mushrooms, soft as full lips, caress my eager tongue in primal passion. The lotus root. Yes, the lotus root—pink and delicate, glorious fragments of lucent dream.

Heaven.

Lian beams, enjoying my shameless zeal.

"By the way, I'm sorry." I take a swig of my tea. "I can't find anyone to take us back to Hong Kong."

Her smile drifts into a frown. I hate that, but it's time to tell her. "We have to stay overnight," I say.

"We can't."

"Why not? You love this island."

"We must go back."

"We can't. Nobody will take us."

"There is no place for us to stay."

"Actually, there is." I pull out the flyer and show her. "It's called the Pacific Inn, on Lai Ling Street."

"A boarding house?"

"Is that what it is? It says 'inn' here."

"It isn't exactly a hotel."

"As long as it has a bed and a shower, I'm happy."

"Greg."

"Please don't fret. It's only for a night." I crunch on a stalk of bok choy, thick juice seeping down my throat. "You can call Mr. Cowen and tell him what happened. He'll understand."

She looks away. I know she has no choice but stay a night with me.

She turns to me again. "We leave in the morning."

"First thing in the morning." I place a hand over my heart. "I promise."

I load my plate for the second time.

Maybe a second chance.

Heaven.

# Tai Ping Inn

The rain has stopped. We find the Pacific Inn on Lai Ling Street, a grim alley about two blocks from the restaurant. A decrepit three-story row house with four small, wretched windows behind iron bars and blotchy yellow cloth curtains. Water-stained walls. A shopworn sign with two oversized red Chinese characters—Tai Ping—hangs in a corner. Through the translucence of the curtains, a dim red glow.

Straight out of a Dickens novel, had Dickens been Chinese.

Through a black folding gate, I knock on the door three times. No answer. I dart my tongue out at Lian. She shakes her head. I knock again. The door slowly squeals open, meeting the ample hip of a runty Chinese woman with white hair, wrinkly face, and a stupendous mole dead center in her forehead. She stares, her eyes narrowed into two slits, at the two strange faces emerging from the night.

"Yes?" she asks, a thick regional accent.

"We'd like to stay here for the night," I say. "Do you have any rooms?"

"One room."

"We need two rooms."

"One."

"No, we need two. Two," I say, holding up two fingers. "One, two. Two."

Lian pushes my hand down. She speaks to the old woman in Cantonese. "That is quite all right. We will take the room."

"But," I protest.

"Greg, this is fine. I am tired and cold. We both need to get some sleep. We will think of something."

The old woman unlocks the gate, folds it, and slides it aside to let us in. The place reeks of incense and mothballs. A humble altar for Gwun Yin—Goddess of Mercy—emits the faint red glow from a corner. The rest of the space is dark.

The old woman squeezes through a narrow gap between a counter and a wall and flicks on the florescent lights. Blinking in the glare, I see a small, square room, a concrete floor as hard and cold in color as it feels beneath my feet. A tattered brown leather couch lurks in a corner, torn down to foam at the edges, next to a large, empty fish tank. Across from the couch, a decades-old Panasonic television perches on a wooden stand, leaning slightly to the left. I look around, frowning—it's crummier than my bachelor pad at Berkeley.

"One night?" she asks from behind the counter.

"Sure. Looks like a long one, too."

"Hundred twenty dollar."

I hand her the money. She drops a heavy brass key in my hand.

She squeezes herself back into the room. "Come," she says.

Lian and I follow her around the corner, up two flights of dimly lit stairs. I take Lian's hand and pull her close to me. The corridor is narrow. At the end, the old woman opens a door and switches on a ceiling light. What a lovely closet. At least it's clean, bright, and neat—a single bed, a pillow, white sheets, a thin brown blanket, a tiny wooden desk, a green plastic stool. The flimsy red rose-print curtains are drawn. I look around and stick out my lower lip.

"There's only one bed," I say. "Don't think it's big enough for two."

Lian frowns at me and asks the old woman for a cot. The old woman shuffles away to find one. I sit on the bed, bounce on it twice. Surprisingly, the mattress is firm and comfortable.

Too bad it's not big enough for two.

"I'm so sorry about this," I say.

"This is fine. I don't expect much."

"No expectations, huh? Tell me, how do we go through life without expectations? I don't need the Grant Hyatt or the Ritz, but staying at a place like this is not what I'd call a good thing."

"What is not to love?" she says, peeking out the window through a chink between the curtains. "The bed seems comfortable. We have a view of a lovely alleyway. We have air in our lungs and food in our stomachs. We have a dry, warm place away from the rain." She chuckles, catching herself uttering all those clichés. But they're true.

"Nothing fazes you," I confess. Peace is contagious. I hop off the bed and step up to the desk. A pad of yellow notepaper and a black ballpoint pen lie neatly in the center. "Paper and pen. What's not to love?"

I write her name on a piece of paper, tear it out, and place it on the bed. I write my name on another piece of paper and put it on the floor.

"In case you complain about the bed, just so you know, the floor is mine."

She laughs. I laugh with her.

There is a knock on the door. The old woman enters, carrying a small blue-green nylon cot, a pink pillow, a green blanket and two thin bath towels. She unfolds the cot, lays it on the floor, and piles the rest on it. The thin, short cot is clearly too small for me, but I keep my mouth shut.

"Need something more?" the old woman asks.

"Where's the bathroom?" I ask her.

She gestures. "Bath and toilet end of hall. Breakfast seven morning."

"Thank you so much," Lian tells her. The old woman nods and leaves the room.

Lian takes the piece of paper from the bed and places it on the cot. She puts my name on the bed.

"No, no. You take the bed," I say, switching the names again. "Don't be silly."

"It is too small for you."

"I'll manage. Just one night."

I sit on the cot, plop my arms over my knees and gaze at her. I have her right here, next to me. What's not to love?

"How is your leg?" she asks, pulling her hair up.

"I almost forgot about it. Still hurts a little."

"We should clean it up. I will see if I can find some bandages and iodine."

"I'm fine. Don't."

"Greg, don't argue with me."

"Yes, ma'am."

"Now, go and take a shower. You smell."

I lift my right arm and stick my nose into my armpit. "Do I really?"

"Greg."

"You're such a fuddy-duddy, you know?"

"And you are a spoiled brat."

I flash her a goofy grin and grab a towel.

"Don't go anywhere," I say. I step out, closing the door behind me.

The communal bathroom at the other end of the hallway is barely large enough for one person. Rusty pipes crawl their ways around the corners to the bottom of a sink spun with a web of hairline cracks, next to a toilet with a dulled wooden seat. An opaque glass window, jammed shut, does nothing for ventilation. The shower stall is marginally sanitary, however freshened with the smell of chlorine. In a corner, a mop leans up from the checker-tiled floor. The Ritz this isn't. But somehow, I feel comfortable here.

It reminds me so much of Lian's old place on Waterloo Road.

I take off my clothes and socks, lay them on the toilet seat, then loosen the soiled scarf and lay it on my clothes. I step into the shower and turn on the water. Shit. It's freezing. Not a drop of hot water. There's not much water pressure to speak of either. I guess this will have to do. The gash stings under the running water. My muscles begin to shiver, then to ache.

As I shake in my nakedness, I start to think—is it really true that every cloud has its silver lining, or rather, every cold shower feels warmer by the second? Here I am, under the icy trickles in the crummiest, most deprived place, happy. Rather, content. I'm so content that I just want to curl up by Lian's side and let her read me a story—a story of a fair princess who awakes the sleeping prince with a kiss. A story without witches or monsters or fires or dark cages or dungeons or sicknesses or heartbreaks or betrayals or blood or death. A story about love.

Then I think of my fair Kate.

"I found some things," Lian says as I enter the room. "Let me take a look."

I roll up my pants leg and show her. The cut is throbbing red.

She frowns. "I hope it didn't get infected."

She cleans the cut with a cotton ball soaked with alcohol, then re-bandages it with a piece of gauze and some medical tape. All the while, looking at her, I remember the cap, the dress, and the white belt wrapped around her slim waist.

I can love her now. I never stopped.

"You are all set," she says.

"Lian," I whisper.

She catches my gaze. She grasps a clean towel, rushes out of the room before I can warn her of the cold water.

I sit at the desk and tear out a piece of paper.

*Dear Kate,*

I hold the pen to my lips. That's all I can think of.

I crumple the paper into a ball. No wastebasket. Nothing to drink either—Chinese food makes me thirsty.

I shove the pad of paper and the pen in my back pocket, step out and tiptoe past the bathroom, down to the first floor. It is quiet. The chilled concrete sticks to my toes. A dim yellow light shines like a beacon around the corner and I follow it to a small kitchen in the back. The refrigerator door is open. A silhouette hovers in front of the light.

"Oh, hello," the shadow speaks to me, a deep voice.

"Hello," I say, squinting. "I'm looking for something to drink."

"You can't drink out of the faucets. Not much in the refrigerator either. I suppose we can brew some tea," the shadow says in a languid British accent. It steps aside, leaving the fridge door open so we can see. My eyes adjust to a man's white buttocks—he's buck-naked. I lean against the wall and feel around but can't find the light switch. He bumbles about, opening and closing the cabinet doors, banging them loudly. He fills up a dark kettle, places it on the stove, and turns on the gas. He turns around and extends a hand to me.

"Timothy Harding," he says. He's about thirty. Curly hair. A tall, taut, naked man.

"Gregory Lockland." I nod instead.

"American?"

"California. You?"

"East Sussex originally. But I haven't been back for some years now. I lived in New York for six years. How do you like this place?"

"Here? It's a dump, to be honest."

He hoots. "Yes, yes. But it's cheap. Perfect way to travel."

"You travel much?"

"All over the world. I'm on sabbatical. It's just me, my backpack, and the world."

"Sounds like a good life."

"It is, but you get homesick once in a while. And sometimes you'd just die for a hot bath."

"I know exactly what you mean. What did you do before this?"

"I taught history at Columbia. Now I write. Well, I still teach English while traveling. Pocket money."

"Naturally."

"And what do you do?"

"Management consultant." I shrug.

"Management consultant? What're you doing in a dump like this?"

"Long story. But I don't mind. Really. I have air in my lungs."

"Ah yes, Chinese food in your belly, and a warm blanket on your feet." He nods. "That's the spirit. It's the best part of traveling poor. You get to see how people really live, eat their real food. You appreciate things."

"Been on the road long?"

"Almost six months now, and I may go on forever," he says, touching his nose with a finger. "You see, I've seen sights only an angel should see and heard sounds deep inside Mother Earth. I've eaten the strangest food. Have you ever tried *Doo Doo*? I did, in Malaysia. Fried noodles with taro paste. Delicious." He kisses the air. "I've met so many people from all over—Cairo, Istanbul, Buenos Aires, the Amazon, Malaysia, Ho Chi Ming City. It is a life."

"I'm envious."

"It's not for everyone, though. It gets lonely sometimes." He brushes a coil of hair away from his stubbly face. "You come across a perfect moment and draw your breath, then realize there's no one next to you to share it. It passes." He cups his chin and grins. "That doesn't make it any less magical. You miss something, nonetheless."

"You're a romantic."

"And a loner, most of the time." The kettle whistles. He turns and sprinkles a handful of tealeaves into a white teapot. "I do enjoy meeting people, though, and sharing a carriage or a hut or a few slices of prosciutto, preferably with a hot cup of tea."

He picks up the kettle and pours the hot water into the teapot. He takes two teacups from the cupboard above him.

"Can you make that three?" I ask.

"Ah, a companion, I see."

"Where're you going next?"

"I came from the south, South Pacific to be precise. I'm going north now, first the southern China provinces, Tibet perhaps, then hopefully ending up somewhere in Mongolia."

"Doesn't that take a lot of planning?"

"Planning? What for? Life's at its most precious without plans."

"That's a lot of risks to take, not knowing where exactly you're going, or what's going to happen."

"What's life without risks? You take risks, don't you?"

"Only calculated ones." I grin. "What about language? It must be nerve-racking not to understand a thing."

"Oh, you learn as you go, a little bit at a time. Cursing is easy. In Cantonese, it's *Dil Lei*. Isn't it?" He sniggers. "Colorful stuff. Then there's *thank you*, the numbers, and *how much*. You can go quite far with those. Actually, it can be very invigorating. New languages, new cultures. If all else fails, you can always draw pictures."

"So you don't expect much."

"Expectation is the death of happiness."

"I've heard that."

"Believe it."

He pours me two cups of tea, himself one. Jasmine.

I nod. "Mr. Tim Harding."

"Mr. Greg Lockland." He nods.

The fridge door slams shut. The light is out.

I raise my teacup. "To happiness."

"To happiness."

We sip our tea.

"When you have a chance," he says, "go up on the roof. There, you will feel better."

The room is dim when I return. I slip through the door. In the small light I see Lian curled up under a blanket on the cot, a butterfly in its cocoon. The rain chimes on the tin roof.

"Lian, are you awake?" I whisper, leaning against the cot, touching her hand. She stirs.

"Hey, come on, you're taking the bed. You hear me?" I say.

"Greg, I am tired," she murmurs. "You take the bed, all right?"

"No, I told you the cot was mine. You tricked me."

She sits up. "It is small even for me. You can't fit into this."

"No, you must take the bed. I insist."

"Are you sure?"

"I'm very sure. Hey, I brought you some tea. Your favorite, jasmine."

"Oh, thank you."

She takes the cup from my hand and presses her lips against the brim. I've dreamed of those lips for days now. To see her like this, wrapped vulnerably in a lean sheet of wool, prompts me to think unsacred thoughts.

I kiss her.

She pulls away.

"I can't. I am married."

I kiss her fingers. "I don't care."

"I do." She withdraws her hand from mine. I grasp it again.

"But you love me. You still do. I know."

"What difference does it make?"

"It makes a whole world of difference to me. I want you back."

Our eyes stay on each other's. The chimes above us are soft and rhythmic.

"You can't."

I let go of her hand. She pulls the blanket closer.

"I think I should go," I say.

"Greg—"

I slip out the door, not looking back.

The view from the roof is magnificent: roof upon roof and the slumbering harbor on one side, a peek of the indolent Tung Wan Beach on the other. The storm clouds have finally cleared. A half moon hangs high, its twin trembling in the black sea. Chains and bells clank randomly in a distance, soft and lazy. Whiffs of seawater and incense drift with the breeze.

*Upon this roof that is my stage*
*The water is my music and the stars my lights*
*A pen my instrument*
*I have sad songs to sing*

I sit on the edge of the roof, my right foot dangling freely. If I fall, I'll most certainly break my neck. And maybe that would be it. All the world's troubles are only that—the world's troubles, not mine.

*There is an ocean out there I cannot cross.*
*There is an ocean within I cannot sail.*
*There is a woman here whom I cannot love.*
*There is a woman I can love who is not near.*

I write feverishly. The paper pad becomes thin and the ink heavy. My fingers are stiff and cold. But I keep writing.

*Pig says to Oscar, why are you sad?* <u>Because the moon is not rising and the wind is not mild and my ears are not warm and my feet are not rested and my friends are not here.</u> *Am I not your friend then?* <u>You are a pig.</u> *But I am here...*

I don't seem to be able to stop now. I pull the crumpled ball of paper from my pocket, flatten it, and continue where I left off.

*Dear Kate,*

*By now you must be thinking, what's wrong with that horrible man? I don't blame you if you think negative thoughts about me...I realize, once again I've failed you. I left.*

*I don't know why I left the way I did, and why I didn't call or write. I just couldn't seem to tell you the truth...I could have told you simply that I was going to Hong Kong...yes that's where I am now...I didn't have to keep that from you...but to tell you that, I would have to tell you everything, and I wasn't ready to do so...I guess the easiest thing for me is always run...*

*I don't know...*

*I found two letters in my father's safe deposit box. From a woman named Lian. A woman I've never really forgotten. Kate, I know this will hurt you, but the truth is, I still have feelings for her, even after all these years. It's absurd, and I don't understand it myself but it's true. I was sad and ashamed about the way I left her. Maybe that's why I couldn't tell you...and now I have found her...I realize I still love her. I do. Oh Kate...I'm so sorry...I don't know why I'm writing you this...I guess you've always been there for me...I want to tell you everything...I want you to understand, but I'm afraid...I'm so confused...I'm with her now...she's asleep...*

I fold the letter in half and scribble Kate's address on the back. 1935 Roselyn Drive. San Marcos. California. U.S.A.

I put the letter in my shirt pocket. I don't know what to do with it.

I return to the room, only a shred of moonlight outlining her shape. The tea on the desk is cold. She hasn't touched it.

In the light I watch her sleep. Her breaths are gentle.

I watched her sleep many times, years ago. The same way I am watching her now.

The same way I watched Kate sleep.

# Tea or Coke

I open my eyes to a pale-green wall splattered with thin strokes of sunlight. I hear no sound other than the creaks of the cot as I move. I yawn and stretch my arms, realize I'm snug inside two layers of blanket, two soft pillows under my head.

I scramble up, tip the cot and fall over. The floor is frigid under my feet. I look at my watch—I've overslept and it's after nine already. The bed is made.

She is gone.

I put on my socks and Nikes, pull open the door and dash through the hallway, past the empty bathroom, down the stairs and into the common room. Two young white men in their parkas are sipping their coffee on the leather couch. I turn the corner into the kitchen. Instant coffee. Tim Harding stands by the fridge, fully clothed in a lime-green pullover and brown khaki shorts, chewing on a large piece of Spam.

"Hello, good morning," he chirps.

"Did you see her?"

"Who?"

"My companion. A beautiful woman with long black hair."

"No, and I'd have noticed."

"Shit. Where has she gone?"

"Ask Wing Po."

"Who?"

"The innkeeper."

I turn to leave.

"Wing Po!" he shouts into the air.

Wing Po enters the kitchen. "Tim Ha Ding, what you want?" she asks.

"Yes, Wing Po, have you seen this gentleman's wife?"

"Actually, she's not my wife," I say.

"Whatever. Significant other, then," he says, and turns to Wing Po. "Have you seen her? The beautiful woman with long black hair?"

"Leave at seven," she says.

"Where?" I ask.

She shakes her head.

"Damn. When's the first ferry, you know?" I ask.

"Six, I think. Then once every hour," he says.

"Shit." I turn to leave again.

"Greg, did you two have a fight last night?"

"No," I say. "I—we were fine."

"Don't worry, maybe she just went out for some flowers or fruits or something."

"Wing Po," I say to her, "if she comes back, please keep her here until I return. I'm going out to look for her."

"She leave."

"She's probably out shopping, like this gentleman said."

"She leave."

"Just keep her here when she returns, okay?"

"I'll help keep an eye out for her as well," he says.

"You can't miss her," I say. "Nobody can."

I run around town, desperate for Lian. The Praya, the docks, the stores, the beach. I even run up the hill to the cemetery again, hoping that she's paying her respects. But she eludes me.

I've lost her again.

I return to the Tai Ping Inn about two hours later. Tim Harding sits on the couch reading the *South China Morning Post*, chewing on another piece of Spam.

"Oh, hello," he says. "Did you find her?"

"No. I suppose she never came back?"

"I'm afraid not."

"Shit."

"Sure you two are all right?"

"Well, not exactly."

"Lovers' quarrel? Maybe she really went home."

"Yeah." I scratch my head. "The problem is—I don't know where she lives."

Tim raises an eyebrow. "You two just met?"

"No, no. It's a long story." I slump in the couch. "I need to find her. I need to find her husband first."

"She has a husband?"

"And he was my good friend."

"Oh my. Foolish, foolish, foolish."

"Don't even start."

"What are you going to do?"

"I need to call my friend Choy."

"Wing Po!" he yells.

Wing Po appears from nowhere. "Tim Ha Ding, what you want?"

"Wing Po, Mr. Lockland'd like to use the telephone."

"Long distance?" she asks.

"No, no. Just Hong Kong," I say.

"Two dollar."

"She charges for everything. Unbelievable."

"But the Spam's free." Tim laughs heartily and takes another salty bite.

I burst into the apartment shortly after two. Agnes, dressed in a pink muumuu, sits on the sofa, reading a *Readers' Digest*. A pot of tea and a plate of shortbread cookies sit on the coffee table.

"Good gracious, what happened to you?" she asks, dropping her magazine.

"A little accident. Don't worry, nobody died."

"Where did you go? Old Chow told me you didn't come home last night."

"I went to Cheung Chau with Lian."

Her eyes glint with excitement. "Oh, tell me."

I sit next to her and tell her everything. This time, I'm totally honest with her. It's actually liberating, even though I'm afraid that she'll judge me. For some reason, I care about what she thinks.

She listens intently, not interrupting me—not even once.

"So," I say, letting out a long sigh. "She ran away the same way I ran away from her."

She tilts her head at me. There is an impish twinkle in those squinty eyes. For an instant, I see my mother.

"Say something," I say. "Laugh. Tease me. Do whatever."

She presses her lips on the teacup and takes a long sip.

"You're in love with her," she says.

"Isn't that obvious? I came all the way across the Pacific—"

"I mean the other girl."

"Kate?"

"Yes, Kate. You never told me about her."

"It didn't come up." I shift my body, stuck in the gap between the sofa seats. "I'm a private person."

"I notice." She sips her tea. "Is she pretty?"

"Kate? She's nice. Approachable. Girl next door. She's smart and fun. She has this funny habit of touching the back of her ear—what?"

"I didn't say anything," she says, smirking.

I clear my throat, feeling tight and uneasy.

"You were with the most beautiful woman in the world, and you thought of Kate," she says.

"But I kissed Lian. I wanted her."

"Yes, yes. I'm not trying to disregard your feelings for Lian. But we're talking about Kate here."

"But I'm still in love with Lian."

"Don't confuse obsession with love."

"What are you saying?" I grab a shortbread cookie and sink deep into the sofa.

"Oh, you home." Old Chow comes out of the bedroom, wearing only his boxer shorts, scratching his large belly. "Look shitty."

"Feel shitty, too," I say.

"You find girl?"

"He stayed a night with her," Agnes says.

"Lucky boy." Old Chow laughs.

"But he's in love with someone else."

"Oh, lucky boy."

"Not really," I say. "I don't know. I have no frigging idea."

"Old Chow had two loves," he says with glee.

"Really?" Agnes perks up, pressing a finger on her lips.

"Mei Fong. First love. Beautiful," he says. "Too beautiful. Like lily flower in spring time. Pick the wrong wife la. Ma wife, Siu Yuen a bitch. Bitch. Bitch."

"So you got rid of the beautiful one and married that pig? Why, for Heaven's sake?" Agnes asks.

"No want competition. Old Chow very young. Stupid."

"Not so young anymore. Still stupid," Agnes says.

"But happy."

"I wish I could say the same," I say.

"Tell Old Chow la. Your two loves," Old Chow says.

"Not much to tell," I say.

"Men," Agnes chides. "You all bolt at the first sound of a heart-to-heart chat."

"No me. I tell everything," he says. He plops himself on the sofa between Agnes and me. He pats my leg. "Tell Old Chow la."

Agnes proceeds to tell the story for me. Old Chow coughs incessantly, amused.

"You love two womans," he says. "Clear like water."

"How is that going to help me?"

"Not everything is about you," Agnes says.

I draw a breath. "You know, Lian said exactly the same thing."

"Have you ever asked the question, 'What does it mean to them?'"

"What?"

"Ask them what they want."

"I don't even know what I want."

"Ah, once again, it's all about you, isn't it?"

"I no ask Mei Fong," Old Chow chimes in. "I no ask her what she want. Big mistake."

"What are you talking about?"

"Tea or Coke?" he asks.

"I'm not thirsty."

"No, you choose tea or you choose Coke?"

"What? I like both."

"Ah. But if you need to choose, which would you choose? Tea or Coke?" Agnes asks.

"I see where this is going," I say. "But it's not simple like that. I like tea and I like Coke. I can choose one over another anytime I want. They're things. They're not people."

"Bingo!" Old Chow cries.

I stare at them.

"You're a dim bulb sometimes," she says, patting the back of my hand. "You will learn."

"Teach me."

"I can't teach you," she says. "You have to experience it, learn from it, and maybe suffer from it, just like Old Chow and I did."

"Show me, then."

"Well, let's see. Do you have the letter you wrote to Kate?"

I grab at my pocket. "Oh shit."

"What's the matter?"

"It must have fallen out of my pocket when I slept. I think Lian might have read it. That's why. Crap."

"What exactly did you say in that letter?"

"I have to find Lian."

"I find her," Old Chow says.

"No, no. I can find her myself. I already have a lead."

"What about Kate?" Agnes asks.

"I have to go. I'm a mess. I smell like mothballs."

"You're running again."

"Really. I have things to do."

I surge up and toward my room, crumbs of shortbread falling like snow from my lap.

I call directory assistance. Tai Ping Inn. After six rings, a young man's voice answers, "Wei, Tai Ping."

"Oh, hello. Is Wing Po there?"

"Hold please," he says.

"Ah-Ma!" he shouts. His voice comes on again, "Sorry. My Ah-Ma has problem with her ears."

"You're her grandson?"

"Yes, my name is Hoi."

"You gave me the flyer yesterday."

"I pass them out every day. I made them on my IBM Aptiva. I visit my Ah-Ma almost every day."

"You must know Cheung Chau pretty well."

"I know everywhere. I grew up here. Hold, please. My Ah-Ma is here."

"Yes?" It's Wing Po.

"Hi. This is Greg Lockland. Remember me? I stayed at your place last night with the woman. Beautiful. Long black hair."

"Lok Lan. Yes?"

"I have a favor to ask you. I think I left a note in my room this morning. Did you find something when you were cleaning?"

"Note?"

"A letter, actually. A piece of notepad paper. Address on the back."

"Letter? Yes."

"Great. Wow." I let out a whoosh of air. "That's great. Can I ask you another favor? Please throw it away for me."

"No. Send already."

"You what?"

"Wife give me letter to send. I ask Ha Ding to send."

"Tim Harding? Can I speak to him, please?"

"He leave afternoon."

"Oh, God," I moan.

I thank Wing Po and hang up.

I can't believe Lian would do that. I can't let Kate know about Lian, not this way. I was a rambling fool, going on and on about Lian and my feelings for her. "She's with me now...she's asleep..." Jesus. What would Kate think?

I have perhaps three days to intercept the letter before it crosses the Pacific to San Diego.

But first, I must find Lian and Martin. Unfinished business, here.

# Dear Kate

"Hi, Kate here. Leave me a message and I'll catch you later."
Beep.
"Kate? Kate, are you there? Pick up the phone, please. Kate? I need to talk to you."
Silence.
"Kate?"
Beep.

I lock myself in my room and pull a white sheet of paper from the desk drawer, its clean surface smooth like Kate's face. I trace an edge, pressing it against my thumb. I pick up a pen. I chew on the cap.

*Dear Kate,*
*By now you must be thinking, what is wrong with that horrible*

I crumple the paper, pull out another and start again.

*Dear Kate,*
*I worry about you. I tried to call you but you were not there. Where are you?*

*I miss you. You may not believe me, but I do. I feel isolated here. I think about you all the time. I think of you at the strangest moments, when I least expect it—it surprises and comforts me. The frequency is urgent now. Constantly I imagine your smile, and I ache to see it.*

*I dreamed of you last night. It was so vivid I thought it was real. You were standing by a fountain, your hair down and your hands stretching out like an angel's wings. I reached for you, but you took a step back and disappeared into the wall of water. I yelled out your name, but you didn't answer me. Why didn't you answer me? I went into the water after you, and I saw a rainbow. Yellow daisies and pink tulips. But I couldn't see you. I yelled out your name again. That's when I woke up.*

*Kate, I never dreamed of rainbows or flowers before. The strangest thing was, I was desperate to find you, but at the same time, I was calm. I felt warm in my dream. It was as if I knew you were there, even though I couldn't see you after you disappeared. It was as if you were looking out for me, touching me, holding me. Loving me.*

*I wish you were with me now. The moon is so high and bright, like your smile when I put that Mickey Mouse hat on you. Or when you saw those shooting stars. Or when you stumbled into me when we were slow dancing. Those were the magical moments for me. Because you were there.*

*You are my moon, my rose, my rainbow, my angel.*

*I miss you.*

*Greg*

I start over again. This time, I go for the simple truth:

*Dear Kate,*

*I love you. Always.*

*Greg*

# The Party

Choy greets me at the door, a big grin on his face.

"I am so glad you called the other day, you know?" he says, shaking my hand with vigor. "So glad to see you again."

"Me too," I say as he ushers me into the harbor-view apartment. Outside the floor-length windows, the Kowloon Peninsula glistens like a diamond hill.

Choy drags me around the place on a quick tour. It's spacious: two bedrooms and a cozy office, a sizeable living room, and a modern chrome-heavy kitchen. Carefully arranged but minimalist Swedish furniture and leafy plants fill the place along with a plasma HDTV and state-of-the-art Japanese electronics. The Choys must have paid top dollar for the apartment, but it is well worth the price—Causeway Bay is the perfect place, the majestic harbor only one block away. Location, location, location.

"Can I get you a soda? Beer? Wine?" Wendy pokes her head in the office as Choy shows me his coin collection.

"A Coke would be great," I say. "Yeah, a Coke."

"You don't drink?" Choy asks.

"I'll be good this time. Hey, the whole gang's going to be here, right?"

"I hope so. David is dying to see you, you know? And you remember Ringo Hui, Simon Fong, and Kelvin Lo, right?"

"Sure," I lie. "What about Martin Cowen? Is he coming?"

"He said he was. He was eager to see you."

I fake a smile.

"What does he do again?" I ask casually, flipping through a booklet of collector's coins.

"A curator at the Hong Kong History Museum. Ten years, I think."

"Met his family?"

"I saw his wife once, many years ago. A stunning woman, if you ask me."

"Any children?"

"A daughter, I think."

"A daughter."

"Yeah. Hey, why don't you save the interrogation for him?" he says. "You want to see my new Playstation?"

People are arriving. I can hear their voices outside the room. There's a knock on the door, and a bald man's head pops in.

"Knock, knock."

"Who's there?"

"David Kwan!" he screams. He comes in and crushes me with a bear hug. "Holy shit. You're unbelievable. Fourteen fucking years. Look at you."

"You look great."

"What drugs are you on? I'm bald and fat. I used to be a big stud."

"You were never a big stud," Choy chides. "Greg was."

"I've been so excited about this evening," David says. He takes a step back and studies me. "Man, you look fantastic."

"This is fantastic." I grin. Choy, David and I high-five.

David plops his big ass on Choy's desk. "Hey, hey. Remember the soccer tournaments? The girls at St. Mary's?" he asks. "I had such a crush on Polly Yuen. Remember her?"

I don't feel like telling him that I went out with Polly. Twice.

"The camping trips on Lantau Island?" Choy says.

"The fire in the chemistry lab?" David howls. "And Ms. Boobies' panties?"

"Don't forget Bulldog's," I say.

"Oh shit. Yeah, Bulldog's. We got so stinky drunk every time." David bursts into an infectious laugh—a living Laughing Buddha.

"We went back a few times after you left," Choy says, "but it was not the same. You were our ring leader, you know."

"I thought Martin was," I say. "Speak of the devil, is he here yet?"

"You seem awfully anxious to see him," Choy says, narrowing his eyes. "You know, he is married."

David giggles like a little girl.

"Shut up," I growl. "I'm anxious to see the whole gang."

"Seventeen. What were we thinking?" David muses.

Wendy comes in and hands David a bottle of Heineken and me a glass of Coke. I sip as David and Choy reminisce. Spit flies as Choy talks about a soccer semis, when Martin got so upset with What's-His-Name that he punched the kid with a full fist, breaking his nose. Martin was banned from the rest of the game. Miraculously, I made a successful long pass to Choy and he scored a last-minute goal to win the game. We went to Bulldog's afterwards. I went home in the wee hours of the morning, a skunk named Johnny Walker. Never fight with your father when you're drunk.

Gosh, the four of us.

Choy throws a vivacious party. We gather around the dining table, munch on scallion pancakes, veggie sticks, stone crab dip and *maki* rolls. The piquancy of pan-fried turnip cakes forges its full assault. U2's *Joshua Tree* thrums in the background. Wendy buzzes around, refilling glasses, offering snacks and napkins. Choy fusses with the Karaoke machine. Simon Fong and his extra-large front teeth are vaguely familiar. Kevin Lo was the scrawny, effeminate kid who once told me I had beautiful eyes, but I reckon he's now a bodybuilder with a wife and three children. And Ringo Hui, whose thin, long skull and small nostrils remind me of a ferret's—I should recognize that face, but I don't.

Ultimately, it's a party for Choy, David, Martin and me.

David elbows me as I nibble on a piece of soy-marinated wing. "What do you think of Wendy?" he whispers.

"Wendy? I think she's very nice."

"That's one way to say she's homely."

"You dog. Are you married?"

"No."

"Are you gay?"

"Fuck you, Greg."

"You really have a potty mouth for a college professor."

"I don't talk like this at school. I'm a professional."

"You're a fucking fraud." I howl.

He shoves me.

"You know," he says, "it really is great seeing you again. Really is."

Choy comes over and shows me an oversized book with a hard, black cover.

"Yearbook?" I say.

"It came out after you left," Choy says, flipping through the pages. David leans on my back and peeks over my shoulder.

"Remember this?" Choy points at a picture of Martin and me holding the Finnegan Cup at that year's Joint-school Swimming Championship. Martin's broad shoulders and thick chest put mine to shame, but his massive legs are a distraction. Fortunately, I looked better in Speedos. I study the picture of us together—both young, handsome, tan and fit, both grinning with deep dimples.

Both ended up loving the same woman.

Choy flips to another page, and reads loudly:

*A soldier lays his head*
*On a white patch of dead*
*Roses and thorns*
*Broken pieces of a sacred heart, torn*
*Between a life that has gone*
*And a love that lives on*
*—G. S. Lockland*

"I give up," I crow, throwing my arms in the air.

"This guy was my hero, you know," Choy announces to everyone. "There was almost nothing he could not do, you know? He could swim. He kicked a mean soccer ball. He wrote poetry. He was good looking. Just about the only thing he could not do was sing." He grins.

"He opened his mouth and the girls fled," David chimes in.

"He was so tone deaf that we thought he rapped."

"A girl he sang to joined a convent three days later."

"You guys are brutal," I say. "Should join a comedy club."

"Do you know what time it is?" Choy asks, loud and excited. "It is Karaoke time! Greg is first."

Everyone eggs me on, hooting and cheering, as I flip through the laminated pages of the karaoke songbook. I'm their token idiot. It amuses them to see a six-foot-one *gweilo* in designer clothes make a fool of himself.

"I don't know any of these songs," I whine. I sit on the hardwood floor. Someone thrusts a microphone in my hand.

"How about *My Way?*"

"Oh God."

"Here is a good one—*You Light Up My Life.*"

"Oh God."

"How about *The Sounds of Silence?*"

"No. Hell, no."

"Don't be difficult, Greg."

"I'm not. I don't know any of these songs."

"Everyone knows *New York, New York.*"

"Stop this madness."

"Greg, pick something already."

*"Total Eclipse of the Heart?"*

The DVD spins and a lovely rose garden appears on the TV screen. A young Asian couple runs hand-in-hand along a stone path, in slow motion, flipping their heads side to side. They're so incredibly happy together that it seems they'll turn into giant clams. The cheesy orchestration swells, and the words bubble in purple across the screen. I start out pretty well—one note at a time, I can pretty much keep up with the annoying synthesizer music. Then the chorus picks up and I'm quickly lost. The music rushes like a roller coaster in a downhill spiral. I try to keep up. Eventually, I give up and just belt it out. By the last stretch of crescendos, I'm rowdily screeching at the top of my lungs.

The music stops. I stretch out one arm, the other anchored on my hip. Elvis. Then I realize where I am, and suddenly my face and ears feel like hot irons. Kevin Ho convulses under a large pillow. Choy and David roll on the floor. A few others are polite enough to cover their mouths. As Choy's coarse laugh turns into a wheeze, David grabs my hand and pulls me up. We dash into the kitchen.

"That was so fucking funny," he spumes, still giggling.

"Yeah, at my expense."

"Don't mind them. You were great."

I chuckle.

"Look, Greg," he says, glancing out of the corner of his eye, "I have something to ask you."

"What now?"

"Something about women."

"David." I cross my arms. "What's going on?"

"Don't tell Choy—he doesn't know yet. Her name is Joanna. She teaches freshmen e-Business at UST."

"That's wonderful."

"You know, you were my hero when it came to women. You always knew what to say and what to do. Give me some pointers, okay?" He scratches his shiny head. "I really like this woman. I am clueless."

I don't think he realizes how little I actually know. My own romantic life is a mess. I'm only a myth. They've idolized a fucking fraud.

"Tell me more."

"We met at a faculty function. She had short hair and the gentlest smile. She wore these cute sixties eyeglasses." He grins. "You know how shy I usually am around girls. But this time I don't know what came over me. I must have been possessed. I actually talked to her. We talked about our classes, the upcoming outcomes assessment, new e-books. One thing led to another, and I asked her out. Out of the blue. I couldn't believe it."

"You did well. I'm proud of you."

"And I couldn't believe she said yes."

"She likes you."

"I hope so. What should I do now? Help me."

"Go to dinner. Don't forget to bring a nice bottle of wine. Be a gentleman and pick her up. That way you know where she lives without being invasive, and if the date goes well, you can ask to give her a ride home. Maybe a little nightcap. A goodnight kiss. Don't call her the next day. Send her flowers instead. Sunflowers are excellent."

"You make it sound so easy."

"It is. I can coach you."

"You da man."

"The most important thing is, be yourself and be honest."

I catch myself giving out the one piece of advice I haven't followed.

I dip a piece of shrimp into cocktail sauce and pop it into my mouth. The phone rings, startling David and me. It stops after two rings.

"I have so much to learn." David grins and picks up a piece of chicken wing. "Choy told me you're in a relationship. Finally, the playboy's settling down."

I rub my neck and smirk. "Well, to tell you the truth, I'm not sure how she feels about me."

"Tell me about her." He nibbles on the wing, juice dripping from his mouth.

"She's a lawyer."

"And?"

"And she's great."

"And? Is she beautiful? Wait, of course she is."

I grin and hand him a napkin.

"I don't understand, Greg. You're always so secretive," he says, wiping his mouth. "Even back then, we knew you were fooling around but you never told us anything. What's the matter with you?"

"A gentleman never kisses and tells."

"So that's the trick, huh? Casanova never brags."

I push him in the chest. He steps backward, chokes on the wing. I hand him his beer.

Choy pokes his head in. "I have bad news," he says with a frown.

"What?" David and I say simultaneously, David pulling chicken off his lip.

"That was Martin on the phone. He is not coming. He said he had an emergency at home."

*Emergency my ass.*

"What's so important he has to miss this?" David grumbles.

"He did not say. He was in a big hurry or something."

I know the name of that something: Lian.

"Damn," David whines. "I haven't seen him for years."

"I know." Choy rolls his eyes. "What a jerk. Party pooper."

"Choy, got his address?" I ask. I have my backup plan. If Martin's not coming to me, I'm going to him.

"I think."

I follow Choy to his office. He fires up his computer, then points and clicks a few times, and Microsoft Outlook comes up. He presses a key and the inkjet printer whirs, spitting out a piece of paper.

"Here you go." He hands me the paper. "You know, maybe we should all go over and raid his house." He shuts down the computer and turns to me. "What is wrong, Greg?"

My face is purple. I can feel it.

"He...they live on Cheung Chau?" I ask.

"Yes."

"Since when?"

"Since forever. What is the matter, Greg?"

I shake my head.

Lian lied to me. The perfect woman lied to me.

"You know where the house is?"

"No."

"David," I call out.

"What? What?" David rushes in, his face a red, plump tomato.

"Do you know where Martin's place is?" I ask.

"Never been there."

"What is going on?" Choy asks.

"Nothing," I say.

"What's going on?" David asks.

"Shut the fuck up."

"What is going on?" Choy's not giving up. "Why are you yelling?"

"I'm sorry." I wave my arms in the air. "Sorry guys. I don't mean to get all excited...I've been...just that...crap, I'm disappointed, that's all."

They look at each other, eyes wide. They know my shit too well.

I need to get out of here.

David stares at me.

Choy stares at me.

The air conditioner kicks in.

The printer is whirring, shutting down.

I look around for an escape route.

Then someone belts out *Yellow Submarine* in the living room, his pitch-perfect, Pavarotti-inspired rendition only adding to the oddity of the moment. David frowns, crinkles his nose, and pushes his lips into a *What-the-fuck-is-that?* pucker. Choy bursts into his wheezing laugh.

We are now in complete hysterics.

The yellow submarine sails on.

We take a few deep breaths, composing ourselves. "You don't have to go now, do you?" David asks.

I shake my head, catching my breath.

"Wonderful," Choy trills. "Let's put Ringo out of his misery."

As we march out of the office, Wendy walks past with a tray in her hand. I grab her by the arm.

Johnny Walker. Double. Straight up.

# Return to Cheung Chau

"Mr. Lockland?" Hoi asks. He twirls a twig, then flings it into a bush.

"I'm sorry. Yes?"

"You like Cheung Chau?"

"Uh huh."

"I grew up here."

"Yeah, you told me already."

"My Ah-Ma said you are good person."

"Uh."

"Mr. Lockland, are you listening?"

"Yes. Sorry. What?"

"My Ah-Ma said you are good person."

"I thought Wing Po didn't like me."

"No, she said you are good. But you are—what is the word?"

"Cranky? Crazy?"

"Chinese word: *ma fan*."

"Cranky. I guess I was kind of cranky."

"You are good person. A lot in your brain."

The familiar road leads us up the hill. The same exotic birds croak around us. The sun is out, casting a gray mesh on the ground all the way to the hillcrest. Unusually warm for November—the heat draws beads of sweat on my forehead.

"You're sure you know where it is?" I ask Hoi.

"I know everywhere here," he says, annoyed.

I pick up a pebble, its chestnut shape reminding me of the long walk just a few days ago.

"What you looked for at the cemetery?" he asks.

"Nothing in particular. Nothing, really."

"Why you want to come here?"

"The Cowens are my good friends."

"But you don't know where they live?"

"Hard to explain. You're way too young to understand."

"Why you old people say this always."

"I'm not old people." I chuckle. "How old are you?"

"Fifteen."

Fifteen. I was that age when I had my first kiss behind a rock at Stanley Beach.. Her name was May. Or was it April? The kiss was urgent and wet—I had no idea a good Catholic girl from St. Stephen's could kiss like that, her tongue wrestling mine. It was also the first time I kissed a girl's breasts. Hers were small but soft, fragrant like strawberry ice cream.

"Something funny?" Hoi asks. I must have been grinning.

"Ice cream," I say. "Do you have a girlfriend?"

"No. Too much school."

"Where's school anyway?"

"St. Stephen's."

I grin.

"I don't like it there," he continues. "Have to take one-hour boat to Stanley. But it is good school. My Ah-Ma says I must go to university some day because I am to be marine biologist."

"Is that what you want?"

He tilts his head at me. "Very much," he says.

Somehow, I realize, this kid is mature beyond his years.

"Mr. Lockland. This way." Hoi points at a forked path off Peak Road—the exact place where Lian picked the dandelions and told me that she was happy.

"You're sure?" I ask.

He nods.

"Where does it go?"

"The other side of Sai Wan. You can see the pirate cave from there."

"Is that right?"

"You know the pirate cave, Mr. Lockland?"

"Yes, very well."

"It is closed now. But my friends and I always went there when we were little."

"Ever brought any girls there?"

"I don't know girls."

"Well, let me tell you, it's a great place to steal a kiss."

The path to Lian's place is a quiet, narrow one—the kind that I'd miss if I don't pay attention, seeing only a woman and her dandelions. A wall of shrubs and vines spreads on each side, ripe with late season's wilt, the overhangs framing the path in a grand archway. We cool under the shade. A loud frog groans nearby—there must be a creek somewhere. The asphalt cracks in places, then gradually turns into a long stretch of gravel and sand, slithering its way further into the deep recess of the hill. A world away from the world.

"Do you know the Cowen family?" I ask Hoi.

"No."

"You never met them?"

"I saw the little girl a few times. She is crazy."

"How do you mean, she's crazy?"

"She is crazy."

"How?"

"She did not speak to me. I tried to talk to her. She did not talk. She is crazy."

"Maybe she's just shy. Is she pretty?"

"Yes. She has big, beautiful eyes."

"How old is she?"

"Younger than me. Twelve, thirteen? I don't know."

"Do you know her name?"

"No. She did not talk. She is crazy."

Around a bend, we come to a shackled steel gate. Behind it, steps against a great wall, eventually curving left and disappearing under a lintel of the same granite.

"We are here," Hoi says.

"You're sure?"

"Mr. Lockland, I know everywhere. This is the address." He waves at me. "I must go now. Homework to do. Bye."

He turns and races down the hill, not looking back. It suddenly occurs to me that he's been afraid. It's almost as if he's running away from a ghost.

I ponder, my eyes following the granite steps. My palms are sweating. I've come so far. Up these steps lives a man who stole my life. I thought I hated him, but now I'm not sure. Perhaps *hate* is too strong a word. These could have been my steps—our steps, Lian's and mine. Instead, they lead to a place, and a life, that may have existed for us only in my dreams. This life is real for Lian— and for that little girl. And for Martin.

Bastard.


I climb over the gate and trot up the steps, passing under the lintel and through a tunnel of ivy. Yellow angel's trumpets flop here and there, decayed petals ground into the stones beneath my shoes, their scent pungent as perfumed hair on a sultry day in the summer. It's almost nauseating.

I push open a cedar gate and enter what looks to be the Garden of Eden—a narrow stone path wrapping its way around rainbow mounds of geraniums, mums, petunias, daylilies, gladiolas, azaleas and flowers I have never seen before: snowflakes and butter clouds amid the rain of stars and river of sapphires. A few banana trees flank the path, their fruits plucked and leaves pruned. On my left, a lily pond sprawls by two falcate beds of pearl acanthus. The path stops at the far end, at the foot of a small incline where another set of steps cuts through a waterfall of vines, dappled with lilacs and yellow roses, beyond which the pale blue sky stretches wide—a canvas for this masterpiece.

Perching above the incline is a cottage with a green tiled roof, red bricks peeking through plastered walls, under an eminent camphor tree the shape of an old man hugging the sky. It's simple architecture—humble, bland even. The vista, however, is magnificent. Set on a lush tract of meadow at the edge of a cliff, the cottage overlooks the broad sea—a glistening, rolling sheet of blue silk. To the left, a few roofs peek through the trees at the top of a hill, which drops abruptly and tapers into the desolate cove below.

Indeed, I can see the pirate cave from here.

Something chirps in the tree. I walk toward it and look up. A cardinal roosts on a fat branch, praising the day. I pick up a camphor seed and place it under my nose—its raw scent tells of a lost summer, rich and full.

I come around to the front door. I knock.

A wind chime flutters.

I wriggle the doorknob. It jitters like a scab about to fall off an arm. The door is locked. I step aside, cup my hand over my eyes and peer into a window. Blackness. As I step backward, I catch my own reflection in the glass.

A man stands behind me.

# Martin Cowen

"Crazy son of a bitch."

I turn and see Martin Cowen standing on the grass, between two shrubs of marigolds in their last glory, carrying a shovel in his left hand. His wavy salt-and-pepper hair hangs loose, framing a set of deep, dark eyes under straight brows. He has aged considerably. He looks older than thirty-four, but still handsome in a gray Henley which hugs his broad shoulders and thick chest. His arms are large and muscular. Both hands are covered with dirt.

"Is that how you greet an old friend?" I ask.

His lips curl into an uneasy smile. He cocks his head and squints, then bursts into a familiar broad laugh.

"Can't believe you," he says. "Actually tracked me down."

He wipes his right hand on his soiled workman jeans a couple times, then extends it to me. I step forward and shake his hand. His strong grip surprises me, but I return the favor.

Eventually our hands get tired, and he lets go of mine.

"Good to see you again," he says.

"Missed you at the party."

"Family emergency. Didn't Choy tell you?"

"What happened?" My voice challenges him.

He grabs the shovel with both hands and plants it on the grass. I fix my eyes on the shovel.

"Had a booboo. My daughter," he says. "Had to take her to the hospital, but she's fine now."

I frown.

"Just a minor accident." He brushes his hand over his face. "But what about you? What are you doing here?"

"Seeing an old friend, of course."

He grins. I can't tell if he's sincere or not. At least he's not bludgeoning me with the shovel. Not yet, anyway.

"Want a beer?" he asks. I won't move. "C'mon, join me." He gestures toward the house, then turns and walks toward it.

I follow him around the corner to a small hut behind a patch of bright purple butterfly bush—I haven't seen such beauty since my mother stopped planting them about ten years ago. He cracks open the padlock and pulls open the hut door.

Inside the hut scatter hoes, shovels, pitchforks, drills, saws, wires, a workbench with two large vices and a sander, hoses, metal pipes, jars of nails and screws, and other odds and ends. He steps over a pile of lumber, slogs over to a corner, opens a small fridge, and pulls out two bottles of Heineken. He hands me one.

I twist open the cap and take a big swig. The liquid sends a chill down my chest. Here I am, drinking cold beer and shooting the breeze with my rival, almost as if we are the best of pals.

Like old times.

"Did you plant all that out there?" I ask.

"I helped. Mostly my wife's miracles."

I almost blurt out, "Lian didn't know anything about gardening." I swallow my words with a gulp of beer.

"Yip." He nods to himself. "All hers. My girl helped, too."

"Who would have thought?" I say. "A daughter and a wife."

"Life is good."

I stare at my beer bottle. Clear my throat.

"You know my wife," he says.

The beer feels cold in my grip. I look him square in the eye.

"She worked at your dad's hospital. Years ago." He wipes the sweat off his forehead. "First saw her there. Lian."

"Huh."

"You don't remember?" He squints. "That one time I broke my ankle? Believe it was the semis at St. Joseph. Anyway, went to your dad's hospital and you got pulled away for something. That's when I saw her. Didn't think she noticed me. But there she was. Sure you knew her."

"Huh."

"You don't remember her?"

"You never mentioned her."

"It never came up."

The bastard's lying. Something doesn't make sense.

"So, you asked her out or something?"

"Nope. Never saw her again until a few years later."

"She never talked about me?"

He stares at me. "Why would she?"

Liar, liar.

"Umm, you said she knew me," I say.

"No. I said you knew her."

"No, I didn't," I lie. "Anyway, how's your daughter?"

"She's doing great. Sweet girl. A little headstrong."

I look over at the garden, its late autumn colors garish and arrogant.

"Yip," he says, "a perfect life. Just perfect."

"How about a tour, then. I'd like to see your cottage, the ocean view and all. That perfect life of yours."

"Well…" he hesitates. "Maybe next time. Got to pick up my wife and daughter."

I take another swig of my beer. "Some other time, then."

"Yip. Some other time."

I finish the beer and set the bottle on a stool. I shake his hand and step out of the hut. The sun blisters—I can feel my skin burning. I feel a little dizzy walking down the stone path toward the steps down the incline.

I look back. The hut door is shut. Martin has disappeared.

What's just happened? What was that whole charade about Lian? He knows something but he's not telling me. I expected the shovel. I expected a confrontation. Instead it was only a quiet something. He was sly. Where was the Aussie guy with the temper—the guy who broke someone's nose just because?

I can't leave without finding out.

Walking around the garden and past the lily pond, I notice a trench behind a few large ferns. I look around, making sure that nobody's around, and plunk myself into it.

Martin scuttles off about ten minutes later. I wait a few more minutes, then climb out of the trench and head back toward the cottage. I come around the tree and reach for the front door. I look behind me and see only trees and flowers. Thinking back on what Kate showed me, I take out my American Express card and repeat the trick. The door opens without a hitch.

# Perfect Lies

A wedge of sunlight unveils part of the living room like the first swipe of cloth reveals glass from dust. The first thing I notice is the faint scent of tangerine. Then, in shadow, the enormous carved wood statue in a corner. I walk over and run a hand over the surface. It's coarse, intriguing—a seven-foot column of oak sculpted into an array of flowers and birds and mountains and streams. The craftsmanship is amateur, but the intent is true. Something my father would have loved.

Otherwise the room is decorated with minimal frill. A beige sofa leans against a long wall, offsetting an oval oak coffee table. The hardwood floor is oak as well. Almost every piece of furniture is oak or ash or some kind of light wood. Some kind of rustic. Some kind of peaceful.

A baby grand piano sits in another corner. I glide my fingers along the black lacquer, lift up the keyboard cover and strike a few keys in the upper octaves. The crisp sounds echo like faded memories. My eyes well up—my mother's piano had the same mellow voice.

Then there's a whole world out there. The glorious flowers. The nauseating smells. The dirt. The soil. The water. The trees. The sky. Life.

Like my mother's greenhouse: her sanctuary outside of her cage.

I close the front door and move, like a ghost, through the rest of the cottage. The spacious kitchen, perfect and functional in birch and stainless steel, is spotless and serene. I wonder if Lian spends a lot of time here—she always liked to cook. The arched hallway creates a sense of grace, and the skylight is a nice touch. I wonder if Martin built this himself with his bare, farm-bred hands. One thing I can't do is build Lian a cottage. With my inheritance, I could buy her a few.

At the end of the hallway is a door to, I suspect, the master bedroom. I reach for it. Footsteps outside. I freeze, then pull open a closet door next to me. I slip inside, pull the door shut and hide behind a rack of winter coats.

At first I hear only some rustling sounds, shoes clacking on the hardwood floor, paper bags dropping on surfaces. I lean forward against the door slats. And I hear Lian.

"You didn't have to do that."

"But I wanted to," Martin says.

"Why, suddenly?"

"Meaning what?"

Silence. I press my ear against the door.

"Well—thank you," she says. "That was very nice of you."

"The doctor said anything?"

"Her fracture is fine."

"Guess you're not going to sculpt for a while," he says impatiently, a rather authoritative tone.

"She knows that," Lian says. "She isn't a baby."

"Did you get the eggs?"

"Yes." She sighs.

"Just asking."

Paper bags rustle and water runs. A door squeaks open then shut. I shift my body and sit on the floor, next to a pair of sneakers, my ear still pressed to the door.

"It turned out a nice day," Martin says.

"It is. Unusually hot."

"You saw the flowers? Still blooming. Unbelievable."

"The butterfly bushes are beautiful this year."

The water keeps running.

"Want one?" Martin asks.

"No, thank you. I already ate."

My breaths are fast but silent. Outside, shoes continue tapping. Paper crinkles. Doors shut and open.

"Martin," Lian says.

"What?"

"We haven't spoken for two days."

"We're speaking now."

"You know what I mean."

Another door creaks open. I press my palms together in front of my mouth and breathe into them, trying to quiet my heart.

"Go out and play," Martin says, his voice on edge.

More footsteps. A door shuts.

"Please don't yell at her like that," Lian says.

"Did I?"

"It was your expression."

"Expression. You never liked my expression."

"Martin, why are we fighting?"

"Are we? Didn't realize we were fighting. Just eating my sandwich."

"Something is bothering you."

"I feel fantastic."

"What is wrong?"

He doesn't say anything. The water stops running. Someone drags a chair across the floor.

"Martin?" Lian asks again.

"So, about that night."

"What night?"

"You didn't come home."

"I told you. I stayed at Victor's."

"You never missed the ferry before."

"I lost track of time. Why do you bring that up again? We already discussed it."

"Because," he says. "I don't believe you."

"You don't?"

"I don't."

I hear a slight thud. Maybe she's whispering. Maybe she kicked him. Or maybe she just killed him—a hard blow in the back of the head. A hammer. A steel pipe. A watermelon. I'll come out of the closet, hold her in my arms, then help her clean up and bury his body. The back of the hut is a good place.

"Martin."

"What now?"

"You are so unhappy."

"We had an intruder today."

"No, I mean in general." She sets something down. "An intruder?"

"Just some stupid jerk. Nothing to worry about. Just telling you, that's all."

"When?"

"About an hour ago."

"What happened?"

"Really. He won't come back. I'll make sure of that."

I hear footsteps getting closer. I retreat behind the coats and cuddle myself in a corner.

"She should be back inside the house." Lian is now about a foot away, a thin door separating us. I can see her shoes through the slats.

"I don't want you to leave," Martin says.

"I will just be a minute."

"No, I don't want you to leave me."

"Martin—"

"What do you want from me?" He's right outside of the closet now.

"We talked about this."

"You didn't even put up a fight."

"You are not happy here, and I know. I so want you to be happy."

"What does it have to do with anything?"

"You have all these things you want to do. And you should. You must."

"I didn't know what I was talking about. I want you. I want her."

"But you see—it is not possible. You want something else. You made it very clear."

"Not anymore."

"You've changed your mind?"

He lets out a heavy sigh. "Those things. They're not that important."

"But they are."

"This is what I want now."

"Bullshit."

"Lian."

"Is that what you always say? Bullshit? You asked for a divorce. Twice."

He pauses. "So eager to see me go, huh?" he sneers. "Is it him?"

"What are you talking about? You think I am seeing someone? You are jealous?"

"You didn't come home the other night."

"I told you already."

"And I don't believe you."

"Ask Victor, then."

"He's on your side."

"What do I have to do to make you believe me?"

"You can't."

"Why are you acting so strangely?"

He pauses again. "Don't think you're telling me the truth."

Silence again. I lean forward, the tails of the coats hanging on my head. I can hear them breathing.

"Take a walk with me," he says. "Just you and me. Down to Sai Wan. The cove. Like old times."

She's quiet.

"You said we needed to talk," he continues. "And I agree. But I need some fresh air. We need some fresh air."

"We can't just leave her here."

"She'll be fine inside the house. Come with me."

He walks away from the closet. I can still see Lian's shoes.

"Martin, wait." She too walks away.

A door squeaks open.

"I do love you," she says. "I want you to know that."

The door shuts.

It's just me again, sitting in the dark. I take a long breath and lean my back against the door. The air is getting stale in here, but I want to wait a few more minutes before I make my next move.

A vein throbs in my head. I place my thumbs on my temples and press hard.

*Squeak.* The door pulls away. The weight of my body pulls me down. As I fall back, a slither of light blinds me. Something hard and coarse hits me on the face, knocking me onto the ground. A loud thump rings in my ears as I close my eyes.

When I open my eyes, the flush of light turns into a dithered shadow. I blink and push myself up. Something hits my head again. I lie on the floor and look up. The shadow becomes a person standing just inches away from me. Two bare feet, a small scar on the right knee just below the hem of denim shorts. I look up further. It's a face of a girl—twelve or thirteen, short black haircut just below the ears, straight eyebrows and big, dark brown eyes. Beautiful eyes.

"Wait, I can explain," I say. I wave a hand and cup my face with another—my face burns with pain but I don't think anything is broken.

She tilts her head and stares at me for a few seconds. Her shocked expression gradually eases. She jerks her hand forward. I wrap my arm around my head and duck. When nothing happens, I peek through the crook of my arm and see her right hand extended in front of my face. Her left is encased in a purple cast with a bunny sticker on it.

She smiles.

# The Girl Who Is Crazy

"I can explain," I say.

She shakes her head, grabs my hand and pulls. With her help, I manage to get to my feet. I look around. No Martin or Lian, just the girl and me.

"Hi," I say.

She smiles again, her teeth straight and white. She should be screaming for help by now.

"Hi," I say.

She twists the fingers of her good hand in a bizarre way, as if she's molding an air sculpture.

She's signing.

I shake my head to let her know that I don't understand. She nods. She takes the sneakers out of the closet and closes the door. She slips them on, then grabs my hand again and pulls me toward her and leads me to another door on the left side of the hallway.

"Wait," I protest.

She opens the door and pulls me inside to a small room, not at all neat. Large posters of The Powerpuff Girls grace the walls. Small blocks of wood scattered around the floor and the desk—actually, more like a workbench—by the large-paned window. The bed is crumpled layers of wheat-colored sheets and a blanket in a heap. A wall of books and magazines: Harry Potter, Dr. Seuss, the Hardy Boys, *National Geographic*, *The Great Outdoors*. The kind of little girl's bedroom I've always imagined. Right.

She sits on the bed and stares at me, examining me all over.

"Hi," I say again, moving my lips slowly so she may read them. "My name is Greg. I don't mean any harm. I'm your parents' friend. I just—well, I don't know how to explain. Do you understand anything I say?"

She nods, begins to sign again. I shake my head. She places her hand over her mouth and nods. She turns around and grabs a piece of paper and a pen from the desk, scribbles something. I look over her shoulder.

*She's so young.* She looks like Lian, though with stronger features, very boyish. She reminds me of someone else, but I can't put my finger on it. Something about her demeanor, confidence and directness. Why did she pull me, a stranger, into her bedroom?

She hands me the piece of paper. It reads:

*You know Uncle Stephen? You look just like him.*

Uncle Stephen? I look up and frown. Then I nod. "Yes. I'm his son."

She tosses me a wide grin, as if she's just seen Santa Claus. She leans forward and wraps her arms around my waist. I'm taken aback, my own arms hanging in mid-air. Then something lurches through my chest, deep and unexpected and inexplicable and sad and warm and sweet and difficult and full and subtle and grand.

I used to hug my mother this way. Long ago. I'd forgotten. I've grown up and moved on and wandered, trying to prove that I'm a man, master of my own kingdom. Someone to be wanted, admired, envied. Loved.

When all I needed was a hug from my mother.

I place my hands on her hair. She lifts her head up and looks at me with those big beautiful eyes. Then she utters, "Ma naim-ee Eh-en."

"Your name? Erin?"

She shakes her head. "Eh-en."

"Karen?"

"Eh-en." She's frustrated.

"I'm sorry. I can't understand you."

She lets go of me and grabs a pen again. She scribbles on the piece of paper and hands it to me:

*Helen. My name is Helen.*

I take a step back and suck in a long breath. I put my hands on her shoulders and crouch down. The words stumble out.

"Do you know my mother?"

She frowns.

"Uncle Stephen's wife?" I ask again. Time has stopped.

She points her finger at me. "I no-oo."

"You know me?"

She nods, then runs back to her desk, flips through papers and books, scouting for something. I sit on her bed and study her. Who is she? Really, who is she?

She returns to my side with a small box in her hand. It's made of fragrant wood, a dragon wrapped around a corner—the same box as the one in my father's study. The same box I broke many years ago during one of our fights.

I look at Helen again, and this time I see my father's face.

*Lian lied to me.*

"How old are you?" I ask.

She stretches out ten fingers, then two fists, then two more fingers. She gestures that I should follow her lead. I flash her thirty-two fingers: ten, ten, ten, two. She laughs, loud and vivacious.

Twelve. *She has to be my father's.*

I take her good hand and pat it gently. I point to her cast. "What did you do?"

"Broka bon."

"How?"

"Mad."

"You got mad? And you hurt your hand?"

She has a dazzling, confident smile.

"Does it hurt?" I ask.

She shakes her head.

"So, you're a sculptor, huh?" I point at the wood blocks and small sculptures on her desk.

She nods. She points at the wooden box. "Oo lie-keet?"

"Yes, very much," I say.

She grasps my hand, leads me toward the back of the cottage and pushes open a narrow screen door. We hop down three steps. To our left, the cliff is only about fifteen feet away and the sea shimmers in the late afternoon sun. Under the camphor tree's expansive canopy, we walk past the back of the hut and to a three-foot-high wire fence.

Within the enclosure of the fence, two small rabbits, one black and one honey-colored, perch on two wooden boxes, twitching their noses, enjoying the shade. They perk up their ears as we approach, otherwise unfazed by our presence. I crouch down and look at them. They don't seem to mind.

"Bunnies. Are they yours?"

She doesn't understand. I face her and mouth the words again. She nods. She bends down, seizes the honey-colored one by the ruff and scoops it up by the rump with her cast. A brief struggle, then it rests in her embrace. She holds the animal out to me and I pat the creature on its head and long, flopping ears. The fur feels soft and warm.

"What's his name?"

"Er. Er naim-ee Unee."

"Honey? That's a cute name for a bunny."

"Peh-er."

We sit by a bench close to the fence. I pat the rabbit again. Helen kisses it on the nose, then pushes her own nose against its chin. Her face lights up as I continue to pat the rabbit.

"Oo-af peh?"

"Me? No. I don't have any pets."

"Why?"

"I don't know. I'm a grown-up, I guess."

She tilts her head at me, a sympathetic look.

I glance over my shoulder. No sign of Martin and Lian.

"Helen, can I ask you something?"

"Uh."

"Did you see Uncle Stephen often?"

She shakes her head. "Naw."

"But you're close to him."

She nods.

"Do you know who he is?"

"Unko."

"What kind of an uncle? Your father's friend or something?"

She shakes her head again. Not a friend.

"Does your dad know about Uncle Stephen?"

"Seekreh," she says. She pulls out a pen from her back pocket and writes on her cast:

*Daddy doesn't know. Uncle Stephen came to see me at least once a year. He took me to the Ocean Park, the zoo, the beaches. And he bought me ice cream and hamburgers. He bought me these bunnies too.*

After I read it, she quickly blacks the words out with the pen. She writes again in the space below:

*He told me a little about you. You work for a big company in America, travel lots. I've never seen your pictures though. And I'm glad. You're so cute.*

Cute? Rabbits are "cute."

I should be angry at the situation—the lies, the deception, the relationship between Lian and my father, the sister I never knew I had. Strangely, I am not. I'm sitting on a bench, patting a pet rabbit with a girl about whom I know almost nothing, and I'm not angry—just sad. I could have gotten to know this sister of mine. I could have learned sign language so I could communicate with her. I could have done many things—given her gifts, sent her birthday cards and flowers, taken her to parks and beaches, watched her grow up. Loved her.

Instead, I don't even know how to tell her who I really am.

But it feels oddly right to be here, halfway around the world, sitting under a grand tree, patting a furry creature, next to my sister. And she thinks I'm cute. Okay, cute.

I wrap my arm around Helen's shoulders. Looking out at the shimmering sea, I have trouble holding back my tears.

Helen and I sit there for half an hour, maybe more. In her arms, Honey's drifted into a trance. Inside the fence, the black rabbit, its white nose twitching and straws of hay quickly disappearing into its maw, seems a little jealous.

"Helen," I say, tapping her shoulder. She looks up. "I have something to tell you."

She keeps patting the rabbit.

"It's about Uncle Stephen."

"I knaw."

"You do?"

She lowers her head, looking at her rabbit, and sighs. "He die-ed."

I tap her shoulder and she looks up again.

"Your mother already told you?"

She nods. I squeeze my arm tighter around her shoulders.

"Do you know who Uncle Stephen really was?"

"Ur dad."

I look at her closely. She continues to pat her rabbit. I swallow hard.

"Yes. My father."

She needs to know, but I'm not going to be the one to tell her.

"Mad," she says.

"You got mad because he died?"

She looks at her cast and nods. She loved my father. She broke her hand because she was mad about his death. I didn't even touch his casket.

"Come," she says. She puts Honey back inside the fence. The dun rabbit hops to the black one, and they cuddle, touching noses with each other.

I follow her back into the cottage and her room. She sits me on her bed, places my hands over my eyes.

She rummages near her desk. Papers fly. She pulls on my hand and shoves a piece of paper in my palm. I open my eyes. It's a letter.

"You want me to read this?"

She nods.

*My dear Helen,*

*How's my beautiful little friend? Your mother showed me the pictures of you at your 12th birthday and, I must say, what a beautiful woman you've become.*

*I can't tell you how much I've missed you.*

*Unfortunately, I won't be able to come this summer to visit. I'm very sad. Please don't be disappointed or sad or mad. There's something I have to do before I can come see you.*

*Remember, we keep no secrets from each other? Well, Uncle Stephen has a heart problem. The doctor says that I must have a bypass surgery. Do you know what a bypass surgery is? It is nothing to be afraid of. I have seen it done many, many times at the hospital. I just want to get my heart fixed so that I can take the trip to see you. I know you love to see the dolphins at the Ocean Park, and that's where we will go.*

*Sadly, I haven't spoken to my son about this. He is a busy and important man at his job. Anyway, I don't think he has anything to worry about. And neither do you.*

*You know what I'd like to do when I see you? Actually, I'd like for it to be a surprise.*

*Remember to smile. And take care of your mommy and daddy for me.*

*Much love,*

*Uncle Stephen*

The letter's dated three months before he died. I don't think he ever had any illusions about the risks of the surgery. He just didn't want Helen to worry. Ironically, the surgery was a success, but he didn't survive to worry about the heart problem. And he never did tell me. Neither did my mother. Then again, I didn't call them for months.

Oh, guilt.

I close my eyes again and let the pain eat at my stomach. For the first time, I feel lost without my father. Four weeks after his death. And now I've found a missing connection. My sister.

Oh, guilt.

Helen touches my hand. I open my eyes, and she hands me a photograph.

Four people: Lian, my father, a little girl and a baby. The Star Ferry Clock Tower looms in the background. The photo's taken a while ago. The girl's about two years old. She looks almost exactly like Lian.

"Is that you?" I point at the girl in the picture.

Helen shakes her head, then points at the baby. "Me."

I look at her, confused. "Who's this then?" I ask, pointing at the little girl again.

"My ee-ster."

"Sister? You have a sister?"

"Uh huh."

"Where's she now?"

She stretches her arm and points at the window. I shake my head. What does she mean?


"What are you doing here?"

Lian stands at the door, her eyes wide with terror.

I surge up from the bed, dropping the letter and photograph on the floor.

"What the—" Martin barges in, taking Helen's hand and yanking her away from me. "What the hell are you doing in my daughter's room?"

"Who is she?" I ask, staring at Lian.

"My daughter. You fucking creep," Martin yells.

"Who is she?" I ask again, looking from Martin to Lian and back again.

"What the fuck? You're crazier than I thought." Martin puts his arms around Helen.

"Martin, you are scaring Hel—her."

"Helen, you mean," I say. "Who is she?"

Helen breaks away from Martin and starts signing furiously. Her mother's face pales as Martin's reddens.

Lian stares at me. "Please leave now."

"I won't leave until you tell me who she is," I say. "What is it you're hiding from me?"

"She is my daughter. Martin's daughter."

"Bull-fucking-shit," I say. "She looks just like my father."

"What the fuck are you talking about?" Martin barks.

"You have no idea, do you?" I scoff. "Look at her."

"Stop it," Lian screams. It's the first time I've ever heard her scream. Her face is paler than ice and her breaths are short and quick. She signs at Helen and gestures for her to leave the room, but Helen shakes her head in defiance. Lian gestures again. Helen huffs and rushes out of the room.

"Surprise," I cry, raising my arms in the air. "Martin, meet Lian. Lian, meet Martin."

"I already told her about you, about us," he sneers. "Fucking creep."

"Martin, please keep your voice down," Lian says.

"Why? She can't fucking hear us."

"Who is she?" I ask.

"My daughter, asshole," he says, raising his fist. "How many times do I have to tell you? Are you out of your fucking mind? Stay away from her."

"Lian, tell him. Tell him now."

"Greg," she says. "Martin is the father."

"You're such a liar," I say. "No wonder he doesn't trust you."

"Greg, look at him," she says, pointing at Martin. "Look at him."

I look at Martin. He stares back. At first, I don't know what Lian is getting at. Then I remember. How we used to joke that Martin and I could have been brothers.

Helen could be Martin's. There's indeed a resemblance.

"But what about my father?" I ask.

"What about your father?" Martin asks.

I pick up the photograph and toss it at him. He picks it up. His hands shake as he looks at the picture.

"What is going on?" He turns to his wife. "Lian?"

"This is all wrong," she says. "This isn't supposed to happen."

"What's not supposed to happen?" he barks.

She shakes her head and drops to the floor. She closes her eyes.

"Tell me the truth," I say. "I'm not afraid of the truth anymore. Tell me the truth."

"Greg, Martin is Helen's father. And that is the truth."

"I don't believe you."

"What do you want?" he says. "A paternity test? I'm game. I want to know, too."

"Fine, everyone gets a paternity test, and everyone is happy," she says. She clutches her hair in both hands.

"Liar," I say. "If he really is Helen's father, why the name Helen? That's my mother's name."

"I didn't know that," he says. "What the fuck?"

"I liked the name," she says. "That is all. I thought Helen was a good name for her."

"I don't believe you," I say. "I don't believe a word you say."

"Believe what you want," she says. She lowers her head, looking tired. "Martin is her father. And that is the truth. We can do a paternity test tomorrow if you want, then you will have to believe me."

Martin stares at me with his trademarked shit-eating grin. He's claiming victory now, but I'm not about to lie there and play dead.

"What about the other one? The older girl in the picture?" I ask.

"Definitely not mine," he sneers.

"Whose then?" I ask.

"Howard Cape's," he says. He looks at Lian. "And I believed her."

"Is she?"

"You need to leave now," she says to me. "You have brought too much chaos into this house already. Please go."

"Where is she now?" I ask.

"Greg, please leave," she says. She places both hands on her face and begins to sob.

"I can't leave now. I want the truth."

Martin frowns and comes over to Lian, wraps an arm around her and pulls her up. She's choking in her tears. As angry as I am, it breaks my heart to see her sob like this.

"Leave, now," he says, scowling. "Leave. And don't come back."

I head toward the door.

"I will come back," I say. "And I want that test."


As I leave the cottage, I see Helen cuddling the black rabbit under the camphor tree, her tan skin shiny even in the shade. No, she can't be my sister. My father did not deserve her.

I lower my head and walk past her. From the corner of my eye, I see her clenching her jaw, frowning, watching me as I disappear.

# Not Everything Is About You

Olie sees me and nods. I wave. He's swamped, so I tread my way to the back and sit by a drainpipe, under a dim red light. Better not to talk, anyway. A few drinks are what I've come here for. When the waitress comes by, I order four Johnny Walkers and two shots of tequila, just in case I'll never see her again.

As I empty my second glass of whiskey, Olie comes over and slaps his heavy hand on my shoulder.

"How's it hanging, mate?"

"Hey." I shrug. "Haven't you noticed? Usually not feeling the best when I come here."

"It happens."

"Looks like you're having quite a night."

"Yeah, some kind of party. Some bloke's father just kicked the bucket and he's throwing everyone a fuckin' farewell blowout. See that?" He points at the crowd. "That bloke with the clown hat? Fuckin' freak if you ask me."

I ask Olie for two more glasses of Johnny Walker. He studies me for a second, then disappears in the crowd.

The place is so packed and choked with smoke that there's no sanctuary even in this little corner. Fat asses bump into me as they grind through the narrow passage into the dark recess in the back. Some drunk babbles at me—government conspiracy, lost fingers to a loan shark, some stupid shit. I just look up at the pipes on the ceiling and wish for death.

Madonna comes on through the speakers. *Like a Prayer*. A young Latino pup yells, "Mother Shit Fuck!" and smashes his beer glass on the floor. His chums burst into a collective laugh.

A thirty-something woman, short blond hair, sits at the bar across from me. She's been giving me the eye for the past twenty minutes or so. I don't recognize her, but her voluptuous breasts, pushing against a skin-tight black dress, beg for attention. Men gawk at her—vulture eyes circling—but so far no one's lunged for the kill. Her eyes meet mine again, and she twists her red lips, moist with freshly applied lipstick, into a seductive half smile. Too easy.

Way too easy. This is what I do best. I grab the shot glass and swallow the last shot of tequila. I grab my last glass of Johnny Walker, push the table away and strut toward her. She peers away and adjusts her dress, exposing a fine pair of long legs.

"Care if I join you?" I ask. "Or are you waiting for someone?"

"No." Gravelly voice. Her breath is gin and cigarettes.

"No, you're not waiting for someone, or no, you don't want me here?"

"I'm not waiting."

"Shame. You're the sexiest woman in the whole joint."

"Is that a pickup line? It's pretty lame."

"I don't need a frigging pickup line. I don't even have to buy you a drink."

She squints. "Is that right?"

"Listen. You have something I want. I have something you want." I lean in and whisper into her ear. "So cut the bullshit already. If I'm wrong, you can just show me the door. Bye, bye. Don't cry over it." I blow gently on her earlobe, place a hand on her waist. "I'm going to show you the time of your life."

"Don't flatter yourself." She lifts her body, turning away from me.

I turn away. She grabs my arm. Predictable.

She reclines against me. I twirl my fingers around the small of her back, feeling the smooth material of her dress slink over her skin. Slowly I glide my fingers lower, to that sweet spot just below her hips. She coos.

She slips off the stool and signals me to follow her. I finish my drink with one gulp. We push, brush and bump our way into a back room, past the men's room, where three large, middle-aged men are smoking pot. She grasps my hand and pulls me into a dark corner, behind a stack of empty Guinness cases. She backs up to the wall, pulls me close.

"Aggressive. I like that," I say.

"Oh, yeah?" she teases. She takes my left hand and guides it slowly down her hip and thigh. I press against her, hard.

"What's your name?" she whispers.

I press a finger on her lips. "No names."

She opens her mouth, and I slide the finger between her lips. She sucks, rolling her tongue around the tip, savaging traces of salty sweat and sweet whiskey. Smoke, gin and perfume, she smells like cheap Paris and that makes me even harder. I kiss her neck, pressing my tongue on her skin. My lips move along the long arc to her shoulder as my hand cups her left breast, my thumb tracing her erect nipple. She raises one leg, bends it slightly, and pulls me closer. Through the thin cotton of my trousers, I can feel her warmth and softness where she's the most vulnerable, inviting. I press closer.

She pushes me away, catching her breath. I peek at my surroundings—everyone's doing his own thing. Nobody cares. Bulldog's has a reputation: cheap liquors, cheap perfume, cheap women. I pull her toward me, but she pushes me away, her eyes over my shoulder. I turn. A small white man in a Jacksonville Jag jersey lurks next to me, squinting, smirking, smoking a fat cigar. "Scram," I say. "Now." He hesitates, scratches his crotch, then reluctantly disappears in the smoke.

I return my attention to the blonde. She unbuckles my belt with skillful hands. Once the belt's loosened, she slips one hand inside my pants, only my underwear separating her hand and my crotch. "Nice," she whispers, and starts rubbing. I sigh. Her body rises and I grind slowly in her grip. She kisses me, but I turn away from her. She kisses my neck instead, licking my Adam's apple, panting, sweating.

Her breath is intoxicating.

Then I do the—unthinkable in the Book of Greg Lockland. I push her hand away. She throws me a look and grabs me, but I press her back again. She stares at me. I close my eyes as the room spins.

"What?" she says.

"Sorry."

"You want to go somewhere else?"

"No."

"My place's only a few blocks away."

"I'm sorry."

"Sorry about what?"

"I'm getting another drink."

"What is this? A cruel joke or something?"

"Or something." I buckle my belt and turn to leave.

"Come back here." She's glaring.

I push my way out of the backroom.

"Fucking freak," she yells.

She has no idea how right she is.

I am a fucking freak.

Dawn's about to break as I crawl out of Bulldog's, staggering, hot and swollen. The streetlights shine in my eyes, making them throb. I have no idea where I am or where I'm going. The world is spinning and I'm spinning, too, in the opposite direction. I lean on a lamppost, a sickening lump rushing up my chest. I open my mouth—foul liquids and chunks spew out, flooding my face and everywhere. I stomp and plod, grab a railing and steady myself. Then I stumble, fall, feeling as if I'm rolling down a hill. The last thing I remember is the bright yellow light coming toward me.

Hell is a thousand needles in my eyes, and a thousand more in my head. I feel like hurling again, but I'm too tired to turn my head to the side. Finally my stomach settles. The thousand needles become more like a hundred. My throat is clammed shut. As my eyes adjust to the darkness, I look around. I don't recognize my surroundings. It's dark and hot. I'm in a shack or a storage room. Boxes and junk are everywhere. Paper, food wrappers, and a few stacks of *Hustler* litter the floor.

I try to push myself up, but my body is anchored in whatever I'm lying on. I close my eyes and breathe through my mouth. Breathe in. Breathe out. I'm going to make some sense out of this.

Eventually, I push hard enough with both my hands to prop myself up. A thin blanket slips onto the floor. I'm in a small, windowless room, on a worn-out couch, a few empty beer cans strewn around my feet. Heavy traffic outside.

I try to stand but my legs are weak. I wobble, then get hold of a plastic chair and steady myself. The place smells of dirty laundry and two-days-old Chinese takeout.

I find a cordless phone on the table. I need to talk.

Feeling guilty and missing Kate, I dial her number.

Her answering machine again. I hang up.

I call her mom.

"Hello?"

"Emily? This is Greg."

"Greg?" Her voice's sharp—she seems surprised. "It's after two in the morning. Are you okay? You sound awful."

"I'm sorry—didn't realize...was this late." I totally forgot about the sixteen-hour time difference.

"It's okay. Just got off my shift. I thought it was the hospital calling."

"Emily, is Kate there?"

"Kate? No. She's in San Diego."

"You talk to her lately?"

"She called last night."

"Did she say anything? About me?"

She hesitates. "Greg, what's going on?"

"I've been trying to reach her. She's not home."

"Now? She's probably in bed already."

"I'll try her tomorrow then."

"Greg, can I ask you something?" She hesitates. "Is there something going on between you and Kate?"

I sigh. "I don't know."

"She doesn't tell me anything. And you're not telling me anything either."

"I really don't know."

"Uh, I thought so," she muses. "I thought there was something in her voice."

"Like what?"

"Something was bothering her, I thought. We almost got into a fight again."

"Can you tell her to wait for my call? Or call me?"

"Why don't you just go and see her?"

"Emily," I say. "I'm in, eh, Hong Kong."

"Hong Kong? What are you doing in Hong Kong?"

"It's a long story. But I really need to talk to her."

I give Emily the number at Agnes and Old Chow's.

"I'll let her know," she says. "Greg, she's leaving for Seattle on Thursday, for a week."

"Seattle? What for, you know?"

"A case. I really don't know. But I'll let her know that you called."

"Tell her that I want to see her in person before Thursday."

"But you're in Hong Kong."

"Just tell her."

"Greg, are you okay?"

"I have to go now."

Next, I dial Patrick's number. It's after five in the morning, his time.

"Hello. Patrick," he says.

"Greg."

"Greg. Where have you been?"

"I'm still here, in Hong Kong."

"You haven't called for days."

"I know. Sorry. So much going on here."

"Yeah."

"Patrick, you wouldn't believe what I'm going to tell you. I don't even know where to begin. I found Lian. She lied to me. I had all those wonderful images, all those memories of her, and now I know they're all illusions. I can't fucking believe it. You know, she's married to my best friend. My best friend. And I thought she was this perfect woman. I really was blind. And to think, she must have feelings for me, too. I just can't believe what she did. I—"

"Greg—"

"Let me finish," I say. "You know, I might have a sister. Maybe even two. I didn't want to believe it. She and my dad. Jesus H. Christ. Do you know what they named her? Helen. Can you believe that? What an insult to my mother. It's like a slap in her face. I hate him. And I hate her. I—"

"Greg—"

"I know what you're going to say. But I have pride, you know? I just can't help but think what it meant to my mom. I still can't forgive him for killing her, but now this? The deceit, the cheating, the bastard children? So don't tell me that I should forgive and forget and all that bullshit. I can't. I'm so angry now I could just fucking kill someone. I'm going back later and I—"

"Greg, shut the fuck up," he yells. The handset wobbles in my hand. "Shut the fuck up already."

It can't be. My Patrick can't be turning on me now. Not when I'm at the lowest. Not when I need him the most.

"Everything's about you, isn't it?" he yells.

"What the fuck?"

"Me, me, me. Greg, it's always about you. Never fails. It's always about your cars, your job, your girlfriends, your sorry little life."

"Is that right?"

"I love you to death, man. But you can really be such an asshole."

"My folks just died. I'm dying here. And you're calling me an asshole? What kind of a friend are you?"

"Your only friend. And honestly, I can see why."

"Fuck you." I hang up.

I hear keys clinking. Then the lock clicks. As the door opens, the bright, florescent glare outside catches me by surprise. I raise my arm over my eyes and blink.

"Yo, you're up." It's Olie.

"Barely." My voice cracks. I open my eyes, adjusting to the light. "Did you take me here?"

"Couldn't leave you on the fuckin' street, drowning in your own fuckin' vomit." He enters the kitchenette and empties the content of a brown paper bag onto the counter. Glasses clanking.

"Thank you." I settle into the plastic chair.

"Sorry I couldn't kick your ass out earlier—too fuckin' busy."

"I guess I did have a little too much to drink."

"A little?"

"Well. Thank you, anyway."

"I thought I saw trouble the second I saw you. But it was Sunday. We needed the money," he says with a laugh. He comes out with a beer in one hand. He hands me a glass of brown liquid. "Drink this."

"What is it?"

"Bullshot, for your hangover. You do have one, right?"

"What's in it?"

"Just fuckin' drink it."

Lumpy, sour, spicy, slimy, it sticks to my mouth and leaves a thin film of aftertaste. But I'll drink ground-up bull's testicles—maybe these are bull's testicles—if they'll take this pounding headache away. I swallow the whole thing and lay the glass on the table, next to stacks of *Sports Illustrated*, half-naked women on the covers.

"Where am I?"

"My apartment."

"I know. Where is it?"

"Right on Nathan Road, just two bus stops from Bulldog's. Why?"

I wave a hand before my face, take a deep breath.

"I need to go home," I say.

"You can't fuckin' walk."

"Call me a cab, then."

"Hey, mate. Back up. What the fuck is the hurry?"

"I really don't want to talk about it."

He squints. Chuckles.

"What's so funny?" I ask.

"You saw the girl, didn't you? The Chinese banquet girl you told me about?"

I nod. My head hurts. I press my palms on my temples, massaging them, feeling the veins throbbing. Olie continues to snigger.

"Really. What's so funny?" I ask.

"Ah, love."

"It's more complicated than that."

"Like what?"

"My father."

"Huh?"

I wipe my hand over my eyes. I really don't want to talk about it.

"Having trouble with your old man?"

"He's dead. Just bunch of bones and rotten flesh now."

"Sorry."

"Don't be. He was a hypocrite."

He takes a sip of his beer.

"You know?" he says. "I didn't speak with my old man for over twenty years."

"And now you go fishing together and he's your best friend."

"No. He was a religious man and I was a drug user and a convict, among other things. You figure it out." He pushes the stack of magazines aside and rests his elbow on the table. "A year ago he called me. Out of the fuckin' blue. He wanted me to go see him, to help him die."

I glance at my glass.

"I wish I could tell you there was a fuckin' happy ending, that we made up and understood each other, all that bullshit," he says. "At the end, he was exactly the way he always was—the same son of a bitch. And I was the same fucked up, stubborn loser. But I was the only one who held his hand when he died."

I lift the glass up, letting the last few drops of Bullshot drip down my throat.

"What I did know was that I loved that fucker," he says. "I was ready to let him go."

I swallow hard. The lump in my throat becomes a sob, my body convulsing as I slump in the plastic chair.

Olie pats me on the shoulder, gets up and heads for the room in the back. I'm grateful that he lets me have this moment. No man should have to watch another man cry.

I let myself go for a while. I don't know what all the emotions are—they're just there, consuming me, breaking me. Then one thing's clear: anger. I'm angry that I can't let my father go.

I wipe my dirty face with my filthy shirt—puke, smoke and alcohol. I manage to get up from the chair and find my way to the kitchenette. Among the piles of grimy dishes, used Saran-wrap and empty pizza boxes, I find the coffee pot. I rinse a mug, fill it with the dark liquid and take a large bitter gulp. The last thing I need is more dehydration. But caffeine is good for the empty soul.

"Feeling better?" Olie startles me.

"Yeah. Thanks—for the coffee," I say. "Can I take a quick shower?"

"I have some clothes you can change into."

"By the way, I'm sorry but I made a couple of long distance calls. I'll pay you back."

"Don't worry about it. Make yourself at home."

After a warm shower, I change into the oversized flannel shirt and ripped jeans that Olie's laid out for me. Through the closed bedroom door, I can hear his obnoxious snore. He must have had a rough day himself.

I hold a new mug of coffee with both hands and perch on the couch, stewing. I pick up a copy of *Hustler* from the floor and flip through it. The big breasts and bare crotches don't excite me at all. Maybe I'm just too screwed up with the hangover, or maybe I'm depressed. When a man is more interested in an article about some South American piranhas than the parade of North American hooters, something is definitely haywire. Short-circuited. Fried.

I toss the magazine aside, then stumble into and rummage through the kitchenette, only to find a few cans of tuna—I hate tuna—and bags of chicken- and beef-flavored ramen. Nothing but beer and leftover Chinese food in the fridge. I haven't seen such an under-stocked bachelor pad since the one Patrick and I shared at Wharton. I tear open a ramen bag and drop the noodles into a small pot of water. As I turn on the grease-laden stove, I smell a gas leak.

What was wrong with Patrick anyway? I didn't deserve that.

Did I?

I pick up the handset and call again.

"Patrick," I say when he picks up.

"I don't need this right now."

"What's going on? Are you all right?"

"Oh, now you ask."

I keep my mouth shut. This time I should just listen.

He lets out a sigh. "Susan's in the hospital."

His daughter—the most important thing in his life.

"What happened?"

"Her kidney gave out. I had to rush her to the ICU on Saturday."

"I'm so sorry." I feel so small. "Anything I can do?"

"I don't know." He pauses. "It's okay. You have your own shit to deal with."

"My problem is nothing compared to yours."

"Nah, they're the same significant," he says. "Sorry I blew up on you."

"I was an asshole."

"You were." He chuckles. It's good to hear that his sense of humor is still intact. "Really. Nothing for you to worry about here."

"I want to help..."

"Your friendship, your moral support. It means a lot to me," he says. "Hey, I got to go to the hospital. Call me later?"

"Where's she staying at?"

"Children's."

"Hey, bud," I say.

"I know," he says. "Take good care of yourself."

I click off and put the handset on the kitchen counter. The pot is boiling over, ramen noodles everywhere.

A thumb-sized cockroach stares at me from a corner, ready to fly at me any time now.

Olie's snoring up a storm in his bedroom. Horns are blaring outside. Two men are arguing in the hallway.

Seven million people in this city.

One and half billion more in this country.

Endless stories to tell.

And mine is not the only one.

# Susan

"What the hell are you doing here?" Patrick opens the door, his hair a mess, his eyes those of a child.

I step forward. "Hey, I just spent twenty hours getting here. Don't give me this shit."

He wraps his wrestler's arms around me, squeezes me tight and plants a big one on my forehead.

"You're a crazy son of a bitch, you know?" He laughs.

"Yeah."

Patrick and I sit on the back porch. He has a Budweiser and I sip a Coke. The sun has already set and the sky is a sublime, late fall violet. The trees have shed most of their leaves, which rumple across the yard. The limestone birdbath, dry and derelict, leans slightly to the left. I remember Susan staring at a finch bathing in the basin. She was only two then. Everyone was in black—except her, in a frilly pink dress. I don't think Susan remembers her own mother's funeral. Patrick will never forget it.

I look over at Patrick. He stares, lost in thought, at the garage where Susan's purple and white bicycle leans on a wall. I want to say something, but I know that nothing I say can ease his mind. Being here with him is the least and best I can do.

A rivulet of wind sweeps past. The crinkly leaves dance in intimate circles, collecting under the trees. I pull down the sleeves of my pullover, but I still feel the chill.

He turns to me. "You're ready to go?"

I nod. He crushes his empty can and throws it like a basketball into the recycling bin. I follow suit. A perfect three-point shot.

In his pickup truck, we turn up the stereo and let Eric Clapton's soulful guitar fill the space. I push the DVD play button on the dash and *Beauty and the Beast* swells from an overhead monitor—somewhere in the dark forest, the Beast fights off the hungry wolves to save Belle.

"How're you holding up?" I ask.

"Huh?"

"Are you okay?"

"Yeah. Yeah. I'm fine."

"You can talk to me."

He stares straight ahead. I push the CD play button and Eric Clapton sings again. *Tears in Heaven.* Patrick turns the stereo off. Too close to home.

"Greg."

"Yes?"

"I don't know what I'll do if I lose Susan."

He sobs. It's like watching a dam break. First a crack, a leak, then a rumble and all hell breaks loose. I put my hand on the steering wheel and help Patrick pull off to the shoulder.

"Do you want me to drive?" I ask.

He waves his hand. "No. Damn it."

"It's okay."

"Damn it. Fuck."

"She's going to be okay."

"Fuck. Fuck. Fuck. Fuck."

I find a big wad of Kleenex in the door pocket and hand it to him. He glares at me for a second, then wipes his face.

"We're going to go to Vermont to see my dad over Thanksgiving," he says. "I don't know what to tell him."

"The truth."

"The truth." He licks his lips, then elbows me. "So, tell me about your quest for the truth."

"I don't think it's a good time right now."

"Hey, help me take my mind off this shit. Okay?" He starts the engine and pulls off the shoulder.

So I do. I tell him about Lian, Martin and the little girl who could be my sister. I tell him about the concert, the island, the beach, the cave, the Tai Ping Inn, the cliff, the cottage, the camphor tree, the rabbits, the letter, the photograph, the wooden box, the screaming and the yelling. I skip over some of the details—Bulldog's, for example. But I tell him about Kate.

"Holy shit."

"Holy shit's right."

"You should go back. Go to Kate. Why are you here?"

"That can wait." I pat him on the shoulder. He smiles. Then frowns.

Patrick pokes his head in the door of Susan's room. She looks weak but her spirit blooms when she sees her father. She seems surprised but pleased to see me. A woman in her late twenties— short brown hair, dark-rimmed glasses, a light blue blouse and long, black skirt, slightly overweight but pretty—sits next to Susan, holding her hand. She nods at Patrick when we come in.

"Hey, Suzie," I say, patting Susan's small hand.

"Look what Uncle Greg got you." Patrick holds up the big fluffy Garfield I got from the gift shop.

Susan grins as Patrick lays Garfield next to her. She can't talk, a tube stuck in her mouth and an IV jammed in her arm. Bags of fluid are hanging around. A monitor with a green screen by her bed beeps every two seconds or so—a repetitious, lifeless sound. The antiseptic air is heavy.

"This is Susan's first grade teacher, Ms. Jennifer Kretzler," Patrick says.

I introduce myself and shake her hand. "Pleased to meet you."

"Please call me Jen."

"Thank you for being here. I couldn't get out earlier," Patrick says.

"I was going to come after school anyway," she says. "She seems to be doing great."

"Yeah, all things considered," he says, patting Susan's hair. "She's a trooper."

"Well, you're here. I should go then," she says.

"Can you stay just a little longer? Keep her company?" Patrick says. "I've got to talk to the doctor."

After Patrick leaves the room, Jen continues to pat Susan's hand while I take a chair next to the window.

"You really care about Susan, huh?" I ask.

"She's easy to love," she says. "We're both new to the school, so we have a bond. She's a great girl."

Jen has a sweet smile. She brushes a hair away from Susan's face and turns to me. "And you?"

"Oh, I watched her grow up. Patrick and I go way back."

"Mr. Taylor's very lucky to have a friend like you."

The guilt women can inflict. Claire used to do that, like the time when she called me to remind me of Patrick's birthday—the day after the fact. We had a good chuckle when I begged for forgiveness.

I miss Claire.

"It must be difficult to be a single father," Jen says. "And working at the Courant must not be easy."

"He manages," I say. "They manage. But I agree. They need someone."

She fiddles with her hair again. I notice that she's nervous whenever I talk about Patrick. She clearly likes him.

"Patrick's a strong man with a big heart," I say. "I'd have married him by now if I were gay."

She laughs. "And what would your wife say?"

"Me? Nope. No wife. How about you?"

"No wife either."

I like this woman. "Where do you live?" I ask.

"Windsor. You know the Advo buildings? Not far from there. And you?"

"I live all over the place."

"Must be nice."

"Not really," I say. "Do you like being a teacher?"

"I love kids, so yes. And I believe education's very important."

"Amen."

"Do you have any children?"

"I wish. Maybe some are running around somewhere. I just don't know about them."

She chuckles.

I get up from the chair and walk over to her. "Patrick's a good catch," I whisper. "That is, if you're interested."

"Mr. Lockland," she whispers, protesting.

"I'm sorry if I'm a little blunt," I say. "I'm like that. Patrick, on the other hand, is kind of socially retarded now. He hasn't had a date for so long, he's practically forgotten they exist. But I can see that you like him. And he obviously likes you."

"He does?"

"Absolutely. He talked about you on our way here," I lie. A nice, little white lie. "Did you see how he asked you to stay? The fact is," I say, "you'll probably have to make the first move."

"What are you saying?"

"I'm just going to say this," I whisper. "I want what's best for my best friend. And I'm going to do whatever I can to help."

Patrick enters the room in a hurry. His face is flushed and his hands jitter, as if he has just won the lottery.

"Mr. Taylor," Jen says. "I really must go."

"Already?" Patrick says. "Can't you stay a little longer?"

"I'd love to. But I have class tomorrow."

"Ms. Kreztler," Patrick mumbles. "Do you, do you think you can come by tomorrow? It'd be a great help if you could. I have to work kind of late again. Susan'd love to have your company."

"Of course," she says. "You don't have to ask. Maybe we can—well, I'd better go." She kisses Susan's hand and says a quiet goodbye to her.

She turns to me. "Very nice meeting you, Mr. Lockland."

"Call me Greg, please." I wink.

After she leaves the room, Patrick darts suspicious eyes at me. "What was that about?"

"I have no idea." I shrug. "So. What did the doctor say?"

He puts a finger over his lips. He pulls a chair up and sits next to Susan, holding her hand, stroking her hair.

"Were you a good girl today? Did you do what the nurses asked you? Sorry daddy had to work late today. Are you hot? Cold? Are you tired? Thirsty?"

He tucks the corners of her blanket snuggly under the mattress.

"Do you want daddy to read you a story?"

She nods.

Patrick looks around him, flustered. "Shit," he whispers to me. "I forgot to bring the books."

I help him look through the room, even the cracks between the sofa seats. The only book I can find is *Alice in Wonderland*.

"Do you want *Alice in Wonderland* again?"

She shakes her head slowly.

"Well," I chime in. "Uncle Greg has a story. Would you like to hear it?"

She nods.

I pull up a chair on the other side of the bed, and hold her other hand. I begin to tell her a story about a boy named Oscar and his potbelly pig.

After Susan falls asleep, Patrick and I slip out of the room. We find a small bench in the hallway around the corner. He fiddles with *Alice in Wonderland*, flipping it over and over, spinning it on his finger like he would pizza dough.

"So," I say, "what did the doctor say?"

"Well," he says and sighs. "They did what they could. She almost went septic. I thought she was going to die."

He stops spinning the book and holds it tight against his chest. "She doesn't deserve this. She's only six." He closes his eyes. "It seems like transplant is the only way now."

"Do you need a living donor? I have a good kidney. I think."

"Greg." He looks at me and chuckles.

"I do. And I will. I don't know about my liver. But kidney, yeah. I'm serious."

"Greg, I'm touched. I really am," he says. "I could have given her mine, but I wasn't a match." He pats my thigh. "She's lucky."

"Lucky?"

"She's got a donor. We've been on the list for fourteen months and we finally got one. The doctor just told me."

"Really?"

"Really. And just in time, too. Thank God." He sighs. "I feel bad, though, wishing for some poor kid out there dying, so that she can have a second chance. But that's how it goes, I suppose."

"That's good news."

He looks around and frowns.

"But look at this place," he says. "I don't want them to do it in Hartford. I wanted Presbyterian's in New York, Johns Hopkins, even Children's in Pittsburgh. But they couldn't allow it. Too expensive. Those bastards."

"Is LA too far?"

"LA?"

"UCLA has a great pediatric transplant program. And I know people. People who worked with my dad."

"Even if I can transfer her out there, I can't afford the operation, the home care and everything. They won't cover it."

"I will."

"Greg?"

"Remember my parents' will? I'm a multi-millionaire now, you know? Fuck insurance. Who needs insurance when you have money?"

"I can't let you do that."

"The fuck you can't," I say. "You and Susan are like the only family I have now. She deserves the best care in the world."

"I don't know what to say."

"Say you'll haul your ass out there. Stay at the Westwood house," I say. "Let me set everything up and let you know. I'm going to see Kate anyway. And I'm going to pull some strings, visit some old folks at my father's place. Just get ready. It's going to happen."

He clutches the book again. "Greg?"

I place my hand on his.

"I'm scared," he says.

I wrap my arm over his shoulder. I'm scared, too. I'm scared about the future. I'm scared about the past. But I know this fear is not going to stop me from moving forward. I just want him to know that I'm here for him and Susan.

Patrick stares straight ahead, his eyes fixating on something on the wall opposite us. I look over. A mother cradles a baby in a soft blue light, a replica of the Cassatt painting hanging on the wall above them.

I can just hold Kate now.

I lean on the wall and close my eyes. I'm so tired. Patrick mumbles something about Ms. Kreztler. Eventually I drift off—some place where gigantic yellow daisies trample like herds of elephants across the sky. I scramble through the flowers, desperately looking for Lian.

# Return to California

I turn the corner and park the car on Roselyn Drive.

I don't know what to expect. By now she must have read my first letter to her. She knows what a screw-up I am. Was. In the past, I would've just escaped, pretending my tail was not between my legs. I would have run as far and as fast as I could. But not this time. I just want to see her.

I knock. No answer. I knock again. Silence. I knock a third time. It's after ten at night. Where could she be?

I turn to leave. I change my mind.

I take out my American Express card and slip it between the door latch and the frame. I wiggle the doorknob while sliding the card up and down, until I hear a small click.

I push the door open, but it's stuck on a stack of mail—one or two days' worth. I push and pull at the door until it gives way. Her apartment smells clean, a hint of pine. The lights are off. The only sound is the bubbles from the filter in the fish tank.

I close the door and turn on the lights. I pick up the mail and sort through it. My letters are not there. In her bedroom, I rustle through her desk—bills, case notes, CDs, a few keys, a large pile of big paperclips, but no letters from me. In fact, nothing is from me, to me, or about me. It's as if I don't exist in her life.

I scribble on a Post-It:

*Please call or see me at the Westwood house. I miss you so much.* ~~I want~~ *I love you. Greg.*

A door squeaks open. I crumple the Post-It and toss it away. I turn, expecting to see Kate. Instead, the woman staring at me in horror is not someone I know. She's in her mid-twenties, short and thin, dark brown hair and large hazel eyes.

"Who are you?" Her voice is sharp.

"I'm sorry. I'm Greg, Kate's friend."

"I've never heard of you. How did you get in?"

"I have a key," I lie.

"Show me."

"Listen, I was just leaving." I move toward her. "I wanted to see Kate. She wasn't here. Thought I'd leave her a message."

She takes a step back. Her face tightens as she clutches her purse. "Don't come any closer or I'll call the police."

"Kate never mentioned me? Greg? Lockland?"

"No."

I notice that the LCD on Kate's answering machine is blinking a big red 1. "I can prove it." I press the play button on the answering machine.

"Don't touch that."

The message on the machine comes on—as I suspected, it's my message to her this evening before I left LAX, coming straight to San Marcos:

*Kate, please pick up...Kate, I want to see you tonight. I can stop by your apartment after ten? I can't wait to see you.*

"See?" I say.

"Doesn't sound like you."

"Well, it is," I say, getting annoyed. "And if you'll excuse me, I'm going now. Would you please tell her that I was here and I must see her soon? Just give her the message."

"I can't."

"Why not?"

"She's not here. She's gone."

"She left for Seattle already?"

"I don't know about Seattle, but she said she'd be away for a while and she wanted me to take care of her fish for—why am I telling you this?"

"Do you have her contact information?"

"I think you'd better leave now."

."I'm going. But please tell her, if and when you talk to her, that Greg Lockland came by to see her. It's very important that you tell her. That she calls me."

I head toward the door, and she takes a few steps back, away from me, her hand inside her purse—I can tell she's ready to use her mace or stun gun or .44 Magnum.

As I go through the door, I turn and look at her again. "Are you sure she never mentioned me?"

"Never. Now go."

I'm back at the Westwood house before midnight. The damage from the car accident on the east wing stares at me in contempt. Long, dark shadows spread like phantom fingers over the walls—distressing, like a deserted gingerbread house, a big ugly chunk bitten off by some angry old witch.

And little Hansel is back without his Gretel.

I dread this empty place: the hallways grim and hollow, pictures of my past haunting me on the walls. A tall pile of mail sits on top of the dining table—I didn't even think of stopping the mail before I left. The central air is running low, humming in the background. Somebody's been here. Must be Emily. She probably still has a key to the house.

I approach the piano by the French windows in the west wing. I sit on the bench and lift up the lid. The black and white keys of the Steinway are inviting. I strike one, its sound delightful and crisp. I strike a few more, then simply bang on them as hard and as fast as I can, making random, furious sounds.

If Kate's punishing me, she's doing a fine job. What I dread, though, is that she has given up on me, or, worse, that she didn't really care for me to begin with. She's left for Seattle without waiting for me or leaving me a message. An eye for an eye. I left. She left.

Should I stay and fight for her? Or should I let her be?

I don't know.

I can't sleep, so I watch the world, as its shadows shift and shrink, rouse to the sounds of birds and ticking clocks and children on the street. Then I drive to UCLA Medical Center and look for Dr. William Heekin, the chief of staff whom my father mentioned on various occasions. A brilliant surgeon. Somebody who can help Patrick and Susan.

I find him in his office, a nice view of the campus and books all over the wall. He's about my father's age, bald and fully bearded, skin as dark as charcoal, distinguished looking. As I enter his office, he takes a look at me, stands up and greets me with a zealous handshake.

"So great to see you," he says.

"I'm sorry to bother you."

"Not at all. Not at all. Your father and I were great friends."

"I'm not here to talk about my father."

His eyes widen. He looks hurt by my stern statement. He has, perhaps, underestimated the fracture in the relationship between my father and me, no matter what he might have gleaned from personal accounts and gossip.

"I'm here about my friend and his daughter," I say.

I tell him about the transplant, how I want to bring Susan here for the surgery and am willing to pay for everything. He seems hesitant at first, but gradually warms up to the idea. They do have one of the best programs in the country, and a top-notch staff of specialists. Transfer is possible. They can work with UNOS and Hartford. Dr. Rook, one of my father's protégés, is probably one of the best transplant surgeons in California. I'm glad to hear that he'll be available in a week or two. They can admit Susan as early as this weekend.

At least my father's good for something. Posthumously.

"That's such good news," I say. "I'm sure Patrick will be glad to hear that."

"Mr. Lockland," he says. "About your father."

"Dr. Heekin, with due respect, I really don't want to talk about him."

"What about his office?"

"What about it?"

"His personal effects."

"Why don't you pack them into some boxes and send them to me?"

"I suppose we can do that."

"Great. You can just send the stuff to my father's house in Westwood."

"Are you sure you don't want to take a look first?"

"Not really. Nothing I'm interested in there. Nothing."

That night, after talking to Patrick and telling him to pack up, fly to LA with Susan and move into the Westwood house, I lie on my bed and stare at the ceiling for a long time.

Finally, I'm doing something for someone else, someone who really matters to me, and I'm happy. I am. It's like a quest, a fire that burns inside of me, and it gives me life and energy.

At the same time, I am lonely. Envious and sad. At least Patrick has Susan—a cause, a relationship, a reason to move forward. I don't know what reason's left for me. I'm drifting, lost in this grand house, feeling miniscule and bitter about my own existence.

I get up and open the window to let in some fresh air. Below, scattered leaves and dirt litter the swimming pool. And little bugs that wanted only a quick drink. The greenhouse looks on in odd silence, flowerpots stacked and abandoned.

I think of Mom. I think of the last time I watched her walking out the door. I think of the last time she cleaned my room and told me not to leave crumbs on the bed. I think of the last time she pinched my arm. I think of her crazy little farce as she fluttered about after I told her I was moving to New York. I think of how she clutched my hands and told me to be good. I think of many things. Big things. Small things. Insignificant things. Things that aren't around anymore.

I start to cry.

The phone rings. I jump. It might be Kate.

I wipe off my tears and pick up the receiver.

"Patrick."

"Did I miss something?" I ask. "I thought I told you all the details. I even called the home care agencies."

"It's not about that," he says. "I think you should go look for Kate."

"I need to be here."

"No, you don't. Just leave me a key."

"I want to be here for you. So much to do."

"What for? I'm a grown man. I can take care of Susan just fine. Listen, the operation won't be another week or so. There's no reason why you should be sitting around waiting. You should go. Find Kate."

"Why?"

"If you truly care about her, you will go after her."

"I don't know where she is."

"Call her office. Ask. Do something."

"I don't know."

"Fuck, Greg. It's about time you do something for yourself."

"I did enough already. You said so yourself: it's always me, me, me."

"I mean something that really matters. Like Kate. Like Lian. You just can't let things hang like that."

"It's over between Lian and me. Long ago. It's probably over between Kate and me. Maybe we shouldn't have gotten back together at all."

"Don't say that."

"It's true."

He's quiet. Perhaps he finally understands and accepts the truth as well.

"What happened to you?" he says.

"Huh?"

"Where's that cocky, aggressive, super-confident son of a bitch I know?"

"He's gone."

"Bullshit. Remember the time you broke your collarbone playing football? You didn't back down. You fought on. You were fierce. Everyone feared you."

"I'm a different man now."

"Yes, you are. A better man, I may say."

"So what?"

"That's why you need to find Kate. You need to show her. You need to show her how much you love her."

"I don't know how."

"Yes you do," he says. "The way you showed Susan and me."

I drag myself into the kitchen, looking around for nothing, and notice some fresh tomatoes and a tall carton of orange juice. Odd. Emily didn't tell me about her visit. As I take a glass out of the cabinet, I notice a shiny object at the edge of the counter by the sink. I pick it up—a wiry, silver ring with a speck of emerald on it.

So, it was Kate. Two hours away from where she was, taking care of me and my house, even when I was gone chasing after something, someone else.

That's all the kicking I need.

First thing in the morning, I grab a pen and some paper, call Young & Wesley and ask to speak to Kate's boss.

"Jerry Young."

"Yes, my name's Greg Lockland. I'm a friend of Kate Walken."

"How may I help you, Mr. Lockland?"

"I understand that Kate's been sent to Seattle on business. I wonder if it's possible for you to tell me where she is—her hotel? The client she's working with? Et cetera."

"She didn't go to Seattle."

"No?"

"No, she turned the case down. It's an important case and a great opportunity for her. I don't understand. So unlike her."

"But she left town."

"She took some time off, yes."

"You know where she went?"

"I have no idea. She just took off, last minute's notice."

I scribble a big mesh of wiry loops on the piece of paper. Keep scribbling and scribbling. Picture of my mind.

"Is there something else I can help you with?" he asks.

"That's okay. Thank you."

I hang up and dial Emily's number. She picks up after the third ring.

"Emily. Is Kate there?"

"Greg? Where are you?"

"No time to explain. Is Kate there?"

"She went to Seattle."

"No, she didn't."

"She didn't?"

"I just called her at work. They said she took off, but she didn't go to Seattle. And she's not in San Diego."

"How do you know?"

"I was there."

"You came back?"

"I don't have time to explain. I need to speak to Kate."

"She's not here."

"You're not lying to me, are you?"

"Greg." Emily pauses for a long second. "I have a strange feeling. I told her you were in Hong Kong. I gave her your number."

"You don't suppose—"

"It's possible. That girl's always peculiar and impulsive. Who knows how she thinks?"

"Emily, this is very important. If she calls, you must ask her where she is and tell her to stay there and wait for me."

"Why don't you just wait for her here?"

"No," I say. "I must go to her. It's very important that I do."

"Greg, what's going on?"

"I'll explain when I come back. Please?"

"Greg."

"Emily." I pause. "She's all I have."

# Return to Hong Kong

The frequent flyer miles.

I check myself into room 3508 at the Grand Hyatt, the same room I had before, overlooking the harbor and the giant white turtle. The city and harbor span the entire length of my windows. I look out. *Where is she?*

I call Agnes, but neither she nor Old Chow is home. I can't sit still, so I take out and flip through the Yellow Pages, pick up the phone and dial.

"Dr. Cape's office," the receptionist answers. "May I help you?"

I ask for Howard.

A moment later, he picks up. "Greg," he shrieks.

"Howard."

"I'll be damned. It really is you. How long has it been?"

"Fourteen years."

"Incredible. You sound just the same."

"But everything has changed."

He doesn't say anything. I watch the Star ferries shuttling between the shores—slow and relaxed, a direct contrast to the adrenaline-pumped world around them.

"Sorry about your dad," Howard says.

"You've spoken with Lian?"

"Greg, I'm actually very busy right now," he says. "But I'd really like to see you and catch up. We have so much to talk about. What do you say, dinner tonight?"

"Where?"

"At my place. Turtleback Bay. 620 Beckham Road. Let's say seven-thirty?"

Seven-thirty it is. I lie down on the soft, fluffy bed. I fall asleep immediately.

The taxi swerves into a hard turn. Beyond the bend and the guardrails is a vast pane of green jade, carved by wedges of lush hills and fringed by narrow ribbons of beaches. Turtleback Bay is a reclusive, semi-private enclave tucked in the southern tip of Hong Kong Island, only thirty-five minutes from the heart of the city proper. Tiered along the ridges and clustered in the valleys, red and green roofs of Mediterranean architecture thrust through the layers of palm trees and tropical gardens. As we come down the road twisting around the grand pines and palms, the vista narrows into a passage, gated estates on either side, reminding me of, at once, Santorini in Greece, Pattaya in Thailand, and Nice in France.

The driver drops me off in front of one of the black gates. Behind it stands a three-story house, tall white walls and European banisters, spiral staircase and marbled front yard. The bay beckons nearby, waves flung along the cliffs behind the structure. I can see snips of turquoise through the narrow gaps and nooks between the walls. The air is moist with a hint of salt and the sun is low, its orange-cream glow peeking above a hill, the sky sheathed in pink and golden shreds. If I didn't know any better, I'd think I was in a Hollywood movie, Greta Garbo in a long negligee waiting for me by the pool.

I press the doorbell by the gate. I imagine a butler in a black tux greeting me and offering me an evening cocktail before the master summons him to bring the honorable guest upstairs to a grand chair by the crackling fire.

Instead, a barge-sized man appears through the French doors. A white silk shirt and sand dress pants. Black hair, pulled back, and dark eyes. And a beautiful voice: "We meet again."

"Victor?"

"Why, of course," Victor Marcello chirps. He opens the gate and lets me in. "Welcome."

I step inside and shake his hand. "You live here?" I ask.

"Almost seven years. Come on back, we've been waiting for you."

He closes the gate and leads me through an archway to the back of the house. It opens on a small terrace, burled teak banisters on one side and carved alabaster pillars on the other, terra cotta inlaid across the floor. The house sits on top of a precipice, about fifteen yards from the edge, overlooking half the bay and its mouth. A small but exquisite garden extends out, on the left, wrapped by a handsome white fence.

"Look at this place. I should have been a doctor."

"Actually," he says with a laugh. "I make more money than doctors."

"What is it with cliff-side houses anyway? Seems like a trend."

"Yeah. Lian told me about your visit."

"What else did she tell you?"

A voice comes from above. "Hello."

I look up. Howard stands on a balcony above us, in a soft blue Polo shirt, holding a glass of white wine. His hair is more silver than black. He's got that bookish look, still, complete with wire-frame glasses.

"I'll be right down," he says and steps inside.

Victor flicks on a switch near the base of the left wall, and the umbrella-domed gas heater hisses, crimson flames dithering within its steel grilles. "It gets chilly in the evening," he says.

"Greg," Howard greets me as he steps off the last stone of stairway. "Good to see you."

We shake hands.

"Do you want something to drink?" he asks.

"Water's fine."

"Perrier?"

I can't hide the smirk on my face.

"Okay, let's get it out of the way first," he says with a wink. "I'm not gay. But my partner is."

"Every bit of me," Victor says. "All two hundred and fifty-six, heck, fifty-eight pounds."

"I hadn't a clue," I say.

"Come on. Gynecologist? That's the first giveaway," Howard says.

"And opera?" Victor laughs. "Greg, what sort of a self-loathing gay man doesn't like opera?"

"But when? You were always Dr. Drop-dead at the hospital."

"That's *gorgeous* for you," Howard whispers to Victor, winking as he leans over him. "You know, just wishful thinking on the nurses' part," he says. "Seriously, when have you ever seen me with a woman?"

"What about Lian?"

"That's something we should talk about. But first, good God, I'm starving."

# Perfect

The proscuitto slips on the tongue like the finest cashmere, silky and soft, bringing out the fullness of the large strawberries and thick cream cheese. The tuna *tartare* with chives and *gaufrettes* oozes moist and sweet. The *foie gras terrine* clumps on the razor-thin rice crackers, majestic and corpulent, glistening golden. Not to mention the *magret de canard*—grilled breast of duck wrapped in French crepes. Delicate. And these are just the appetizers. The burly Italian cooks as well as he sings.

"Like the food?" Howard asks as he sits next to me on a lounger.

"Love it," I say.

I wrap my fingers around a rolled crepe, tilting it, keeping the juice from flowing out.

"That's why I have this gut," he says, pointing at his waistline. "I used to have a six pack."

"Tell me about you and Victor. How did you meet?"

"Who wants to hear that old story?" Howard says.

"I do," Victor says. "I never get tired of that."

"You tell him, then," Howard says.

"It was a dark and stormy night—" Victor says.

"Be serious," Howard says.

"It was the Children's Hospital charity concert," Victor says. "I sang *Nessun Dorma* for the first time at the Cultural Center—boy, was I nervous. And Howard was there." He starts to sing *Some Enchanted Evening* from *South Pacific*. Then he stops and leans gently against Howard. "And the rest, as they say, is history."

"Actually, I didn't know who he was," Howard says. "I thought he had a great voice. That was about it."

"That was about it?" Victor scrunches his nose, sending up a pout. "That was about it?"

Howard chuckles. "I wasn't a big fan of operas," he says. "Then Lian introduced us at the reception, and that was it—I was in love."

I swallow the last shreds of duck and dab my mouth with a napkin.

"Did Lian know?"

"About me?" Howard says. "Of course. I think she knew before I did."

"But I thought you and she—I mean, she never told me otherwise," I say.

"She knew how to keep a secret," Howard says.

"I guess," I say. *You mean she knows how to lie.*

"I was very much in the closet," Howard says. "She was my great confidant. And beard. She understood me. If not for her, I wouldn't be here, with Victor."

"And it was a beautiful thing," Victor says. "The way she introduced us. It was like, 'Flower, please meet Bee. Now go and make some honey.' And the whole night I was drinking it in. I was a dog in heat."

"Please." Howard laughs. "We were very civil."

"I know," Victor says. "We didn't even have sex until the fourth date."

"Yo, too much information," I say, throwing my hands in the air.

"Please," Howard says. "I listen to straights talk about their sexual problems, and look at vaginas all day, for crying out loud."

I laugh. I lean against the banister and sip my Chardonnay—I wasn't going to drink, but the occasion seems to call for a little wine.

Blue-violet hues wash across the drunken sky. The bay lolls somber, waiting for the moon's kisses. I remember the rooftop on Cheung Chau, where I realized the love I couldn't have and the love I'd forsaken. And here I am—a different sea, a different moon, a different place. Yet it's the same story, possibly the same ending.

"Greg, are you okay?" Howard taps my hand.

"I'm—" I sigh. "I don't know."

"It's about Lian, isn't it?" he asks.

"I don't know how much she's told you," I say. "But yes. I'm baffled. And I'm angry."

"She's not perfect, you know? None of us is," he says.

"But she was."

"What is it about perfection, anyway?"

"I don't know what you mean."

Victor takes over for Howard. He points at a skewer of grilled shrimp, pink and plump. "This can be perfect. A piece of steak can be perfect. By George, my foie gras is perfect. But can a person be perfect?"

"Of course," I say. "She was."

"Was she?"

"Howard, I'm not playing a semantics game with you. You know what I mean."

"Actually, no, I don't."

"For Christ's sake, she was an angel. She's magnificent. You said so yourself."

"She's also human."

"I didn't make her into a saint, if that's what you're getting at."

"Didn't you?"

I look out at the bay. The low horned moon turns into a frown in the shivering water.

"Philosophically, and realistically, nobody can be that perfect," Howard says. "I love Victor to death, but I know he's not perfect."

"I snore like a banshee, for one thing," Victor says, and snorts loudly in demonstration. "And I'm fat. I love food too much."

"And love—true love—is not about perfection. Actually, it's about all the little things that are perfectly imperfect." Howard folds his napkin and places it neatly on the table. "Greg, can I ask you an honest question?"

I shrug. One more question is not going to kill me.

"Were you in love with Lian, or were you in love with perfection?"

"Now, that's stupid," I say.

"Perhaps you were so drawn to that perfection because you wanted so much to be perfect yourself."

"I knew I wasn't perfect. Far from it."

"Ah," Victor interjects, "but you wanted to be perfect. You were expected to be perfect. And being with someone like Lian seemed like a way to have that."

"That's absurd," I say.

"Is it?" Howard asks. "What would your father say?"

"What does it have to do with him?"

"Just think about it."

I gaze into the distance. A few yachts linger in the bay, their long masts wavering gently, like magic wands, flicking the dust into a sea of lights.

"She didn't have to lie to me," I say.

"She did what she had to do," Howard says.

I suck in a long breath. The air chills in my lungs. "She could have admitted to the affair," I say. "I'd have forgiven her."

"What affair?" Victor asks. A piece of shrimp falls out of his mouth.

"Guess you didn't know either."

"Your father," Howard says calmly, gesturing me.

"Right, he and the woman I loved. It's starting to sound like a damn soap opera. I'm ashamed to even mention it."

"What if," Howard asks, "there was no affair?"

"Of course there was."

"Of course?" Victor says. "You're so sure."

"I have letters," I say. "Do you want to read them?"

I reach into my pocket. Victor leans against me, curious as a pussycat. Howard shakes his head and puts his hand on mine, stopping me.

"I know all about the letters," Howard says. "Lian told me."

"She didn't tell me," Victor protests.

Howard darts him a disapproving look. Victor grins and sits down on a lounger, smoothing his wavy hair.

"First of all, she told the truth about Helen," Howard says, twirling his wine glass slowly. "Helen is Martin's daughter."

"How do you know?"

"They did the paternity test. Tuesday. It came out positive."

I let out a whoosh of air. So that's the final answer.

"What about the other girl?"

Howard stares into his glass. He raises it and takes a long, slow sip. "You're curious, aren't you?" he asks.

"Is she yours?"

"What do you want out of this?" he asks.

"The truth."

"The truth." He finishes his wine and sets the glass on the round table. "But. Are you ready for the truth?"

"Yes."

"Then what?"

His question catches me off guard. I never thought of that. "Forgiveness? Redemption?" I say.

"Whose? Whose forgiveness? Whose redemption?"

"Howard, I didn't know. You're so full of crap."

"Welcome to my world," Victor says, bursting into his high-pitched laugh.

"Yes, I can be rather nasty." Howard winks. "Just ask the adoption people."

"Adoption?"

"Yeah." Howard stares at his hands. Victor glances at me and shrugs. He comes over, places his hands on Howard's shoulders and massages them.

"Have faith, Howard," I say. "Some day a child will come along. You'll make a great father."

"He did," Victor says. Howard shakes his head and grabs Victor's hand.

"The girl," I say. "At least tell me her name."

Howard closes his eyes. "Lillian."

"Where is she now?"

Howard turns to me, an immense sadness in his eyes. "You'll have to ask Lian."

"But she won't tell me. She probably won't even see me, after the whole Helen debacle."

"We'll see what we can do," Howard says. He pats me on the shoulder, then hops up and starts toward the house. "It's getting a little too chilly out here."

"Come on," Victor says. "Join us for a cocktail by the fireplace. We have pictures to show you."

# Twelve O'clock Ferry

After a while, I give up asking Howard and Victor for the truth about Lian. Instead, I sit by the French masonry and spirited flames as they show me their seven years together: their honeymoon in St. Maaten, the Parisian châteaux where they spent a whole night devouring mint chocolates, the way they fell in love with this little house overlooking Turtleback Bay, the battle they're fighting to adopt a Cambodian girl, pictures of their trips, dinner parties and an entourage of friends. By midnight, Howard gets a little drunk, so Victor kisses him, then ushers him to bed. I slouch in an armchair, the glowing embers gently consoling me, and grow solemn and reflective, envious of what these two men share.

The evening has been a celebration of past acquaintance and future friendship. A little cognac goes a long way—I'm still warm and full when I return to my hotel room shortly after one in the morning. I plop myself on the bed and reach into my shirt pocket, pulling out the three photographs Victor shoved there before I hopped into the taxi. In these pictures, Howard's the same Dr. Drop-dead I knew, and Lillian's a little angel, a perfect replica of Lian.

I toss the photographs on the nightstand. I decide to call the Baptist Hospital, hoping to catch Agnes on her night shift. The receptionist mumbles something unintelligible, then shuffles off to find Agnes.

"Greg," Agnes quacks. "Where are you?"

I lie on my back, resting an arm across my forehead. "You don't want to know," I reply.

"Kate Walken called."

"She did?" I bolt upright.

"Yes. This afternoon."

"What did she say?"

"She said something about her mum? That you called her?"

"Yes, I did. What else did she say?"

"She asked me where you were. I didn't know what to tell her." Agnes pauses. "She said she was on Cheung Chau."

"Cheung Chau? What the hell was she doing on Cheung Chau?"

"She didn't say. I told her you'd call. She said she'd call back tomorrow morning."

"Agnes, I have something to tell you," I confess. "I'm back in Hong Kong."

"What? When?"

"Yesterday."

"Why didn't you tell me? Where are you now?"

"I just needed some time alone to think. I'm sorry."

"What's the matter with you? You don't like us or something? Come back. Now, and I mean it."

"No time to argue with you, Agnes," I say. "I need you to do something for me, though. Something very important. I need you to tell Kate to meet me at the Ho Won Restaurant, right across from the wharf on Cheung Chau. She can't miss it."

"Ho Won?"

"It's very important. You must tell her. I'll be taking the twelve o'clock ferry. Remember. Noon. I will see her at the Ho Won Restaurant when the ferry docks. Get it?"

"Greg, can you tell me what's going on?"

"I'll explain later. I promise. But I must see Kate tomorrow. Make sure she gets the message. Ho Won Restaurant."

"What if she doesn't call?"

"She will. I know she will."

After I hang up, I reach for the mini-bar and grab a four ounce bottle of Jack Daniel's. I study the label for a few seconds and put it back. I hop on the bed and stare at the ceiling, listening to the air vent droning a lullaby.

I can't sleep. I start to count rabbits.

The blasting sound almost stops my heart. I jump up, looking for the ambulance that goes with the siren. It's only the phone. I roll over to the side of the bed and snatch the receiver.

"Yes?" I ask, my eyes half-shut against the glare of the light surrounding me.

"*It's a beautiful, beautiful morning. I'd love to sing you a song!*"

"Victor, stop singing. It's early."

"Early? It's almost noon."

I jump up from the bed and seize the alarm clock. "Shit—it's late."

"You're right. If you want to catch Lian, you'd better hurry."

"What?"

"She'll be at the Cultural Center in about an hour. I can get you inside. You'll have all the privacy you want."

"An hour? I can't."

"Don't tell me—"

"I can't. Can we make it later?"

"Greg, this isn't a dental appointment—we're going on tour. We'll be leaving for Beijing this afternoon."

"I can't. I have to go to Cheung Chau."

"What for? Greg, this may be your only chance."

"I know. I know. I'll be there. Keep her there."

"I'll do what I can."

"Victor, I owe you. I have to go now."

I frantically dial Agnes, but no one picks up the phone. I don't have any time to waste. I hate people who don't believe in answering machines.

I pull on a pair of mismatched socks and the Nikes, and dash out of the hotel. I haven't shaved for two days and my hair flops all over my face. I really don't care. It's twelve or thirteen blocks from the Hyatt to the piers, and I run as fast as I can. As I cross a street about six blocks down, the light has turned red, but my feet won't stop. I race through the light and a blue double-decker bus screeches toward me, its horn blaring. I don't know how close it gets, just that I'm still alive and barely make it to the piers five minutes before noon.

As I pant and sweat, the Star Ferry terminal on my right and the Central Piers on my left, I know that I can't possibly be two places at once. There's no time to ponder.

Choice.

# Seeing You Again

She's not there.

My eyes sort through the crowd, and she's not there. The place is crowded with tourists and locals, teacups clanking and chopsticks clacking, waiters and busboys busy shuttling around, ignoring me. I scan every table and corner. There's no sign of Kate.

I tug at the sleeve of the maitre d' and ask her about Kate. She shakes her head. I don't think she understands me, or maybe she's seen too many white women with brown hair to differentiate. I wait for another five minutes. I'm about to leave when I see Hoi riding past me on his bicycle.

I run after the bike and grab the seat, jolting him to a halt. He turns around, fists in the air, ready for a confrontation. When he sees that it's me, he lets out a gawkish laugh and relaxes his fists.

"Mr. Lockland. You come back."

"Aren't you supposed to be at school?"

"I skip school. Stupid school. But I get A in my biology exam," he says. "Mr. Lockland, a lady looked for you."

"Yeah? What did she look like?"

"Tall, pretty, brown hair, and tiny dots on her face."

"Do you know where she is? Now?"

"I took her to your friend's house."

"The Cowens?"

"Cowen. I can never remember that name."

I turn to run, then turn back. "How did she find you?" I ask him.

"She stays at Tai Ping Inn."

"How?"

He grins. "Flyer. I make good flyers."

In the ivy tunnel, more decayed petals of angel's trumpets rest on the ground. The sky has darkened and a drizzle begins, landing softly on the foliage, thrumming out a small but quick tune. I trudge up the steps and past the cedar gate, beyond which the garden looks exquisite still. The banana fronds quaver in the fine rain like solemn Hawaiian warriors strutting their feathers. Over the incline, the meadow looks greener than a summer field, yarns of red, yellow, violet and white crocheted over a wide, long patch. There's no sign of Kate. Or anybody. I breathe hard, suffocated by scents of the flora. The wind chime's ringing. I remember the rabbits behind the hut.

Under the grand camphor tree and sheltered from the drizzle, Kate sits on the bench, holding Honey in the crook of one arm, absorbed in patting the smooth golden fur. She wears a straw hat, an oversized khaki shirt and blue jeans. A brown backpack's stowed by her side. She is so beautiful.

"Kate."

She looks up, not recognizing me at first. Then she frowns.

"You look horrible," she says.

I can't help it. I get all choked up. Tears fall before I can stop them.

"Okay, okay. You don't look all that bad," she says.

I break into a laugh. Tears and laughter—I'm a madman.

"I'm so happy to see you." I wipe my sleeves over my face. "I've been looking for you. You're very difficult to track down."

"Me?" She frowns again. "You're the one who went half a world away. God knows what you've been doing."

"Don't be mad. I can explain."

Kate nuzzles the rabbit.

"Who is she?" she asks, her voice tender but firm. I don't think she means the rabbit.

"Lian. Her name's Lian."

"And she's your daughter?"

"Daughter?" Then I realize whom she means. "No, no. That's Helen."

"Helen? Your mother?" She shakes her head. "I'm confused."

"Helen's Lian's daughter. I think she was named after my mother."

"Why?"

"That's what I wanted to find out. That's why I came here."

Kate looks up. Her eyes are hard. "Why did you lie to me?"

"I'm sorry."

"I don't understand any of this, Greg," she says. "She looks like you. The eyebrows are uncanny."

"I'm telling you the truth. I thought she was my dad's, but I was wrong."

"Your dad's? Wait." She shakes her head again.. "I'm even more confused now."

"It's a long story. I'm more than willing to tell you. I didn't feel like I could."

"And now?"

"I just wanted to see you. To be next to you."

"You tricked me."

"Tricked you? How?"

"The letter you sent me. The things you told my mom. And to meet you at the restaurant at noon. You didn't even show up."

"Noon? No." I sigh. "Agnes got it all wrong. I told her I'd be on the twelve o'clock ferry. I didn't get here until one."

"Oh." She shrugs, and her eyes soften a little. "That explains part of the mystery."

"And the letter. I didn't ask you to come here."

"No, you didn't."

"Why did you come, then?"

"It was a spur of the moment thing."

She reaches into her shirt pocket, pulls out a piece of paper and hands it to me.

*Dear Kate,*

*By now you must be thinking, what's wrong with that horrible man? I don't blame you if you think negative thoughts about me...I realize, once again I've failed you. I left.*

*I don't know why I left the way I did, and why I didn't call or write. I just couldn't seem to tell you the truth...I could have told you simply that I was going to Hong Kong...yes that's where I am now...I didn't have to keep that from you...but to tell you that, I would have to tell you everything, and I wasn't ready to do so...I guess the easiest thing for me is always run...*

*I found two letters in my father's safe deposit box. From a woman named Lian...I have to find out the truth.*

*Kate, I really miss you. There is nothing more to hope for than your happiness, and I hope that happiness includes me. I'm so sorry that I left the way I did. I will explain everything when I see you. I need you. I wish you were here with me now.*

*Greg*

I flip the letter over. There's no return address, but Kate's address is written in the same handwriting that resembles mine, only neater. The postmark is "Cheung Chau, Hong Kong."

"I didn't write this," I say.

"No? Who, then?"

"Lian."

"Who's Lian again?"

It's time to tell the lawyer the truth, the whole truth, and nothing but the truth. She listens intently, her expression impossible to read. The rabbit slumps in the crook of her arm, relaxed and entranced. I lean over. She's so close I can almost touch her. But I know not to come any closer.

She's right here, but somehow, I feel like she could at any second disappear before my eyes. I have to make her stay. Have to.

Just as I'm about to tell her about Lillian, the screen door squeaks open. Startled, the rabbit squirms. Kate gently lowers it back inside the fence. Helen leans against the wall, a wooden box in her hand. She hesitates, then runs over and wraps her arms around me.

I hold her for a long time. Kate watches us. I look at her over Helen's shoulders. "I suppose you've introduced yourselves?"

"Not really," Kate says, touching the back of her ear. "We had some trouble understanding each other."

I tap on Helen's head, and she looks up at me with her big, bright eyes. I mouth my words carefully. "Helen, please meet Kate." I turn Helen toward her.

"Ay," Helen says.

"Yes, Kate," Kate says, touching Helen's hands. Helen holds out the box. "For me?" Kate asks.

Helen nods and gestures to me.

Kate takes the box from Helen and carefully mouths, "Thank you."

"Helen, where is your father?" I ask.

She shrugs.

"Did they leave you here alone, by yourself?"

She shakes her head. "Unko Owur tay-kin mee oo ees ows."

"He has a great house. Uncle Howard is a good man."

She smiles.

"Helen, would you give Kate and me a moment alone?"

She nods and heads back into the cottage.

"She's so sweet. Was she born this way?" Kate asks.

"Kate," I say, stepping toward her, "I need to tell you something else."

"I don't know, Greg. There's already too much to digest." She sits on the bench, pushing the box and her backpack behind her. "I'm very confused."

"I'm struggling here, too, trying to sort everything out."

"Maybe I shouldn't have come here."

"No, no. I'm so glad you did. You have no idea how much that means to me. You came for me. All that distance. Just for me."

She stands, suddenly looking pale.

"What is it?" I ask.

She shakes her head and takes a step back. I look over my shoulder, but there's no one behind me.

"What's wrong?" I ask.

"I just—I just—" she says. "I can't."

"What?"

"I understand now."

"What?"

She keeps shaking her head. She draws a breath. "You came here for her."

"Kate."

"You love her?"

"Kate."

"Helen's mother. I saw her pictures on the piano. She's so beautiful."

"You are beautiful."

"Greg, don't. I'm not a fool. Look at Lian—she is stunning. Look at this place. It is perfect. I didn't know at first, but now I do."

"I told you why I was here. I needed some answers."

"Listen to yourself. You're still avoiding the truth."

I stare at her.

"If you were here only for the answers, you would have gotten them and left a long time ago. But you're still here."

"I did leave. I came back for you."

"Don't."

"It's true."

"Greg, it's okay. Everything's going to be okay. You don't have to explain or lie." She grabs her backpack. "I'm a big girl. I can deal with it."

"Kate, listen to me."

"No, you listen to me. I'm not bitter or anything. I'm just realistic. I came here because I wanted to. Hey, I even got a vacation out of this." She grins awkwardly. "I don't blame you. This really is a remarkable place. I think I may even stay for a few more days."

"You will? Stay with me?"

"I'll do just fine on my own."

"What are you saying?"

"I don't need you."

I take a step back.

"Why are you doing this?" I ask. "Don't you know how I feel about you?"

"How exactly do you feel about me?"

I gaze at her, my mouth and throat dry.

"I thought so," she murmurs.

I take a step forward. "I love you."

She takes a step back, almost tripping over the fence.

"You love her."

I can't deny that, and I don't want to lie. *Not everything is about me.* "Do you love me?" I ask. "What do you want?"

She puts on her backpack and adjusts the straps. "I want to go now."

"Don't leave." I lunge forward and grasp her arm. She pulls back and brushes my hand away.

"Tell Helen that I say goodbye, and that I'm very happy to meet her," she says. "Goodbye, Greg." She trots past me and disappears in the rain.

I don't know why I don't stop her.

I lean over the fence and wrap my hands around the black rabbit. I grab its ruff, place the other hand under its rump, and swiftly scoop it up. It struggles vigorously at first, but eventually settles in my embrace.

Resting on the bench with the rabbit, I breathe in the musky smell of dirt and rain—it soothes me. I look down at the floppy ears, twitching nose and helpless posture. Suddenly I want to kiss it, so I do, on the forehead, comforted by the fine fur grazing against my lips.

Leaves crunch behind me. I turn. It's Helen, standing at the foot of the tree.

"Ay?" she asks.

"She's gone. She left."

"Why?"

"We had a fight."

"Be-cause of me?" she asks, pointing at the box still sitting on the bench.

"No, no. She likes you. Very much. She just forgot."

She picks up the box and starts toward the gate. I put a hand on her arm, gesture that she should sit down. I hand her the rabbit.

"But Ay…" she protests.

"I'll take it to her. Please, just sit here. Keep me company."

She wraps her arms around the rabbit, the box still in one hand. "Ay mad eh-oo," she says.

"Yes, she is."

"Why?"

"Because."

She knocks at my arm with her shoulder, urging me to speak up. I stroke her hair.

"Because," I say. "Because I was a jerk."

"I lie-er."

"Me, too," I say. I look up. Through the leaves I can see the ashen sky. "I love her."

I don't know if she really understands what's between Kate and me. But that's okay. I don't expect her to.

Suddenly I don't expect Kate to love me back. Perhaps I really don't deserve her, but I love how I feel when I say I love her. And that's good for me. Kate's happiness means so much to me. I now realize.

I can't let her leave feeling so angry, hurt and sad.

I gently take the wooden box from Helen. I stand. Leaning down, I kiss her left cheek, then her right. She giggles as the rabbit starts to fidget in her arms.

"I have to go now," I say.

She nods. She knows I'm going after *Ay*.

In the drizzle, I trot across the meadow, along the path and past the banana trees, then through the ivy tunnel and down the stone steps. Before I know it, I'm running as fast and as far as I can.

# Lillian

By the time I get to the beach, I'm sure I've lost Kate. I lope through alleys, make a few wrong turns before I come out of one end of the Praya. There are only a few places for her to go. Most likely the Tai Ping Inn.

I cross the street before the Ho Wan restaurant, make three turns and find Lai Ling Street. The street is covered with mud and sand, water streaming from a broken pipe in a corner. I knock on the door and wait.

Wing Po greets me with a knowing smile. "Lok Lan," she says.

"So glad to see you again, Wing Po," I say. "I'm here to see someone. Her name's Kate. A white woman with wavy brown hair. Tall and thin."

Wing Po nods. "She leave."

"She did? When?"

"Before noon."

"Yes. And did she come back?"

"No."

"You're sure?"

"Lok Lan, no ask question two times. I tell you. She leave."

"When's the next ferry, you know?"

"You late. Ferry leave soon. Good luck."

I squeeze her hand in appreciation, and I bolt.

I run back to the Praya and to the wharf, jump over the turnstile and dash through the crowd. I hear a loud horn. My chest tightens as I glimpse the bow of the ferry pulling away from the dock. I peek through the fence, looking for Kate, but I can't see much of anything. The horn sounds again, further away. Yet further away the third and last time.

I've lost her.

The rain has stopped but the sky is gray still. I head back up the hill on Peak Road, not knowing where else to go.

I wander by the cemetery, back and forth near the water fountain. Finally I sit on the bench near the lamppost, catching my breath. An elderly man in a loose, gray traditional Zhongshan suit sits by the fountain, a birdcage in one hand, whistling to his red-beaked finches. He takes a long look at me.

"Are you lost, young man?" he asks.

"I am." I let out a protracted sigh. "Lost. And now I'm just wasting time."

"Cheung Chau is a good place to waste away time."

"You know, looks like we're both alone, on this little island."

"Alone, yes. But not lonely." His little birds rustle in the cage, and he leans forward to whisper to them. He turns back to me. "This is my birthplace, and I was married here after I came back from Cambridge. And now, I wish to die and be buried here as well, with my wife."

"In this cemetery?"

"Right behind you. I have a plot next to hers. I come here often, with my finches. They sing little songs for her."

I turn and look through the gates, at the staggered monuments. I remember Mr. Yee Man Sun. The white urn. The incense. Lian's face.

I think of something else.

"Mister—"

"Doctor. Dr. Szeto."

"Dr. Szeto, is there a special area for children's graves here?"

"They are all over. Many sites throughout the cemetery. Usually smaller, less ostentatious tombstones. So many of them."

I thank him and head inside the cemetery. I'm not sure exactly what I'm looking for. There are many gravestones, large and small. Urns and incense and flowers everywhere. I search one row after another, studying the name etched on each memorial.

Then I see a small stone on a slight hillside, a lone white rose beneath it. My heart thumps hard.

It's well-maintained: swept clean, the headstone polished, the grass neatly trimmed around the edges. The rose rests in the center, fresh droplets of rain on its petals.

I kneel before the grave and glide my hand across the granite, its surface smooth and cold.

Lillian. Born in April, eight months after I left.

I know.

She was mine.

The office smells clean, a hint of lilac. A few patient women wait for the receptionist to call their names. I approach the window and ask for Dr. Cape. The nurse remembers me. She pages Howard and buzzes me in.

Howard greets me at the end of the hallway. He frowns. I'm dirty, scruffy and wet. He gestures me to follow him into an exam room.

He closes the door behind us. "What happened?" he asks.

"I saw Lillian's grave."

He lets out a slight breath and slowly lowers himself into a chair. He is quiet and still, almost a mannequin. I wait.

Finally he speaks. "Lian told you," he says.

"No. I figured it out myself." I sit.

"Okay," he says. "What do you want to know?"

"Lillian was mine."

"I didn't know, not until you came back."

I stare him down. "She told Martin you were the father."

"I offered. She was about to marry Martin." He lowers his head and examines his hands. "For a while she was my daughter."

My breath is heavy. "How did she die?"

"Reye's Syndrome." He sighs. "It's an acute disease, resulting from a viral infection that affects the brain. It develops and kills very quickly, especially among children."

"How could that happen? You're a doctor. She was a frigging nurse."

"She was in Shanghai, in training." Howard lowers and shakes his head. "And I didn't know the severity of it. Martin thought it was only the flu—and it was, at first."

"So he killed her."

"He's not a doctor. He didn't know. He thought he was doing the right thing. He loved Lillian, Greg."

I don't need to hear that. "I can't believe you people."

"Greg, don't be so judgmental. We did our best. No one can control everything. Lian's a good mother. You have no idea what she went through."

"Why didn't you tell me?"

"She should have been the one to tell you."

"Why didn't she?" My jaw clenches. "I feel like a fool. I have this great knot in my heart. I don't know how—"

"I know how you feel." He places his hand on mine. I pull away.

"No, you don't," I say.

"I lost Lillian, too."

"She wasn't yours."

He turns away. I'm a bastard. He's loved Lillian like his own, possibly more than I have ever loved anyone.

A knock on the door. A nurse pokes her head in. "Dr. Cape, your patient's been waiting in room two," she says. "What should I tell her?"

"I'll be right there."

"I need to see Lian," I say.

"Victor. I'll ask him." He gets up.

"Call me at the hotel when you know something. I need to collect my thoughts." I grab his hand. "And—thank you."

He nods, then disappears through the door.

In the hotel lobby, I approach the front desk. No messages. The concierge hands me a large FedEx box. "I signed for you this afternoon, sir," he says.

The package came from Los Angeles. Patrick's handwriting— he and Susan must have moved into the Westwood house.

After a cold shower, I lie on the bed and study the gray sky outside the windows. What a miserable day. A fitting day.

I tear open the box. Inside, another box, a piece of notepaper stuck on the top. It reads:

*Hey bud—Suzie and I settled in just fine! Thanks for the stocked fridge and everything...even the Bud, you're such a pal—a box came for you this morning. Its from UCLA and I thought it was about Suzie so I opened it. I'm sorry! It was from your dad's office. I will put it aside until you come back, but I did see some things that I thought you might want to check out immediately. I don't know—its just a hunch. Anyway, give me a call so I know you're okay. Everything's fine here. Again, thanks for everything you did for Suzie—she says hi—Patrick*

I open the second box, find a stack of white envelopes, carefully bunched together with three black shoestrings. The envelope on the top is addressed, in my father's steady, careful hand, to a Ms. Margaret Hepburn in London.

I untie the shoestrings and fan the envelopes on the bed. There are sixteen of them, also in my father's hand. The first three have been sent and returned—next to the address, a big, red stamp: UNDELIVERED—RETURN TO SENDER. The rest are addressed simply to Maggie—dated, no address, no stamp. I open the first envelope, trying not to rip past the slit.

Here's my father's soul.

# Dear Maggie

My Dearest Maggie,

It's been over a month. I miss you so much—you have no idea. Such foolishness to write you such a letter. But I must make sure that you know how I feel. How much I love you.

We both knew that this was supposed to be only a fling—but it turned out to be more wonderful than we had ever imagined. And I've fallen deeply in love with you. Fool becomes me.

I'm sorry I had to leave the way I did. I promised you that I would hold no secrets from you, and I will keep that promise. The truth is Helen's pregnant, with our first child. I just didn't have the heart to tell her about us, and about my desire to leave her, when a new baby is coming. She's already emotionally distraught, suspicious and accusing me of having illicit affairs while I was in Paris and London. If only she knew.

Maggie, I love you, but I feel so guilty. I have a family and I pride myself on being a family man. That was how I was brought up. I felt and feel a sense of duty, and soon I will become a father. Yet my heart yearns for you, and the pain I feel is the pain of separation and of you not knowing how much I love you.

I do.

Yours Always,

George

My Dearest Maggie,

My letter was returned. Where are you? Have you run away from me? Are you really so angry? I must speak with you. I must hear your voice. I must know where you are, and how you feel. Please write me.

Love,

George

Dear Maggie,

I hope this letter will finally find you. I'm going mad not knowing where you are. Please do not do this to me. I need you right now. I love you.

George

*Dear Maggie*

*I don't know why I feel the need to write you, knowing you'll never read what I have to tell you. I just feel the need.*

*Helen gave birth to a beautiful boy this morning. Oh, Maggie, I wish you could see him. He's the most perfect boy a father could ever hope for. His smiles are captivating. And healthy at 8 lbs and 3 oz. We named him Junior.*

*Although my heart is still full of regrets, at least a shred of light has blessed my life. Junior is that shred of light. That strength I need to go through this life without you.*

*I do love Helen, I realize. Though I love her not the same way I love you, I do love her, in my own way, and I swear to protect and provide for her and Junior. It is my duty, and for once in my life, I feel I may be doing something good, that I've made the right choice.*

*I've decided to go back to medicine. I've applied for residency at UCLA Medical. I realize that being a photographer is a foolish dream, a dream that won't feed a family of three. One must make the right, responsible choice.*

*I truly wish you could see Junior. I know you would love him as much as I do.*

*Love,*
*George*

*Maggie,*

*I think my life is a mistake. Having a family is a mistake. Being a doctor is a mistake. I'm not ready for any of this. I feel trapped. My dreams are slipping farther and farther away, and I'm only getting older and grayer. I'm miserable.*

*Most of all, my life should have been with you.*

*Love,*
*George*

*Dear Maggie,*

*It's been three years to this date. Not a day goes by without me thinking of you. I miss you—if only you knew how much.*

*Junior is growing up beautifully. A perfect boy. He can speak very well now and he's quite a Prince Charming, and all the ladies at his school adore him. The other day he gave me a little matchbox filled with red eraser heads. I asked him, "What are these?" He tilted his head and said, "Hearts. My hearts for you, dada." I almost broke down crying. I can go on and on about him, but I will spare you.*

*Helen's doing better, still not completely well. I think having Junior in school helps her deal with things. She's started to paint and pick up the piano*

*again. Her practicing is driving me crazy, though. She's thinking about going
back to the hospital. I cautioned her about her emotional stress, but she said
she was fine. She looks fine. I hope she is, for Junior's sake.*

*I miss you.*

*Love,*

*George*

*Dear Maggie,*

*Something wonderful happened. We have another boy. He's perfect in
every way. I'm a truly blessed man. When I hold his hands and kiss his face, I
know that all the world's troubles are gone. Love has no limits. And I believe
that now.*

*He's a quieter boy than Junior –introspective. There's a careful aura
about him. We named him Gregory—a good Irish name for Vigilance. I want
him to be watchful of the world around him, be aware, become a great observer
of life's great lessons. I have many hopes for him. I think he'll be very successful
in life. He'll be the pride of my life, as Junior's ever my joy.*

*I feel very fortunate, Maggie, even as I continue to miss you. I'm
beginning to accept this life of mine, and the fact that this pain for you will
never go away. It'll only be lessened somewhat by the grace bestowed upon me.
I'm a grateful man. I don't ask for much. I have my health, my children and a
brilliant career ahead of me. Life can really be grand.*

*I love you, Maggie.*

*George*

*Maggie,*

*Please Maggie. Answer me. Please. Let me know I'm not in hell.*

*Maggie,*

*It's been almost four months now. I'm only beginning to feel better, good
enough to write. My hand still shakes as I hold this pen. Only a drink or two
can steady it now.*

*I don't know how to begin. I feel lost and despaired. I know I haven't
written you for so long, and you probably have forgotten about me. I haven't
forgotten about you. Only life has taken me away for a while, and now death—
oh God—death has taken everything away from me.*

*Maggie. I'm so sad. I feel I'm in an abyss at all times. Deep, dark and
cold, I'm forever sunken in this blackness of pain and remorse. And a dire
sense of hatred and guilt. And questions. Why? I ask. My family's falling
apart and I don't know why. I did my best. Why this cruel punishment? Why
him?*

*Why, Maggie? Why? Why?*

*Dear Maggie,*
*Another two months have passed. Only now can I write again.*
*Something horrific happened six months ago. I'm only beginning to grip the reality of it, as if I have been in a nightmare for the past half year.*
*Junior is dead.*
*He drowned. Because Helen was not watchful, he drowned. A bountiful, bright-spirited boy, he took a swim in the Big Eagle River with Greg. He was never a good swimmer, not like his little brother. The undercurrent was too strong and it swept him under. It almost took Greg away as well. But Helen didn't notice, not until she heard Greg screaming and crying. She was too busy knitting. Who knits in the middle of July in the mountains?*
*I can never forgive her. I can't.*
*So much pain. So much death. First yours, and now Junior's. I still remember, vividly, the day I received the letter from your brother so many years ago. I burned it. I couldn't bear to be reminded of your horrible suffering, and the guilt that I'd abandoned you. And now, I feel like I've abandoned my boys. I wasn't there when they needed me. And now I must be punished.*
*I swear, Maggie, that I will protect my boy from any harm, and that I will live to see that he lives a good and fruitful life. I shall never let my boy down.*
*Mark my words.*

*Dear Maggie,*
*The mosquito infestation here in Malaysia is insufferable. God knows why we're here. But the hospitals need help and I must do what I can do.*
*It's been a long time since I wrote. My apologies. Life for me has taken some significant and strange turns. The World Doctor program is going strong, and I'm part of their effort to educate third world countries, especially Asia, on health issues. They have a crisis here, and every day is a challenge. We manage, though, as a family. It's not always easy, but as long as we have each other, I think we'll be fine.*
*Greg is quite a handful. I forgot what adolescence was like! Hopefully he will calm down and find something he's good at, and do it. Perhaps some day he'd become a doctor, just like me. I know, ego you say. But I still think it's a good thing.*
*As always, thank you for letting me talk with you. I always feel better afterwards.*
*Love,*
*George*

*Dear Maggie,*
*I need some advice.*

*Greg is in trouble. He's in love—or at least he thinks he is—with a girl, and now she's pregnant. He's already left for Berkeley. I don't know what to do.*

*His life's going to be ruined, just like mine. Well, I don't mean I didn't manage to turn my life around. I don't mean my life is a sham, but you know what I mean. He just turned 18, for Christ's sake. What is he going to do with a baby and a family? He can't even be responsible for himself. Abortion is an option, but I'd suggest the girl weigh in against it. I don't believe in it—killing a child.*

*I need to speak with the girl again. I need to know what she wants and let her know what's at stake here. But what should I tell her? What should I do? Maggie, please tell me.*
*Love,*
*George*

*Dear Maggie,*
*The baby girl is… What can I say? I can't find words to describe it. Suddenly, it's as if life is given back to me. I can see the angels smile again. I'm so happy that Lian decided to keep the baby. Lian. What a remarkable girl. She truly is. She understood every word I said about Greg, and she, too, wanted what was best for him. She's strong. She really is an incredible human being. I hate to say it, but Greg doesn't deserve her.*

*I finally let Helen know. She was ecstatic and anxious at the same time. It took me a while to calm her down. Strangely, for once, she understood my reasoning and agreed that it was for the best. She promised she wouldn't tell Greg.*

*Am I doing the right thing? Now there's a baby. I should let him know. Perhaps they really belong together? No, no. Too young. Way too young. Look at the mistakes Helen and I made—and we were very much in love. And then I met you…Life really is too fragile and unpredictable, and I don't want my boy to get hurt. I don't want Lian to get hurt. I don't want the little girl to get hurt. It's best that he doesn't know. And it's best that she lets him go.*

*I'll take care of Lian and the baby. Mark my words, Maggie—until the day I die. It's my duty now.*
*I love you,*
*George*

*My Dearest,*

*Happy 30<sup>th</sup> Anniversary. Thank you for being there.*
*Always,*
   *George*


*Oh Maggie,*
*Why? For Christ's sake, why?*


*Dear Maggie,*
   *There is no God. Truly there is no God. I don't believe anymore. A child's not supposed to die. I've seen so many at the hospitals, but I never thought I'd see my own die. Not Junior. Not Lillian. And please, not Helen—she's all Lian has now. My heart is shattered. I weep for her. Please, Maggie, if you're here—I really don't know anymore...have you ever listened to my pleas? Please protect Lian and her child. Make them strong. Keep them safe. Don't let anything bad happen to them. If you're really there...I beg you. If you really love me as much as I love you...*
   *George*

# Let the River Run

My father.

I slip under the down comforter, wrap myself in it. I breathe hard.

Regret and guilt bludgeon me, crush me under their weight. I took everything for granted. I was a boy. Everyone who loved me knew pain. They tried to shield me, but I resented them. Everything.

I'm no longer a boy.

A knock on the door.

"Greg. Please open the door. I want to talk to you."

I struggle out of the bed, falter to the door and creak it open. Lian. The beauty has come to save the beast.

"Hi," I say.

My dam finally breaks. I drop my head on her shoulder. She brushes a hand over my neck, gently tracing the fine hair there as I cry, then try not to. I lift my head, gaze into her dark brown eyes. I kiss her.

The kiss lasts a long time—solid, deep, remorseful, maybe erasing everything I've done, maybe compensating for everything I haven't.

I take her hand, lead her into the room and close the door. She sees the letters on the floor.

"From my father," I say.

"To you?"

I shake my head.

We sit on the bed. I gather the letters and hand them to her. At first she just holds them——she doesn't want to read them. Then she frowns, takes a deep breath. I bury my face in a pillow as she flips the pages.

She finishes and sets them down. "He loved you."

"I know."

She wraps her arms around me. "Please forgive us."

"No. Forgive me. I didn't deserve you."

As much as I want to hate my father for what he did, I couldn't. I know the truth now. I know they were right. I couldn't have been a father, a husband, at eighteen. Not even a few weeks ago. They did what they had to do. Out of love.

How can I be mad about love?

"How could you have loved me?" I say. "I abandoned you."

"There is no logic to love."

"I'm a big Dodo. A failure to the hundredth degree."

"Now, now." She wipes the tears from my face. "No need to be so hard on yourself."

"Why didn't he tell me? Why didn't he just punch me, shake me by the shoulders? Wake me up? Tell me to face my responsibilities? Tell me that he loved me?"

"He was just like you. You don't know how to express love, through words. You think you can just fix things. You really believe that actions always speak louder than words."

I place my hand on her hair, lean back on the bed. She rests her head on my chest. Her scent is subtle, calming.

"How did you find me?" I ask. "I thought you went to Beijing."

"Victor told me," she says. "I knew I must find you."

"Why didn't you tell me earlier? About Lillian."

"I promised your father."

"Promised?"

"I promised him that I would not tell you or anyone else about Lillian. After she died—" Her voice turns small. "I thought it was best to bury it forever. Then you came back." She sighs. "My regret is that you never got to see Lillian."

"Tell me about her. Please."

She lays her head on my chest. I can feel her heart pounding against my body. Her body starts to shake. She's crying. I kiss her hair again, burying my face in it. "Shhh—it's okay," I whisper. "Tell me."

She holds me tight. Then she tells me about my little girl.

I hear about her dark brown eyes, her soft face, her silky hair, her loves—singing jazz, dancing ballet, patting dolphins. Her first step. Her first word. Her secret pact with Uncle Stephen. How proud she was of being a big sister. Her dream of becoming an opera singer just like her mother. Her laughter, tears, tantrums. How she loved to hear the story of Oscar and his potbelly pig. When she was happy, she said "*wunda.*"

Her life was a short, *wunda*-ful song.

Lian knots her fingers with mine. She sighs. "When Helen was born, I thought I was the luckiest woman in the world. I named her in honor of your mother. Your mother was very good to me. She taught me about gardening and cooking. How to love right. About being a mother."

I kiss her hair again.

"Then Lillian died," she says. She curls deeper into my embrace. I hold her tighter. "It was so hard. I was in shock. And angry. I could not understand. I wanted to blame Martin for everything, then I realized nothing good was going to come of that. He was still Helen's father. I disappeared into China for a few months, trying to hide from everything, even Helen. I knew she wasn't a substitute, but her illness and disability was so difficult. I couldn't handle it. I was so ashamed. I really thought I would just die if I stayed in Hong Kong. That's what I wanted.

"Then I came upon and joined the Huang Shan Monastery. I learned a lot from the monks—about pain, suffering, seeing the light through all of it."

She looks up at me. I kiss her forehead. "Everything happens for a reason," she says. "Lillian's death changed my life forever. I have found my peace. I had to. There was no other way. We must accept the past and embrace the future, find peace and happiness. That is life."

"Even when it deals you a bad hand."

"Yes."

"I hope I can."

"You will." She kisses my hand. "Now that you know everything, you can start to heal, too. And you will understand eventually."

"Understand?"

"Understand what love is all about."

But I do understand. *To give.* "I love you, Lian."

She kisses my hand again. "But there is someone else."

"Martin?"

"Kate."

I stare at the ceiling.

"You love her," she says.

I caress her hair. "I do. Very much."

"Then you should go to her."

"What about you?"

"I did fine for fourteen years. I think I will be okay."

"And you have Martin."

"He left," she says under her breath. "He needed some time. I told him everything. I told him about you and Lillian. We need to work things out. But right now, he needs some space."

"I'm so sorry."

"We will work things through. We will be fine. After all, we still love each other."

I let out a resigned breath. "Do you? Still love me?" I ask.

She snuggles closer. I touch her face.

"Remember the river?" she says. "Look downstream, not up. Let the river run."

"But I want to make it up to you."

"Greg, love is not about guilt or reparation. Guilt is such a useless, consuming emotion. Love is about giving and sharing, remember? Ask yourself. Deep down, you know what you must do."

Deep down, I know I love Kate more than anything. Anything.

"You talk like a monk sometimes, you know?" I say.

"I do."

"Why did you write Kate the letter?"

She laughs. "Because your letter was horrible. You could not send her that letter. Kate would not want to read about your desire for me. I just helped you out a little."

"But why?"

"Because. Your life is in California, not here. With her, not me."

I kiss her forehead. "You're right."

"Greg," she says. "I have made many mistakes."

I turn, pushing my back against her. She loops an arm around me and slips a hand between my face and the sheets.

"But we make decisions, and choose certain paths," she says. "We must always move forward, wherever those paths take us. I have chosen a path, and I can live with that. Think about your paths. Think about Kate. Do you love her? Would you give up yourself for her? Would she do the same for you?"

I stare at the painting on the wall, splashes of red, blue and green in a circular pattern. I realize something: Kate came for me. She flew across the Pacific just to find me.

"Yeah," I say, pulling Lian's hand close to my heart.

We cuddle for a long time, the vent droning in the background. The ceiling becomes a great canvas for our minds to draw pictures—pictures of our past, our present, and our future. Pictures of peace and joy. Love. Families. My mother. My father. Helen. Lillian.

Kate.

Lian and I take a slow walk to the Central MTR station. She has to gather her luggage at the Cultural Center, then catch a late flight to Beijing.

Hurried crowds push and shove around us, determined to catch the next train or bus so they can finally get home and get ready for yet another day of pushing and shoving. We stand at the turnstile, sharing a quiet moment just between us. I drape my arms over her shoulders. I know it's time.

"Are you sure you don't want me to come with you?" I ask.

"I am fine."

"Will I see you again?"

"It is your decision." She winks. "Always. You know where to find me. You still owe me a lemon iced tea."

I kiss her.

"I'll keep my father's promise for him," I say. "Don't you and Helen worry."

She grins. And I kiss her again.

"I love you, you know?" I say.

"I love you, too."

With a final, tender smile, she glides through the turnstile. She looks back and waves at me. I draw a long breath as she turns and walks away, disappearing in the sea of black, sails of white, blue, green, yellow and red—a colorful, rapid, buzzing world rushing in around me. This side of the Pacific.

# Come Full Circle

Then there is the city of angels. A weave of former farmlands skirted by rumpled mountains, Los Angeles is a web of dreams. My dream is to make a life with Kate. But I know now the difference between dreams and reality.

Patrick picks me up at LAX. He seems upbeat, whistling the theme to *The Andy Griffith Show,* sure to stick in my head. On our way up the San Diego Freeway, he grins.

"What's so funny?" I kick off my shoes and let back the seat.

"You look like a chia pet." He gestures to the three days' growth on my face.

"At least I'm not losing my hair."

He whaps me in the head.

"How's Susan?" I ask. "Better?"

"She's holding up pretty well. I think I'm more nervous than she is."

"The operation is when?"

"Next Tuesday. Thank God my dad's here. I'd be a train wreck without him."

"That's good news."

"What's up with that, anyway?" he asks, pointing at the large cardboard box on my lap.

"Nothing. It's personal."

"C'mon, tell me. What's in it?"

"Odds and ends," I say. I look out of the window, watching cars stopping and going. "Some yellow daisies. A new U2 album. Sarah McLachlan. The Grateful Dead. Big paperclips. That sort of thing."

Patrick looks at me funny—he's waiting for the punch line.

"Every time I think of Kate," I explain, "I pick up something that she likes and put it in the box. I want to fill this box."

"A present for her?"

I shrug.

"Man. You're more helpless than I thought."

I grin. "How's it with you and Ms. Kretzler?"

"Right."

"Ah ha. She asked you out."

"Coffee. We went and had coffee."

"And?"

"And you're a big jerk." He chuckles.

"Tell me."

"She calls. She always asks about Susan, but we end up talking a lot."

"That's great. You haven't thanked me yet."

He laughs. "Speaking of thanks, you're staying for dinner, right?"

"I don't know."

"C'mon, it's Thanksgiving."

"I have to find Kate."

"You know, I'll bet she's at her mom's."

"You think?"

"Should we check it out?"

Patrick takes the exit off Santa Monica and heads towards Brentwood. He's good with directions, and I'm a good navigator. Before long, we turn into Amherst and immediately I see Kate's Explorer in the driveway.

"Wait. Stop here," I say.

"What?"

"I don't want her to see me."

"What's up with you?"

"Just drop me off. Go."

"How are you going to get back?"

I throw him a look. He knows when to shut up.

I creep around the back of the house. Emily's busy in the kitchen, chopping carrots and onions. Kate's not with her.

I come around the corner. Kate's old bedroom is above me. The sky reflects on the windows, and the fawn drapes are open. I look around. A steel ladder slants against the shed. I carry the ladder back to the side of the porch, pick up a few pebbles on the ground and drop them in my pants pocket. I climb up the ladder, one slow step at a time. The shingles on the overhang look fragile and I don't want to crack them, so I lean against the ladder, steadying myself on the ledge.

"Kate." I wait a few seconds. "Kate," I call out again.

I take a pebble from my pocket and throw it at the window. I notice some movement inside, but it's just too dark. I throw another pebble. This time I swear I see Kate inside. The windows remain shut.

I'm determined to make a fool of myself. In my wobbly, cracking voice, I sing an out-of-tune verse from Sarah McLachlan's *Angel*. Our song.

The shadow moves closer to the window, lingers, hesitant. The thought of the slightest gap between the window and its frame makes me sing louder.

The shadow now rests by the window, hiding behind a fall of drapes.

I climb another step, flip around and lean over, carefully pressing my behind on a few shingles. I want to be closer to her.

"Kate?"

No response. But the shadow hasn't moved away.

"Kate," I say. "I know you can hear me."

I take out the pocketful of pebbles and clatter them in my palm. It's now or never.

"You know? I'd be dishonest if I told you I didn't love Lian. The problem is not that I love her—it's a different kind of love now. The problem is that I didn't realize how much I loved you, and that you were the one for me.

"Kate, you're real. You're real and fun and intelligent and beautiful and all that—but the truth is I've fallen in love with you, head over heels. I love you for who you are, and not because of some dream or fantasy. You're as true and spectacular as the sunrise or the Grand Canyon or Fourth of July fireworks or shooting stars or the moon in an October sky. I'm not going to take you for granted. I'll do anything for you, to make you happy.

"Kate, I want you to know that I love you. I love you, I love you, I love you. I really love you. I hope that you'll open the window, and your heart, and accept me. But if you don't, I just want you to know, that I love you. God, it feels so great to say that."

The window creaks open. I jerk and lean forward, trying to catch a glimpse of her. Instead, a young girl, about eight or so, peeks out with a giggle.

"You talk too much," she says.

"Who are you?"

"Kelly. Kate's cousin."

"You heard everything I said?"

She nods, then shakes her head. "I don't understand though," she says. "And you can't sing."

"Where's Kate?"

"She went out with my mom and dad."

"When will she be back?"

"I don't know. You can come back later."

"I need to talk to her, in private."

"I already heard your speech."

I laugh. "Tell her to call Greg," I say. "But don't tell her what I said. Don't tell her about the song either. It's between you and me. Promise?"

"Okay."

I wave at her, then climb down the ladder. Feeling a rush of energy, I run.

The cab drops me off at the cemetery. It feels odd standing at the gate. I haven't been back for a month now, but it seems like I just buried my parents. It was a clear, sunny afternoon, just like now. The sky is blue, the air balmy.

I trudge up the hillside looking for their graves. I don't remember exactly where they are. I never expected to come back, a different man. A grown man. I vaguely remember a few cherry trees over a small bend. I walk around the bend, and there they are—a few yards away from the trees, two platinum plaques on the ground, my father and mother resting together. Forever.

I pull out a letter from my back pocket and lay it on my father's plaque. So many things I want to say to him. Two letters brought me back to my past, then his letters to Maggie brought me back here. It's only fitting that I write him a letter to tell him everything, everything that I didn't have a chance to say. Come full circle. Kate said it right: "We circle back to where we started, not to face our past, but our future." My future starts here. Now.

I kneel and kiss the plaques.

I'm ready to let them go.

# Giving Thanks

"Where have you been?" Patrick crosses his arms at the door.

"Am I late?"

"Very. We're hungry."

He pushes me into the house, the dining hall in the west wing. The large cherry-wood table is decorated festively, full of white corn, cranberry sauce, yams, green beans, garlic mashed potatoes, gravy, asparagus, fresh dinner rolls, a cornucopia, seemingly miles of ribbons and gardenias. What it needs is a golden bird.

"Uncle Greg," Susan shrieks when she sees me.

"Suzie," I shriek back. I run over and hug her close.

"Uncle Greg, you're crushing me," she protests. She pushes me away.

"Hey, hey, hey," Patrick says behind me. "What're you doing to my girl?"

"I hate that," she says.

"Better get used to it," I tease her. "Did you do all this? Good job."

"Daddy helped."

Patrick returns from the kitchen with a turkey the size of Gibraltar. Must be at least twenty-five pounds. I gawk. There is karma involved, eating this bird.

Might as well.

"Greg, you sit down over there," Patrick says, gesturing to the chair at the head of the table. "You're the master of the house. Without you, we wouldn't be here."

"No. Without my father, you wouldn't be here." I feel like I should point to a place in heaven, creating a chair.

"True, true. We should raise a toast to him," Patrick says. He points at the old man across from me. "Greg, this is my dad, Taylor. Dad, you remember Greg, right?"

"Of course," Taylor says. "The kid who laughed at my name."

"Dad." Patrick pretends sympathy. "You have to admit—Taylor Taylor is a funny name."

"You should thank him for not naming you Junior," I say to Patrick.

"Very funny," Patrick says. "Well, Greg, carve the turkey already. C'mon, everyone's hungry."

"Yay," Susan cheers.

"I think Taylor should do the honor," I say. "He's the eldest and the wisest."

Patrick looks at me funny. "You're very strange lately," he says. "But I like it."

"I'm glad you approve," I say. "Now, before we eat, Suzie, would you like to say grace for us?"

"Of course, Uncle Greg," she chirps. She then gets all proper and serious. "Please hold my hand."

We link hands and close our eyes. Susan recites her prayer:

*Lord, thank you for this wonderful dinner with my dad, my grandpa, and a very special Uncle Greg, together and happy. I know my dad's very sad about me but I know that I'll be okay because I love him and he loves me. Ms. Kretzler said that good things happen to good people. And I believe that. I also love my grandpa. Lastly, I want to thank Uncle Greg for everything he does. He looks so unhappy all the time. Please God, make him happy.*

*Amen.*

I draw a deep breath. Suddenly I feel full.

Patrick and Taylor are tucking Susan in when I sneak into the study with a glass of red wine. The velvet drapes are drawn and the room smells fresh and clean. I can see my father now, sitting at his desk, a glass of Merlot in his hand, looking at the fragrant-wood box Helen gave me a long time ago.

I pick up the box from the desk. Smiling, I think of Helen and her bunnies. I take a big yellow paperclip and put it in my back pocket. Kate'd like that.

"Greg." A voice startles me.

I turn. My father stands behind me, in his checkered cardinal and golf pants, his silver hair neatly parted on the left. He's handsome—square jaw and the Lockland eyebrows, like a stoic king.

"I read your letter," he says.

"I meant every word."

"When did you start getting so sentimental?"

I shrug. "It's about time."

"I'm still a tough, strict, stubborn son of a bitch, you know?"

"And I still smoke pot."

"Me, too."

"Really?" I laugh. It's been a long, long time since I last laughed in my father's presence—even though I know this is not real. Or is it?

"So, you don't hate me anymore?" he asks.

"No. But I did. You got off easy."

"Easy? It has been fourteen years." He waves his hand. "Your mother and I did what we had to do. We did love each other. You have to believe me. But I guess it wasn't enough. I didn't want you to follow my path. Perhaps I was wrong. Maybe I did it all wrong. Hell, I didn't know everything."

"Me either."

"So—don't you want to know who Maggie was?"

"To be honest with you, no."

"You're not interested?"

"Of course I am. But I respect your privacy. Your rights to your secrets."

"You don't have a problem with secrecy anymore?"

"It wasn't the secrets I was having trouble with. It was the truth." I take a deep breath. "The truth about myself. It was about avoidance. That was how I survived all these years. Avoiding the truth, avoiding responsibilities, avoiding consequences."

"I thought you did pretty well, actually."

"Now you tell me."

We laugh.

"About this writing thing," he says, "did you really blame me for stopping you?"

"Yeah."

"I never objected—in fact, I believe I encouraged you. I even bought you that damn typewriter, for Christ's sake. You used to bang on it at three in the morning, driving me crazy."

"I guess I modeled my life after you, in a way," I say. "I didn't want to disappoint you, but at the same time I resented that. I didn't know what the hell I was doing. I just wanted to be successful, but at the same time, I was afraid of success."

"Interesting."

"Is that all you have to say?"

"Greg, I'm not here to answer all your questions."

"Why are you here, then?"

"To say goodbye. But not in the sense you think."

"Don't talk in riddles, please."

"Excuse me, Greg. What I mean is…" He gestures me. "I'm allowing my old self to say goodbye to you."

I shake my head. I don't understand.

"The father in your head," he says. "The towering figure with the green cape shadowing over you at your brother's funeral. The surgeon. The father who was emotionally detached. The one you tried to measure against. Me. I'm gone now. All you have now is yourself. You have only yourself to answer to."

"So I can let you go."

"I hope you'll still miss me. But yes, you can let me go."

"I can let you go."

"Let go."

He turns to leave.

"Dad?" I say. He turns. "About the writing thing."

"Yes?"

"Did you really encourage me? Were you proud of me?"

"Why else would I have shown your novel to Lian?" He grins. "What you wrote was very good, son. I was surprised that you never finished it."

I clutch the wooden box and close my eyes.

"I will, Dad. I will."

I open my eyes.

He is gone.

# Set Them Free

I've never felt so happy. Except for one thing.

I glance at the phone. It hasn't rung all evening. I doubt that it will ever ring tonight, or tomorrow, or ever.

I'll have to let her go.

I pick up Kate's cardboard box and enter the kitchen. There, I find a small bag of Columbian coffee—her absolute favorite—and put it in the box. Pour myself a glass of iced tea. Then I turn around the hallway and trot up the steps to the rooftop terrace, push the door open, and a rush of crisp air greets me. I roll down the sleeves of my pullover and head toward the edge of the roof. The breeze ruffles my hair and strokes my face. Layers of clouds roll in, gradually masking an otherwise perfect moon. I remember the slow dance and garlic breath.

I grin.

So, this is inner peace. Lian was right. It feels wonderful.

I start to sing *If You Love Somebody, Set Them Free*, off-key and loud.

"You know what I've always wished for?"

That voice sounds so real. I think I'm imagining it, just as I imagined my father. I turn. Kate's standing next to the door, in her purple sweater, her hair down and curled. The same picture I've painted in my mind, many times.

She is real.

"What?" I mutter. I feel my face warming as I lean on the parapet.

"Peace and happiness," she says. "Yours."

I cock my head. I feel grand.

"And a song from you." She smiles. "Hopefully a love song."

"For real?"

"For real."

"How did I do?"

"Terribly."

"Well, at least one of your wishes came true today."

"Twice."

"Oh, that Kelly."

"She said it was the funniest thing she ever heard."

"And you're the most beautiful thing."

She comes forward and sits on a lounger. Her hair ripples in the breeze. The air smells like it's going to rain. A drizzle, maybe. But I don't care. I have her right here with me. What's not to love?

"I have so much to tell you," I say. "I finally spoke with my father."

Kate gazes at me, puzzled. I laugh.

"Or I think I did. I don't know. I finally realized how much he loved me. Kate, he did. I missed him so much—I really thought he was there with me, in his study, his sanctuary. I needed to talk to him, and I did." I take a deep breath. "You must think I'm crazy."

"No," she says. "I did that with my dad after he died."

"You told me."

"And you didn't think I was crazy. Or did you?"

I laugh again. *No, I didn't.* My heart is warm.

"Oh, did Patrick let you in?" I ask.

"Patrick?"

"Ah, right. Breaking and entering."

"And you've learned well. Becky told me."

I amble forward and sit on the other lounger. "So, you believe me now?"

"Believe what?" she asks.

"That I came back for you."

"Why did you do that?"

"Because." I pause. I can say it now. "I didn't want to lose you."

"It's not that simple."

"It is. It can be."

A drizzle starts to fall, gently touching our faces and hands, light as feathers and gleaming like broken stars. She and I do not move one bit.

"You don't trust me, do you?" I ask.

She leans back on one end of the lounger and rests her feet on the other end. I realize she's not wearing any shoes. The raindrops dazzle on her hair.

"I remember us having a similar conversation here," she says.

"We did. Our perfect night."

"It feels different this time."

"How?"

"It feels more real this time."

"And the verdict is?"

"Do I trust you? Well, perhaps I can," she says. She touches the back of her ear again. "I've read your notes."

"Which ones?"

"All of them, even the Post-It you left on my floor."

"So you know my feelings for you are real."

"It's not that simple."

"Simple as you like. Simple as you like."

"This is not a fairytale. It's not all happily ever after and true love conquers all. Life is tough."

"It is," I say. "But you don't have to be."

She lowers her head and stares at her feet. "If I'm not, who's going to protect me?"

"I will."

"Greg." She forces a smile. "Even if I can look past the whole Lian thing, someday you're going to leave, go back to your big job and big life and big dreams. There's no room for me."

"It's me who's actually wondering—is there room for me?" I point at her heart. "And you don't have to answer me now. I want to know, someday. Someday. Right now, as a matter of fact, I feel peaceful and content."

"Why is that?"

"Because I have you here with me, for one thing." I smile. "And I know that I love you. I'll always, always love you. I'll always show you how much I love you, if you'll let me. And I'll always take that love with me, no matter where I go. To my grave."

"You really do know how to talk romantic."

"No, I'm not—I might have tried in the past. But I'm telling you the truth now."

"Really?"

"Really."

"What about your life in New York? Hong Kong?"

"I can write anywhere. San Diego."

"Write?"

"Yeah."

"Really?"

"Really."

"And you'll move to San Diego? Do anything for me?"

"Anything. Everything." I glance at the box on my lap.

"What's up with the box?"

"It's for you."

"A cardboard box? Where's the one Helen gave me?"

"In my room. But this one is more special."

"What's in it?"

"You'll have to find out."

"Now?"

"Someday. Like, in thirty, forty years, when we're all wrinkly and frail, sitting on a swinging chair on a porch by the Pacific Ocean. Then, I'll let you find out."

"Really?"

"Really."

"Really, really?"

"Really, really."

"Hmmm, I just don't know."

"Trust me."

"Prove it to me."

I put my hand in my back pocket and pull out the paperclip. I bend and twist it into a circle—not perfect, but who cares about perfection? I get off the lounger, kneel on the ground on one knee and slip the circle on her ring finger. I take a drop of rain from her hair and place it on the circle.

"Katherine Walken, with this paperclip my ring and the fallen star from heaven my diamond, will you marry me?"

Tears fill her eyes. I gaze into those deep emeralds, and I know I can get lost in them, forever. I kiss her hand. My heart is so full of love for her, no matter what her answer will be. I will always love her. I will die for her.

I will.

"No," she says. "I won't."

The rain is falling fast, still soft and quiet.

She places her hands on mine. "Not until we have a proper date first."

"Dancing?"

"Movies."

"Audrey Hepburn."

"Cary Grant."

"Griffith Park."

"Dinner under the moon."

"Tomato paste."

"Garlic bread."

"Burnt shrimp."
"Burnt shrimp? Do you always have to have the last word?"
I smile. I kiss her.
"Yes."
I do.